TITLES BY JENNIFER J. CHOW

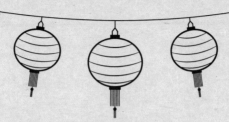

DEATH BY
BUBBLE
TEA

JENNIFER J. CHOW

BERKLEY PRIME CRIME
New York

BERKLEY PRIME CRIME
Published by Berkley
An imprint of Penguin Random House LLC
penguinrandomhouse.com

Copyright © 2022 by Jennifer J. Chow
Excerpt from *Hot Pot Murder* copyright © 2022 by Jennifer J. Chow

ISBN: 9780593336533

First Edition: July 2022

Printed in the United States of America
1   3   5   7   9   10   8   6   4   2

Book design by Daniel Brount

This is a work of fiction. Names, characters, places, and incidents either
are the product of the author's imagination or are used fictitiously,
and any resemblance to actual persons, living or dead, business
establishments, events, or locales is entirely coincidental.

PUBLISHER'S NOTE: The recipes contained in this book are to be followed exactly
as written. The publisher is not responsible for your specific health or allergy needs
that may require medical supervision. The publisher is not responsible for any
adverse reactions to the recipes contained in this book.

For Stan and Steve, who first thought of the Canai and Chai idea

ONE

IT IS A TRUTH UNIVERSALLY ACKNOWLEDGED, THAT a single woman in possession of a good fortune, must be in want of a book. To that end, I strolled with purpose from my residence to The Literary Narnia to retrieve my paycheck a few days early and splurge on a tome. Even after having worked in said bookstore for nearly five years, or perhaps because of my extended tenure, I still recommended The Literary Narnia to family, acquaintances, and strangers. I provided the recommendations not to increase our customer base and secure my financial stability but because I truly believed in the message of our store.

The two Japanese American sisters who ran it, Dawn and Kelly Tanaka, always spread new books featuring female main characters out on the front display table and complemented these with other classic books about women in a prominent placement on a book carousel near the cash register. Both ladies were in their sixties, and although even longtime customers couldn't physically tell them apart, with their petite statures and similar bushy silver hair and wire-rimmed spectacles, I could differentiate between the two based on character traits. I'd even developed my own special way of categorizing the personalities of people around me; I used dim sum characteristics from my years working at the restaurant that Ba owned.

Dawn reminded me of *ha gow*, translucent shrimp dumplings served in bamboo steamer baskets on one of those rolling dim sum trolleys. She never failed to be transparent with everyone she met, and I could rely on her unfailing honest opinion for everything, from books to diva authors. The Literary Narnia had only occasionally hosted guest writers, usually ones local to Los Angeles, but none of the top-tier *New York Times* bestselling authors. The small shop, hidden in a residential strip mall, didn't gather large crowds of readers either. Those who resided in Eastwood Village visited the bookstore, more for nostalgia's sake than for anything else. The Literary Narnia also got a boost of sales from the college students from the University of California Los Angeles who lived only a few miles away from our cute community area.

Dawn's sister, Kelly, resembled *ham sui gok* in personality. Those deep-fried salty triangular bites possessed a savory filling tempered by an outer crispy and glutinous shell that tasted salty and sweet in the same bite. Kelly Tanaka was like that, mostly of a pleasant disposition, but often with a deceptive tang of saltiness that came out unbidden and biting upon reception.

I counted myself as one of the lucky residents of Eastwood Village who had The Literary Narnia as their bona fide local bookstore and frequented it often. Like the rest of our community, developed only ten years ago, the strip mall housing The Literary Narnia still looked freshly birthed. It had sharp rectangular lines with a fake brick façade surrounding each storefront. The coal black asphalt appeared freshly tarred with bright dental-white parking lines. However, it couldn't compete with the sprawling outdoor mall across the street unoriginally called The Shops at Eastwood Village.

Despite it being Friday, the official start to the weekend, only a few vehicles took up any spots in the bookstore's adjoining parking lot. Two pastel-colored beach cruiser bikes, painted in seafoam green and sweet lilac, with attached woven baskets were positioned in the bike rack. I noticed that the owners hadn't bothered to lock up their bicycles.

The door to The Literary Narnia was already open, perhaps in a subtle attempt to entice customers who'd come to the strip mall to get groceries from the organic produce mart or visit the hairstyling plus eyebrow-threading services salon.

I sauntered inside and took a moment to literally breathe in the air. The heady rush that came to me whenever I sniffed the pages of older books and even new books washed over me and filled me with contentment.

From the checkout counter, Kelly waved to me. "Yale Yee," she said, giving me a slight shake of her head. "Coming in even when you have the day off. Didn't I tell you to enjoy the weekend away from this place?"

"I can't help it," I said, spinning around in a theatrical twirl. "I'm lured by the siren call of the work of a thousand authors."

"Yeah," Kelly said. "The ones always languishing on our shelves." Even though she'd started off in a joking manner, a layer of underlying verbal acid tinged her words.

I took a look at the small space around me, marveling at the tall towering wooden bookshelves with their various handmade signs in calligraphy done by Dawn. Beyond the usual sections like "Children's" and "Science Fiction," other quirkier spaces were labeled with such titles as "Stories Written from a Pet's Perspective" and

"Books with Exquisite Interior Art." It did seem like none of the inventory had moved since I'd been in the day before. It took less than five minutes to wander down the aisles of The Literary Narnia, and I didn't find another soul browsing the volumes or lurking in our hidden corner with the overstuffed plaid armchair, flipping pages.

When I returned from my scouting, Dawn had joined her sister near the register.

"Uh-oh. I'm your only customer," I said.

On hearing my words, the lines around Dawn's eyes seemed to crinkle with worry. "Yes, dear. That's why we had to—"

"I haven't told her yet," Kelly said.

"Told me what?" I moved to stand in front of the counter.

"We'll explain after the weekend," Kelly said, using a brusque tone.

"I'm here today to pick up my paycheck," I said. "Might as well tell me now."

"I'll get that check right away for you," Dawn said, scurrying to the back room where we kept even more unsold inventory and books we planned on returning to the publisher, their covers ripped off.

Kelly looked beyond my left shoulder. "How's your father doing nowadays? Still busy running Wing Fat in Westwood?" She'd pronounced the name of it correctly, making the "fat" sound more like "fought." The phrase meant "Always Prosperous" in Cantonese, but none of my schoolmates in sixth grade had known or wanted to know the significance when my dad had started running the restaurant. This was after he'd poured in years of savings from waiting on tables and being a line cook until he achieved his dream of owning his own business.

"Ba's doing great," I said. "The wait is out the door during dim sum hours, and people love his other dishes.

He's even testing out a few new snack foods I recommended, but he's not sure his clientele will want to try them, so he's going to introduce them at the local night market happening this weekend."

Dawn returned from the back room with my paycheck in hand and thrust it at me. "I can't understand why you won't do direct deposit, but here you go. Guess we'll see you on Monday. Bye now," she said.

I folded my paycheck and stuck it in my back pocket. Purses were the bane of my existence, and I made do with many pockets and the occasional wallet when needed. "You can't shoo away a paying customer like a pigeon," I said. "I'm going to select one of your fine literary products to purchase."

I wandered over to the display table, again scanning the newest titles we'd received. A domestic thriller was getting a lot of starred trade reviews recently. I picked up the novel with a cover of a shadowy female silhouette.

At the cash register, I noticed that only Dawn stood at the counter to ring up my purchase. Maybe Kelly was taking a break in the back room. Sometimes she napped in the uncomfortable metal folding chair we had there.

I plunked down the domestic thriller on the counter and idly looked at the paperback classics on the book stand. My eyes were immediately drawn to my usual Jane Austen favorite. I loved *Pride and Prejudice*, and my old copy was all tattered with the words almost rubbed off of the title. Should I add it to the pile? It wouldn't be a prudent purchase, since I was also considering getting takeout from that new kebab place for lunch on the way home from the bookstore. I gripped the edge of the counter tight to stop myself from temptation as I said, "Just the one book, please."

Dawn picked up the huge tome and flipped it around to

reach the back cover. She aimed the scanner at the barcode and hesitated. "This is a lot of money, Yale, and I know that you're on a tight budget. Are you sure you don't want to reconsider, given . . ."

I gave Dawn a pleasant smile. I tended to pretend I knew what people were blathering about to cover up the fact that I didn't have the slightest clue.

"You're really taking the news well," she said. "It's only because of the lack of customers. We love your presence . . . but my sister and I can barely make ends meet as it is. We had to cut corners somewhere. I don't think *we* even make minimum wage at this point."

I opened my mouth to speak, closed it, and then opened it again. "Are you telling me that I no longer work here?"

Her cheeks turned an alarming shade of pink. "Oh. I thought Kelly already told you while I grabbed your paycheck."

"When is my last day?"

"Monday." She fiddled with her spectacles. "I'm so sorry. We ran the numbers yesterday and just couldn't figure out how to keep you on. People don't really walk into bookstores anymore, and we've never been good with that internet thing."

Monday would be my last day in this beautiful shop that I called my home away from home. I almost staggered from the sudden physical pain in my gut.

Dawn blinked. "Me and my big mouth. I'm really sorry about this, Yale."

"Right." I nudged the hefty novel away from me with a clenched fist. "On second thought, I think I'll get the Austen."

She scanned the paperback and slid it inside a plastic bag stamped with The Literary Narnia's logo, a faun holding a book under a lamppost. In a soft voice, Dawn said, "You know, Yale, you could take this time to explore what you really want to do with your life. Maybe go back to college . . ."

I shuddered and grabbed the plastic bag away from her. "Hope more customers come in today, Dawn, and I'll see you on Monday."

The credit union was located only a few stores away from the bookshop, and I paused there to deposit my check. Afterward, I marched over to the main intersection and pressed my finger on the crosswalk button with one firm push. When the pedestrian sign flashed at me, I made sure to turn my head to the right and left to check for traffic hazards before I crossed.

To get to my apartment, I could go around the block or cut straight through The Shops. I decided to follow the shortest route and got an eyeful of polished stores flanking either side of me. They towered above me because of their multilevel construction. The shops on the bottom level had faux mosaic tiles and neon signs that lit up at night in startling scarlet or piercing purple. The residential units placed above the stores were colored in fruitier tones like avocado, lemon, and pear.

A huge plaza lay in the middle of the open mall, a design of interlocking cobblestones for pedestrians to amble along while browsing the high-end and chain stores located there. A steady stream of people walking around added a festive buzz to the air. A few of them wore costumes, in anticipation of Halloween happening in a few days. I darted by Harley Quinn, Rosie the Riveter, and a zombie bride. Finally, I reached the far end of the plaza and moved past the large two-tiered circular fountain with its strong gushing water. Anyone who lived in the area (and those who visited) soon found out that water splashed far beyond the overhanging lip of the fountain. People gave it a generous berth to avoid getting drenched.

My apartment lay just beyond the water feature and

abutted a small residential street. Fountain Vista was a tall complex painted in a delicate eggshell hue and offset by brilliant blooming orange bird of paradise plants near the front entrance. I entered the foyer through its automatic doors, nodded at the security guard, and scurried across the slick floor. The lobby was set to a chilly sixty degrees despite being in the middle of the fall season. Not bothering to pause at the collection of metal mailboxes—I only ever got spam mailers, and once a week sufficed to retrieve those—I continued to the bank of elevators.

I lived on the third floor in a two-bedroom "apartment home," as the brochure had described the place. It catered to modern tastes, with its monstrous stainless steel appliances, slippery hardwood floors, and an overabundance of swirled granite countertops. I wished it came with antique furnishings, but I managed to disguise its lack of personality by adding my own touches. I stuck handmade artisan magnets onto the refrigerator, tossed cheerful patterned rugs on the floor, and draped lace runners made of crocheted doilies over the counters.

The minute I hung my set of keys on the rustic wooden hook near the entryway, my stomach grumbled as a reminder that I'd missed an opportunity at trying out the new kebab eatery. I reflected on the paycheck I'd deposited at the credit union. Even though I technically lived alone, the amount would cover my "share" of the rent with little left over for extravagances. I rummaged in my alabaster white pantry and perused its bare shelves. Doll noodles would have to do for lunch.

I'd survived on doll noodles, or ramen, in my short-lived stint at college. I filled a pot with water and placed it on the stove. I flipped on the switch to ignite the gas burner and watched the blue flame lick greedily at the underside of the pot. As the water bubbles commenced, I remembered how many times I'd made this same meal in college before my sudden unplanned departure.

I'd also eaten it a lot as a child. Ramen was cheap, and even though the instant noodle packaging had changed over the years and didn't have the same doll figure that had inspired its original name in Cantonese, the food to this day reminded me of my parents and how they'd scrambled to feed me before Ba got his big break to open up his own restaurant. I plopped the block of ramen noodles into the pot, a little water sloshing over the side and sizzling away in the heat. I watched the noodles transform, change from a hard brick into soft tendrils bobbing in the boiling water.

At my country-style dining table with turned legs, I slurped my noodles and read at the same time, immersing myself in the happenings between Elizabeth Bennet and Darcy. I didn't bother to check the vintage clock ticking away like a steady heartbeat until I'd finished half the book and closed it with a happy sigh. After I hand-washed the bowl, chopsticks, and pot, I glanced at the clock and studied its Roman numerals to find that the entire afternoon had passed between the pages of a book. The best way to while away the time. I smiled.

I wandered over to the study, the second bedroom of the apartment. Besides a never-been-used daybed for guests, it held a wide cherrywood bookcase, which featured three shelves. Two-thirds of the bookcase was filled with novels, while I left the bottom shelf empty for future literary acquisitions. I squeezed in the new copy of *Pride and Prejudice* under the "A" section on the first shelf and added it next to my more battered copy of the novel. I stood back to admire the effect, and as I did so, my gaze was attracted to a blinking red light.

The very top of the bookcase also served as a resting place for my Victorian-style rotary phone with answering machine. It must be a message from Ba. Nobody else contacted me on my landline, although he never called in the middle of the day if he could help it. The restaurant hours were long, starting from opening at ten in the morning to locking up at eleven at night. I was used to calls at midnight or even one in the morning, but I didn't mind since I was a night owl.

I blinked at the bright flashing light and clicked the playback button.

The clanging of pots and pans assaulted my hearing. Then Ba's voice filled the air. "Yale, your cousin is flying in this evening. Sorry, couldn't warn you earlier. Celine got on a flight at the last minute. Can you pick her up—I mean, greet her—at LAX? Eat dinner together or order takeouts . . ." My dad sometimes mixed singular and plural nouns, the only tell of him having emigrated from Hong Kong to the United States to attend college. He gave me the details of her flight, and I jotted them down on a notepad with a harsh scribble of my pen.

Poor Dad. This trip had been sprung on him, and he was busy enough at the restaurant without needing to act as a tour guide. It was just like my cousin to not breathe a word to us in years and then waltz into our lives again. Celine had the long-awaited-for-child status, which meant her parents catered to my cousin's every whim, so I shouldn't be surprised at her spoiled actions, but I felt irritation brewing inside me.

I'd have to plan early to get to the airport because sometimes public transit could be finicky. The bus didn't always arrive as exactly scheduled on the timetable. Besides, Celine's flight might arrive earlier or later than predicted. I hoped the latter were true. The less time spent with my only cousin, the better.

To check on Celine's flight status, I would have to go to the local clubhouse since I didn't own a cell phone. It had to do with my preference for the past, with its unrushed pace, like flipping through the pages of a paper book rather than quick tapping at the screen of an electronic reader.

I rushed out of my apartment and hurried to the building down the block. The clubhouse was made of sandstone and seemed to take up a third of the street. It sprawled in size, funded by the fee we paid to be a resident of Eastwood Village, and the clubhouse was the center of the community. It boasted a large pool surrounded by palm trees and cabanas, a party room with ivory tulle cloths draped over banquet tables, a fitness area, a screening room, and a business center.

I only used the clubhouse for its computers and printer in the business center. Sometimes I did need to use the internet to search for things, like flight schedules, but it wasn't often. I'd thought about moving out of Eastwood Village, but I liked how everything was within walking distance in the community: grocery stores, the park, and my soon-to-be-terminated job.

When I logged in to the computer and checked Celine's flight, I realized it would arrive early. Of course it would. Everything always worked out for my glamorous cousin. It seemed like she'd been gifted a tailwind all her thirty-two years of life.

I needed to hurry to meet her plane but wanted to change my clothes first. Back at the apartment, I picked a new outfit. None of the clothes in my closet were what I'd call fancy, but I made do with a cardigan paired with a floral dress—of course, I'd checked for pockets before splurging on it. I also made sure to brush out my chin-length hair and straight bangs. On the way out the door, I even snatched a tiny lip gloss in "Stardust" that I saved for special occasions.

The ride to the airport was uneventful, and I kept playing with the lip gloss in my pocket. Rolling the tube around, I realized that initial impressions lasted a long time.

For me, I'd carried the image of Celine etched in my sensitive ten-year-old mind for the past twenty years. Celine and her parents had only visited the United States that one time, and our trip to Disneyland (upon the insistence of Celine) remained a montage of tumbling images in my mind.

We'd been sitting in the back of the family sedan, my seat belt tucked tightly around me, while she'd sneakily unbuckled hers on the highway. She plucked out a lip balm from her tiny sequined bag, which looked like a sparkling mermaid's tail. Celine uncapped the lip balm and proceeded to roll it over her lips.

I'd imagined asking her, "Can I try?"

She'd respond back with, "What are cousins for?"

Or even better, she'd say, "What are *sisters* for?"

In reality, I hadn't been brave enough to ask, so the scent of Dr Pepper floated in the air between us. When I leaned toward her subconsciously, trying to whiff the delicious soda, Celine snapped the cap over the lip balm. She stowed it in her little purse and scooted away from me, almost squeezing herself against the other side of the car.

We'd explored a number of exhilarating rides that morning, but after the spinning teacups made my stomach heave, I'd needed to sit down on a bench between my parents. They both fussed around me, checking my temperature and giving me sips of water. Meanwhile, Celine ran off with her parents to enjoy further delights of Disneyland, including a special lunch at the exclusive Club 33. As she skipped away from me, her light blue dress looked like a petite version of Cinderella's gown floating around her frame. She didn't look back, not even once, to check on me. That was the last time I'd seen her in person, although her parents had mailed a few sporadic letters and photos over the years.

With less than five minutes to spare until the bus reached the airport stop, I extracted the lip gloss and traced my mouth with its soft brush wand. I smacked my lips together a few times to spread the gloss evenly. Then I squared my shoulders as I got off.

I couldn't miss Celine even if I'd tried as she sauntered into the arrivals area. She seemed to own the entire space. A few people standing around me blinked at her, as though trying to place her face and determine whether they'd seen her on some television show.

Celine didn't look frazzled at all from the international flight. Her hair, honeyed strands mixed in with a darker espresso color, brushed past her collarbone in gentle waves. Her wide Bambi eyes went well with her bow-shaped full lips. She pulled along a stack of three royal purple suitcases tethered together, and when she noticed me, she smiled and flashed brilliant white teeth I'd only seen before in toothpaste commercials.

"Yale," she said, giving me a quick once-over. "You haven't changed a bit."

"I was ten when you last saw me," I said.

"You've still got those adorable chubby cheeks."

If she tried to pinch them, I would make a run for it.

Celine continued, "And that cute schoolgirl haircut."

I honestly didn't know if she was trying to rekindle childhood memories or make disparaging comments about me, but my dad had asked me to play hostess. I could at least be civil to my cousin for one night. "Ba said we should get dinner together or takeout."

"So kind of Uncle to suggest," she said. "Let me stash my luggage in your car, and then you can drive us somewhere good."

"I don't own a car," I said.

She scrunched her nose. "How is that even possible in L.A.? Even I own a car in Hong Kong, and it's frowned upon there. Pollution and all."

I scrambled to create a better impression. "I've heard about the cool restaurant in that spaceship-looking building outside. It overlooks the city."

"A panoramic view. That would be nice. Let me first check the reviews and the type of food they serve." She pulled out a sleek metallic pink phone and spent a few minutes searching. "Um, that place closed down in 2013."

I hadn't heard that, but then again, I didn't keep up with the news. Scratching at the back of my neck, I said, "We could eat inside the airport?"

"No. Never mind. I'm not that hungry anyway." Her fingers danced over the screen of her phone. I watched, mesmerized by the tips of her polished nails.

"What are you doing?" I eventually asked.

"Getting a Lyft to take me to the Four Seasons." She bit her bottom lip. "The driver should be here in a few minutes. I'd better go and wait outside."

Then she waltzed out the sliding glass doors, her hair bouncing against her back, as she again darted away from me toward better and more exciting prospects. Again.

Back at home, when my clock struck midnight, I called Ba from the comfort of the settee in the living room. I had my delphinium-blue chunky knit blanket tucked around me for soothing purposes. He picked up on the first ring.

"Ba," I said, "I messed up with Celine."

"Did something happen tonight? Is she all right?" His voice held a hint of alarm. He and I were both well acquainted with sudden tragic news.

"No, nothing like that. I tried to welcome her at LAX and offered to get dinner together, but . . ." I explained the mishap at the airport and how Celine had ended the night by calling a rideshare service and slipping away.

"A small misunderstanding," he said. "Perhaps she really wasn't hungry. Remember the time difference. They're sixteen hours ahead."

My dad was so kindhearted that he'd given my cousin the benefit of the doubt, but I said, "I don't think that's why she ditched me."

"Remember, relationships are the essential heartbeats

of life," Ba said. "Family should be together. After a good night's sleep, Celine will want to eat something tasty, and I know a great way to make things right between the two of you. Come by Wing Fat around three tomorrow."

I promised him I would.

TWO

WING FAT USED TO BE MY HOME AWAY FROM home. I'd grown up in its kitchen and dining room from the age of twelve up through high school graduation. Of course, it'd evolved along with me over the past decades. What used to be a small operation of one dingy dining room now boasted additional banquet space for lavish weddings and parties. My dad employed a staff of five dim sum cart ladies (all fierce aunties and grandmas), five waitstaff, three bussers, one assistant cook, and a hostess. I'd run the gamut of all the outside positions, including ringing up bills and greeting customers as they entered the establishment.

I didn't recognize the young woman acting as hostess now, but Ba often hired UCLA students, and they stayed only until graduation (at the most). She stood behind the oak podium with its attached microphone, calling out a number in English and then repeating it in Cantonese and Mandarin. The young woman wore the requisite cheongsam of the position. Her dress with a traditional high collar was in vibrant red, and silver blossoms trailed diagonally down the front panel.

As a favor to my dad, I'd taken on the role of hostess for about a week before I begged off. I couldn't stand the body-hugging discomfort of the dress. Besides, my mom had been hostess, ever since she'd started feeling short of breath my second year in college and had to give up her demanding role in the kitchen. No one else could ever take over as the optimal hostess in my eyes, not even me, her own flesh and blood.

I glanced at the young woman with her hair put up in a high and elegant bun, secured with metal chopsticks. She was pretty in a girl-next-door sort of way, but my mom had possessed true radiant beauty. It went beyond her glowing skin that she pampered with honey facials and past the shiny hair she bathed in homemade coconut milk shampoo. She had an open generous face and kind eyes that spread warmth with their trusting gaze. Maybe that's why her heart had grown too big, because it could no longer contain all the goodness inside her.

The hostess continued calling out the same number. Right before she moved on to the next guest, a family of four burst in through the doors, waving a ticket in the air. She collected it with poise and directed them to a waiter wearing a white button-down shirt with a burgundy vest, who had a stack of menus clasped in his hands.

I followed behind the family, but I knew I wouldn't find my dad or cousin in the main dining area. Instead, I located the banquet room hidden behind a sliding screen door. I pushed the partition open and found them at one of the round tables, already seated before a lazy Susan laden with dim sum goodies.

Celine snuck a look at her sleek phone, already out, and her nose twitched. My dad stood up from the table and welcomed me in a loud voice. "Right on time, Yale. It's good to see you here. Been too long."

I ignored his last comment, and making my way to the table, I tried to sit down on the other side of my dad, with him as a physical buffer from my cousin, but Ba pointed to a chair right next to Celine. After a slight pause, I settled in it.

"Would you like some tea?" my cousin asked, her manicured hand reaching toward the teapot.

"No. That's my job." I held up my palm in rebuttal. A row of empty white porcelain cups sat lined up on the lazy Susan. As the youngest person at the table, I knew it was my role to pour the tea. Why had Celine even asked? Had she assumed that I wouldn't pay heed to cultural tradition?

I glanced at the stainless steel teapot and made sure not to touch its hot metal side and burn myself. With a tilt of the pot, I poured its steaming contents into my dad's cup first. The earthy fragrance of *boh lay* black tea scented the air. I offered the full cup to my dad with both hands as a sign of respect. Then I poured Celine a cup, deliberately using one hand to pass it to her. As duty indicated, I served myself last.

Ba clicked his chopsticks together and said, "Don't be shy, you two. Dig in."

It was a feast for the eyes and the senses. He'd outdone himself in giving us a variety of the best dim sum dishes from the restaurant. They weren't even the remainders, the unwanted leftovers at the end of the dim sum service, which ended in the late afternoon. All the contents of the bamboo steamers looked piping hot.

A few of the dishes were my hands-down favorites: *cheong fun* steamed rice noodle rolls, oyster sauce drizzled over *gai lan* Chinese broccoli, and deep-fried *wu gok* taro puffs. I noticed Celine reaching for the bamboo basket holding the chicken feet. I could understand why she'd prefer something with talons; she was like a peacock herself, strutting around in her riches. I think her parents had ties to the booming casinos in Macau, which explained her extravagant lifestyle, being able to jet overseas on a whim. I bet she'd even flown first-class.

I studied Celine grabbing the bird's feet with a pinch of her chopsticks. I'd known her prior to my dad running Wing Fat, so she hadn't been dim sum categorized by me yet. Would chicken feet be an apt description of her personality?

My dad noticed me staring at the dish and asked, "Oh, Yale, do you also want some *fung jao*?"

I frowned at the Cantonese nickname for chicken feet. "Phoenix claws" sounded so much better than their English equivalent. Maybe I'd wait until later to come up with a better dim sum dish to represent Celine.

We all dined with gusto. My dad ate with the rapidity of a restaurant owner who could only take a quick break from his work. I stuffed my mouth with the deliberate determination of a woman intent on avoiding conversation with her distant cousin. Maybe Celine ate like someone who had only nibbled on room service the night before.

When we'd finished with the meal, with enough leftovers to stock my empty fridge, Ba sat back in his upholstered chair with its red silk cushion and wiped his mouth with a white cloth napkin. His dark brown eyes looked at both Celine and me, seeming to gleam with unbridled joy. "I have a proposition for the pair of you."

"Yes, Uncle?" Celine leveled her doe-like eyes at my dad.

"Yale's been hounding me to make these new snacks for the restaurant, but I know most of my customers want traditional dim sum and Cantonese dishes. I've decided instead to sell them at the new night market being held tonight and tomorrow at Eastwood Village. It'll be in the shopping plaza near where Yale lives. What's it called again?" Ba turned toward me.

"The Shops at Eastwood Village."

Celine fluttered her long lashes at the possibility of a bustling night market or a shopping expedition, I wasn't sure which.

Ba continued, "Anyway, I'd have to cut short closing duties at Wing Fat for me to even make it and set up before the eleven o'clock opening time. Since you're in town, Celine, why don't you and Yale run it together this weekend?"

I managed to stop short of choking on my boh lay tea.

"A night market?" Celine said, tapping one manicured nail against her pointy chin. "That would be so much fun. And I assume there will be different foods to check out."

Ba nodded with enthusiasm. "Of course. But not only food stalls. Also games, crafts, and even entertainment."

Celine seemed to catch my dad's excitement. She whipped out her phone and said, "Sounds fab. I'll get so many great shots for Instagram!"

My dad looked at her in confusion. His flip phone didn't make him a huge expert on tech.

"Is that a social media?" Ba asked. "I heard you want to make things go sick on it."

"Er, you mean, viral," Celine said. "And I'm a food-stagrammer. I take pictures of food."

"Ah. That's why you were taking photos of the dim sum earlier. It's for your job," Ba said.

"Kind of," Celine said, averting her gaze and sliding her phone back into her slouchy leather purse.

Maybe I wasn't the only one who needed to hunt for gainful employment. Of course, Dawn and Kelly still had three days left to change their minds.

Ba beamed at the both of us. "Naturally, you two would keep any profits made."

I couldn't pass up a chance to pad my meager savings account.

My dad started clearing the dim sum and putting them into takeout containers. "Celine, you can handle the social media and marketing side. Yale, you're in charge of the food and drinks."

My stomach lurched, almost like that time during the teacup ride at Disneyland. I hadn't really tried cooking since about five years ago, when Wing Fat had been short-staffed. I got called into the kitchen and began making dishes, working in an easy rhythm at the stove, the same way I'd seen my parents do after they'd opened the restaurant.

But when I realized I was working side by side with a burnished wok next to my dad, like my mom had done for so many years, a distinct sourness rose inside me. A few days after the epiphany, I couldn't handle being at Wing Fat any longer. The sharp sizzle of the oil and the heady smell of stir-fried vegetables flooded my senses and grabbed me by the throat until I couldn't breathe. I'd quit and found a safe haven at The Literary Narnia. Though I'd often purchased takeout from Wing Fat, I'd never darkened its kitchen space since then.

Ba placed a calloused hand on my shoulder. "Don't worry, Yale. I already made cold foods to serve for tonight. You just have to take care of the drinks."

I could do that. Beverages seemed an easy enough task. "You can count on me, Ba." Besides, I'd make sure to do plenty of drinks research.

My dad bagged all the containers and gave the leftovers to me. I could fit in hours of research before opening time tonight.

I turned to my cousin. "Meet you at ten in the plaza to set up the stall, Celine?"

"I'll be there with heels on," she said.

"I think you meant with 'bells' on."

"I know what I said. See you then." She thanked my dad for the delicious meal and strolled out of the restaurant.

Ba wandered over to the kitchen and returned with two

large aluminum trays covered in clear wrap. "These are the chilled snacks," he said. "I made batches of soy sauce eggs and spicy cucumbers salad."

"Thanks, Ba."

"One more thing." He hurried out of the banquet room and came back with a portable stove unit and a canister of gas. "This is in case you change your mind about cooking this weekend. Do you know that you used to hum while you cooked? I miss that happiness . . . and the good food." He patted his rotund stomach.

I felt my face grow warm, from both the praise and the embarrassment of him having caught me humming before.

"This is too much to take using public transportation, so I'll drive you," Ba said. "I already have someone who will cover me for the quick trip."

My dad drove me back to Eastwood Village and even helped me carry the items into my apartment. After we filled up the fridge, I said, "You're always welcome to come by. And to sleep in the other room."

He shook his head, and I noticed how his hair had thinned out, and the bags under his eyes looked more pronounced with the overhead track lighting. "I don't want to be a bother."

"It's not an imposition." I bit my tongue after that because I didn't want to straight up tell him that he paid for the lion's share, more than half of the rent *and* the community amenities fee. It was a right and not a privilege for him to drop by whenever he wanted.

"I'm comfortable at the house," he said. "It has a lot of good memories."

I nodded, not knowing how my voice would sound if I replied. He referred to the quaint two-bedroom 1950s home in the Palms neighborhood that I'd grown up in. It was a house of fond memories for my dad, but a residence where those same recollections threatened to overwhelm me. After I'd removed my box of childhood stuff from its premises after the accident and its aftermath, I'd never crossed the threshold again. I preferred to have Ba visit me at my apartment.

"I'd better let you prepare for the night market," Ba said.

"Thanks for this opportunity," I said. I meant it. It would provide me with a fun distraction for the weekend and help me to avoid dwelling on my upcoming unemployment status. *Too bad I have to do it with Celine*, I thought as I walked my dad to the apartment door.

I decided not to look for drink recipes online. Besides, I'd already visited the business center last night to figure out the transit options to the airport, and I tried to eschew technology for days, if not weeks, at a time.

From my home library, I grabbed the well-worn tomes already on my shelf. I flipped through their yellowed pages and perused the accompanying glossy food photographs for inspiration.

After I'd scoured their dog-eared pages for different variations on beverages, I visited the Asian mart around the corner from my building and purchased ingredients for the tapioca drinks I planned to make that evening.

I ate a quick dinner of dim sum leftovers before diving into the test batches for the night market. I puttered around in the kitchen, wanting my first foray back into the food industry to at least be palatable to customers. The tea would be easy enough to brew in my electric water kettle and then cool down in my refrigerator. I even splurged a little by juicing some fresh grapefruit to add to the mix of options.

Several hours passed by with me testing the flavors of the different tapioca balls I'd bought: lychee, brown sugar, and regular black pearls. I also experimented with how long to boil the tapioca to achieve the right amount of chewiness for the drinks. As a backup, though, I'd purchased several bottles of aloe vera drinks in case my own concoctions failed to impress.

When I'd finished experimenting in my kitchen and had cleaned up, I placed the cold food Ba had prepared, two pitchers of chilled tea, the portable gas stove, plus all the ingredients and supplies I'd purchased onto a rolling utility cart. I added the stack of cookbooks on top just in case. One never knew when a book might come in handy.

It was nine thirty when I rolled the laden cart out of Fountain Vista. Even though night had fallen and blanketed the community in darkness, the lampposts placed around the residential streets cast a warm glow on the sidewalk. A few passersby walking their pooches or enjoying the night air gave me curious looks as I strolled toward The Shops at Eastwood Village with my cart.

The plaza had been transformed into a mini festival. I passed by the spouting fountain and snuck under some velvet ropes blocking off entry from that side of the road. At the end opposite from me, I could see a stage set up with spotlights and a sound system. An athletic man was breakdancing, balancing with his head on the ground, legs up in the air but bent at his knees, and spinning in a circle. Behind the stage stretched a large section labeled "Arts and Crafts." Facing the stage on the left side was an area designated "Fun and Games" with carnival games set up. I spied balloon popping, ring toss, and pachinko pinball, among other festivities. Several hawkers had decorated their counters with Halloween flair by using black and orange streamers, bubbling mini cauldrons, and scattered wrapped candies. Maybe I should have brought some decorations for our food stall to attract attendees.

On the right-hand side of the stage was a "Food and Drinks" space. There were four vendors in the front row: three stalls and a food truck. Signs for grilled kebabs, fried potato swirls, and roasted corn stretched out in the background. I hoped I wouldn't have to go through too many aisles to locate our booth.

I first scanned the tables and awnings before me. Ba had mentioned registering the stall under the name of "Yee Snacks," but I couldn't find any such banner. A sharp piercing whistle drew my attention to a table in the middle. Celine was standing in front of one of the stalls. She took her fingers away from her mouth and struck a pose, using an exaggerated flourish of her hands like a game show hostess to point at the sign above her head. She'd replaced my dad's suggested title with a banner reading "Canai & Chai."

I pushed the cart across the short distance and almost rammed it against the table. "You changed Ba's name for the food stall?"

"I'm in charge of marketing, right?" She tossed her striated honey locks behind her. "This is definitely a cooler name."

I glanced up at the banner. "How did you get a sign made so quickly anyway?"

"Expedited printing," she said. "It can be done if you pay for it."

"But, Celine, we're doing cold foods tonight," I said. "No *roti canai* flatbread in sight."

She shrugged. "Whatever. 'Canai and Chai' rhymes, and the words both have that catchy *ch* sound to them."

I maneuvered the cart around the edge of the long table and behind the two opened folding chairs and parked it in the food prep area. Then I took out the cooler with the bag of ice and deposited it on the ground. "I'm also not making any chai tonight. Just boba drinks."

"It doesn't really matter. As long as they come to our stall to check out what we have."

"Which reminds me. I'd better start on the tapioca balls. Can you help me set up the stove?"

She tapped one finger on the top shelf of my cart, the one with the cookbooks on it. "Why'd you bring these?"

"Books are essential," I said. I'd memorized the recipes, but it provided me comfort knowing I could recheck the instructions in case I forgot a step.

She arched one thinly plucked eyebrow at me. "I brought what we'll really need."

"You brought more food?" I said, looking around and sniffing the air in case she'd already cooked her items.

"Of course not. Our outfits."

"I don't have time for this right now," I said as I set up the stove and the pot I needed to boil the water. I wanted to make the tapioca pearls fresh, so that they'd have a nice chewy texture to them. I concentrated on boiling the balls, grateful that I'd purchased the kind that would cook in five minutes and not one hour. Afterward, I'd still need to steep them in a sugary syrup base to create the sweetness most people associated with the starchy pearls.

As I worked, I noticed Celine puttering around. She tried to arrange the folding chairs and create some sort of aesthetic look by draping fairy lights across a fancy brocade tablecloth.

When I finally had all the drinks and dishes prepped and ready for customers, she took out a mini whiteboard and shoved it in front of my face.

"What do we have on our greatest hits list tonight?" she asked.

I wiped perspiration from my brow with the back of my hand. "We have spicy cucumber salad and soy sauce eggs for food. Green milk tea, black milk tea, grapefruit green tea, and aloe vera drink on tap for beverages. Plus, boba in flavors of standard, brown sugar, and lychee."

"Excellent." Celine used a fine-tipped dry-erase marker to create a faux calligraphy script for our menu.

"You are pretty creative," I said, not managing to keep the surprise out of my voice.

"I didn't get my bachelor's in fine arts for nothing," she said.

I swallowed a sudden lump in my throat. "That's quite an accomplishment."

She gave me a dismissive wave. "My parents aren't too impressed with my degree. And even if I hadn't majored in art, undergrad education is practically worthless now." Celine snuck a side glance at me. "Unless you graduate from a university like your namesake."

I suppressed a groan. How many times had I explained to curious people about my name? Ba believed in higher education and had actually been sponsored by a family to attend college in the States. He'd graduated with his undergrad degree and had also intended to get his master's in business administration eventually, but the arrival of baby me had permanently derailed his plans.

Oblivious of my discomfort, Celine continued, "Did you actually attend Yale?"

"No," I said.

"Harvard? Stanford? Um, what are the other Ivy League schools again?"

I didn't let her know that I'd barely scraped by with an associate's degree from college because of the family emergency. Anyway, I'd supplemented my formal education by reading boatloads of books in my spare time.

I picked up a cookbook from the utility cart, not even opening the volume, but brushing my palm across its cover to calm myself down by feeling its smooth texture. After a few seconds of this, I turned to Celine. "What was that you said about having outfits?"

She did a shimmy with her shoulders. "Wait until you take a look at these."

I noticed that she had already deposited a huge box in the back corner of our stall. She undid the flaps on it, reached in, and pulled out chef coats. These were not the usual formal white coats I'd seen before, but bedazzled ones with fancy embroidering, pearl buttons, and a touch of glitter.

As Celine soon demonstrated, when she put one on, they were also slim fitting and cut to accentuate the figure. She did a mock catwalk in our cramped space.

"I can see how they're essential . . ." *To your vanity.*

"It's all about branding. Standing out from the competition," she said. "When we're wearing these, everyone will flock to our stall."

I wore the bedazzled smock, but it didn't seem to work any miracles when the attendees started arriving. More than half of the night market participants wore costumes, probably in celebration of Halloween, but none of them headed toward our booth.

Instead, a large group gathered around the stage and clapped for the breakdancer wearing a black beanie, flipping and spinning to blaring hip-hop music. Others opted to approach the game booths to try their luck and win prizes. A swarm of people approached the food region, but they walked past us, wanting to try the vendors farthest away first. Adding insult to injury, potential customers who headed to our small section started at the ends of the rows, attracted to the other stalls beside ours.

Two people finally wandered our way. The first asked if I'd offer him a discount because of his pirate costume. When I declined, he sniveled. "But they gave me two dollars off on admission since I wore this thing. You should give me a discount, too."

How would we make any money tonight if I offered the food at cut-rate prices? "Sorry, no can do," I said.

The next customer, dressed as a witch, asked if we actually served piping hot roti canai bread and spiced chai tea, with excitement in her voice. I glared at Celine, but she had her back turned to me and didn't notice. "Sorry, not today," I told the witch, who hurried off faster than if she'd been on a speeding broomstick.

Celine started rummaging in the large box she'd brought. "I got some neat beverage containers. They might do the trick and get us new customers. Let me find them."

I started shouting into the crowd: "Cold drinks! Cold food!"

Nobody came by. A half hour passed in this melancholy way.

I stood up and tried another variation of my announcement by hawking the boba, advertising that we had "pearl milk tea" in Cantonese.

Finally, a ninja stepped up to the booth. The figure matched my height and was swathed in black from head to toe, except for a rectangular slit in the face hood. "You serve cold food?" a female voice asked.

I pointed to the offerings listed on the whiteboard. "Yes. That's our specialty today. Take your pick."

"Perfect. A grapefruit green tea with regular boba would hit the spot. Extra ice, please."

"Coming right up." I turned around, scooping boba and adding green tea with fresh grapefruit bits into a plastic cup with a domed lid. I'd needed a container that would fit the large straws required to suck up the tapioca balls.

"Ooh, I can't wait to drink it," the woman commented.

I appreciated her compliment about my homemade bubble tea and looked into her eyes with gratitude. "Thank you very much." She had an unusual eye color, an enchanting violet hue.

The woman gave me an extended wink. "It looks real *yum.*"

"Wait," Celine said from behind me. "You need to make the drink even more spectacular, present it better." She grabbed the cup from my startled hands.

In the meantime, I gave a weak smile to the woman before me. "We're still ironing out a few wrinkles. First night and all." Then I proceeded to ring up her purchase. She pulled out a pretty silk coin purse with embroidered flowers and paid.

After I finished, Celine thrust an actual glass light bulb—but filled with my tea—into the ninja's hands.

"Wow," the ninja said. The light bulb was inverted in her hands, with the rounded part resting against her palm. A wide straw went through a hole in the middle of the metallic-looking screw part.

"Bon appétit," Celine said to the woman with a long wink of her own. "I hope this both looks and tastes great."

The ninja retrieved her special drink, walked a few steps away, took her phone out, and snapped a picture. Did everybody take photos of their food and drinks nowadays? Then she slipped away, her black figure disappearing like a shadow into the crowd.

"Was that an actual light bulb?" I asked Celine.

"Yeah, it's all the rage. I didn't have a chance to add an LED component to it, but I would've if I'd had more time to shop."

To Celine's credit, business did seem to pick up after that. The ninja must have recommended our stall to others because people showed up asking for our "light bulb" drinks. In the beginning, Celine tried to take photos of every single snack and beverage served, but I told her to put away the phone when we started getting swamped by an increasing number of people.

There was only a brief pause in the customer line when the hula dancer went onstage—and started twirling fire. Everyone, from attendees to vendors, seemed to stare at his mesmerizing act until it was over.

I lost count of the customers after a while, and when we closed up at two in the morning, we'd depleted most of the food and drinks. At least my cart wouldn't be too heavy to push back home. "Thanks for your help, Celine," I said. "That light bulb idea really worked."

"Yeah," she said with a straight face. "It was *brilliant*."

She must be so tired she was making up puns and thinking I'd laugh at them.

I stored away my materials and organized them on the cart.

"Hey, Yale?" Celine said.

"Yes?" I glanced at my cousin standing there in a glittering chef's jacket, wringing her hands. "Do you need something?"

"A tour guide for the Los Angeles area. Are you willing to show me around?"

"Maybe. How long are you here for?"

She smoothed her unwrinkled coat. "At least for the weekend."

I drummed my fingers against the pile of cookbooks on the top shelf of my cart. It'd be nice to feel like a resident expert. Plus, it sounded like Celine would only be here for a short while. I could handle her company for that long. "Okay, I'll do it."

"I rented a car, by the way. Uncle gave me your contact info, so I'll come by your place tomorrow morning around eleven. Sound good?"

I nodded, and we parted ways. Celine carried her box and moved in the opposite direction from me. All the other vendors seemed to amble toward the parking garage, too.

I made my solitary way back to my apartment complex. The stores had closed down in the plaza a long time before, so there weren't blazing neon signs to light my way, but I knew the familiar route well. I pushed my mostly empty cart along the pedestrian pathway. At the fountain, I hit a sudden snag in the road. These cobblestones sometimes didn't make for even walking. I shoved the cart, but it seemed lodged against something.

I bent down to examine the stubborn wheel and noticed that my cart had hit an obstruction near the fountain.

However, it wasn't a jutting stone. I'd run into a shoe. Who would've walked off with just one sneaker?

Then I noticed a foot attached to the shoe. An unmoving body lay half-hidden under the large overhang of the fountain.

Why hadn't the person woken up when I'd accidentally rammed into them? I touched the person dressed in black and tried shaking them awake. Even as I did so, I recognized this stiffness of body. I knew I'd touched death.

THREE

I STARED AT THE BODY AND TREMBLED. MY LEGS shook, but I knew I needed to move. I debated whether to run to my apartment or secure help from any night market stragglers. Celine was probably long gone by now. I glanced back across the distance to the deserted plaza and realized that the vendors had all packed up. Perhaps a few remained in the parking garage, but I doubted I could catch up to them before they started up their cars.

Leaving my cart behind, I bolted inside the Fountain Vista complex. At the elevator bank, I kept jabbing the up button, hoping that would make it come faster.

My hands sweated on the phone as I called the police department. I wiped my palms against the fancy chef jacket I still wore. When I got through to the cops, they ascertained the situation and told me to stay at the scene.

I hung up and sprinted back to the fountain. Nothing had changed, although the darkness seemed more ominous. A cloud covered the moon, and it looked like shadows were reaching out for me.

Finally, a uniformed cop approached where I sat, several feet from the spouting fountain, on the side away from the very still body. He questioned me about the incident, but I had no answers for him. I didn't know the person or how they'd ended up at the fountain.

Time seemed to stretch out as he secured the area and took photos. I waited in silence and exhaustion for other officials to arrive. The paramedics came and tried to revive the person on the ground, to no avail. Then the detective showed up.

In the dim light, I couldn't make out much beyond a suit and tie and a strong jawline. He introduced himself as Detective Greyson Strauss and crouched down to be on the same level as me. "Can you describe what happened in your own words?" His voice sounded soothing, as refreshing as the aloe vera drink I'd served earlier in the evening.

"I was at the night market selling food. Then I packed up my supplies at the end of it, but when I was walking home, I hit a bump." I pointed to the wheel of my nearby cart. "I realized it was a body . . ."

"You don't know the victim?"

"No, not at all." I didn't have anyone in my close circle of contacts besides Ba, the Tanaka sisters, and my newly arrived cousin. How could I know the person curled up near the fountain?

The detective took down the rest of my statement, consisting of the same answers I'd given to the patrol officer. He asked for my contact information and, in exchange, gave me his business card.

"Call me if you remember anything else," he said.

I nodded and started pushing my food cart away as the forensics team arrived. As I wheeled it down the residential street toward my complex, I heard one of the team members announce, "Hey, there's an interesting light bulb lying here."

Did he just say light bulb? I shuddered. Was it the

regular kind or . . . I'd also handed out drinks using those special containers. Could something have been wrong with them? Had the victim been one of my customers? I wondered if I should turn around and let the police know.

No, I was overreacting. I went over the drinks menu in my head. Everything I'd made had been fine. None of the ingredients I'd used could have caused injury. And maybe the light bulb was just plain trash that had been left behind and totally unconnected to me.

⊏━━━━━━⊐

It seemed like I hadn't gotten much sleep before the chime of the doorbell woke me. I padded over to the front door and looked through the peephole. A distorted version of my cousin stared back at me.

I swung open the door and let her inside while I stifled a yawn.

"Sleeping in, I see. Fountain Vista is a secure place," she said. "Had to show my ID and match our last names before coming up. I really dig the marble lobby and the—wait, did you sleep in my special customized chef's jacket?"

My brain had been so muddled last night, I'd barely managed to put the leftover food in the fridge. I hadn't even organized the cart but had left all the nonperishables out, including the scattered pile of cookbooks threatening to spill over the edge of the top shelf.

"Is everything okay?" Celine peered at me with her beautiful face. Up close, I could see her dewy complexion with a hint of peach blush highlighting her cheeks.

I wondered how I looked in contrast. Stumbling onto a dead body in the middle of the night did not lead to restful sleep. "There's something I need to tell you—"

"First, take off the jacket. Where's your ironing stuff?"

I unbuttoned the coat, handed it to her, and showed her my laundry supplies.

She proceeded to set up the board with efficiency and plugged in the iron. I watched her for a few minutes as she worked on the jacket.

Finally, the bottled words burst out of my mouth. "Celine, somebody died last night."

She stopped, holding the iron up in midair. "Is it Uncle?"

"No, it's not my dad." I took a deep breath and continued, "When I was walking home last night, I found a body near the fountain at the edge of the plaza."

She resumed ironing until the creases in the fabric had disappeared. "Maybe it was somebody sleeping off their partying."

"I tried shaking them. They were so still." I couldn't help but give a shudder.

"Well, did you call the police?" Celine asked with a briskness to her tone as she unplugged the iron and let it cool down.

"Yes."

"Then they'll take care of everything. That's their job." She left the ironed chef jacket lying across the board.

"The odd part is . . ." I turned to rearrange the cookbooks on the cart into a neat stack. "A light bulb lay near them."

From my peripheral vision, I saw Celine shrug. "So what?"

"Do you think it was one of our glasses? I mean, it could have been a regular light bulb, but if not . . ." My voice cracked. "That means we'd just been talking to this person, and then a few hours later, they were *gone*."

My cousin blinked at me and put a hand on my shoulder. In a soft voice, she said, "I know you've seen death up close before . . . I remember my father telling me the sad news about your mother."

To put distance between us, I turned toward the hallway. "Let me splash some water on my face, and then we can start your Los Angeles tour."

She gave me a startled look. "You can just rest today. Get ready for more night market in the evening."

As I trotted to the bathroom, I said, "No, I'll feel better after I go to Lake Shrine."

I'd stumbled on to Lake Shrine while trying to sort my feelings after my mom had passed. Her death had been sudden, even though we should have noticed the warning signs before. She'd passed off the troubled breathing as allergies affecting her, maybe from the Santa Ana winds that blew with hot ferocity across Southern California. Besides, she didn't have a chance to take any time off to see a doctor, given the heavy work schedule at Wing Fat. Ba and I didn't realize her breathing issues were tied to a heart condition until the tragic incident with the car.

When I finished making myself presentable, I followed Celine to her vehicle. I stared at the shiny royal blue Porsche Boxster that she'd chosen.

"I've always wanted to rent one of these babies," she said as she settled into the driver's seat.

I consoled myself with knowing that Celine had opted for the most modern of models. It even had that lingering new car smell in the air as I sank into a leather seat. She punched our destination in the touchscreen navigation system, and I sucked in my breath. "This is safe, right?"

She gave me a strange look. "It's one of the latest in the line and can go from zero to sixty in four seconds." That snippet of information didn't inspire any more confidence in me.

Celine put the car into gear, and we soon found ourselves heading west. We ended up on the Pacific Coast Highway. Glancing at me as we drove on the road with its marvelous ocean view, she said, "Time to really enjoy the fresh air. Watch this."

We paused at a stoplight, and she pushed a button. The soft rooftop disappeared, and I found myself in a convertible, the wind whipping the bangs across my eyes and obscuring my vision. In contrast, Celine looked stunning beside me, with her hair streaming behind her as she raced down the road. I didn't let myself peek at the speedometer to see how fast she was driving. I knew the wind rushing past made it feel even speedier and more dangerous, but I still hugged the edges of my seat until we made it to the serene Lake Shrine.

This place was an oasis, located in Pacific Palisades, right off Sunset Boulevard. Lake Shrine, the property of Self-Realization Fellowship, was a wooded area that shielded its meditation garden from prying eyes.

We stepped past its gates, and Celine halted in her tracks and sucked in her breath. "What is that beautiful archway across the water?"

The first time I'd seen the stark white frame made up of a big rectangle and flanked by two smaller rectangles with golden features on top, I'd also been in awe. "That is the Golden Lotus Temple."

She took several steps forward on the pathway through the gardens, strewn with different colorful plants and flowers. Celine tilted her head toward another unique structure in sight. "Is that a . . . windmill?"

"Windmill Chapel," I said. "You can go in to meditate if you wish." I'd been sorely tempted to go inside after the incident, but in the end, I'd decided against it, not wanting to reflect even more on what had happened to my mom.

I gestured all around us to the quiet environment with its abundant fragrant flowers and half-hidden placards filled with wise sayings. "Go look around. I'll be at that bench over there."

Celine moved over to investigate the various areas. There were influences from Islam, Christianity, Judaism,

Buddhism, and Hinduism around the garden. I wandered over to a mosaic bench with swans on it to sit and reflect on the huge lake the path encircled. Of the five elements of metal, wood, earth, fire, and water, I'd always felt most in tune with the liquid substance.

I dropped my head and gazed into the water, trying to make myself as smooth as its glassy surface. Then a ripple spread out around the spot I was observing. A single swan glided across the lake, breaking my concentration. I glanced up to check on my cousin, in time to watch Celine approach the distinctive windmill structure and tug at its doors. The chapel must have been closed, and I remembered that sometimes they offered limited hours for visitors to enter the space. I wondered what Celine had to think about. Her life seemed as elegant and carefree as the swan gliding on the lake.

Celine peeked over her shoulder. Before she could catch me spying, I dropped my gaze to the ground. For some reason, I sensed that she didn't want me to see her.

Five minutes passed, and I heard her coming up the path. "I like this hidden-places tour that you're taking me on, Yale. Although the whole quiet-zone mood is getting to me. Plus, I'm hungry. Any food recs?"

Free admission to this sanctuary was one thing, but I wasn't sure if I could afford a foodie tour, especially since Celine was some kind of food photographer on social media.

As though sensing my unease, Celine said, "My treat."

"Gladstones it is, then."

I knew that if we went west on Sunset, we'd soon hit Gladstones on PCH. They were known for their spectacular location, steps away from the beach.

We, of course, ordered seafood dishes. Celine took her time setting up her shots with her phone's camera, and I asked her how Instagram worked. She talked about tagging her pictures to make it easier for other users to search by using keywords like #foodie or #forkyeah. She even showed me a shot from last night of the grapefruit boba drink I'd concocted. With Celine's creative lighting, the contents of the glass seemed to almost glitter.

"It looks magical in your picture," I said.

"All about the presentation, like I say."

I deliberately didn't finish my meal when lunch ended. As per tradition, the server ended up wrapping my food to take home in a tin foil extravaganza. Instead of a rushed job, he made sure to create an artistic masterpiece that resembled a mermaid when he twisted up the malleable aluminum. Even though it wasn't an actual food dish, Celine still took a picture of it with her phone, and I didn't bother to hide the grin spreading across my face. This was how I'd imagined us bonding before, like real cousins and friends. I wanted to freeze time and keep this special lunch moment.

I didn't even mind the ride back on PCH with the top down on the car, although I asked Celine to go slower. The excuse I came up with was that we could better see the waves of the Pacific Ocean and those tanned athletic volleyball players at the nets if we took our time coasting along.

In my apartment, she lingered on the threshold and said, "Don't forget to hang up that chef's coat to keep it from creasing."

"Thanks again," I said as I motioned toward the ironing board. "You didn't have to do that."

Her shoulders stiffened. "Like I said before, I'm a stickler about presentation."

Although my home wasn't very presentable, I figured I should play hostess since she'd treated me to a lovely meal. I deposited my tin foil mermaid in the fridge and then said, "Do you want a quick tour while you're here? I was too sleep-deprived to do it before."

"I'd love one."

She followed me along and praised all the modern elements I'd previously dismissed. "Hardwood floors," she said, "make for less trapped dust and last longer. Granite countertops are heat resistant and easy to wipe clean."

She almost sounded like a real estate agent assessing my home, but it did make me see the contemporary amenities in a new light.

When we entered the study, she gasped. "You have an extra bedroom. Nice. Do you have a lot of guests?" She peeked around the corner of the door frame back toward the foyer. "Or a roommate that I haven't met yet?"

I bit the tip of my thumb, a nervous habit from childhood I'd never overcome. It'd be a long time before I could get sleek painted tips with gold nail art like Celine's without ruining them in five minutes flat. "It's for Ba," I said.

Her lips twitched. "Doesn't he have his own place?"

Since my parents had never sold off my childhood home that I'd been born and raised in, I bet Celine and her family still remembered it. "Yes. He's in the same small house in Palms."

"Why don't you two live together? That's what I do."

I gave her a blank look, which she must have misinterpreted.

She tilted her nose in the air. "There's nothing wrong with living with your parents. It's cultural."

"Practically speaking, it'd be great to be with Ba—I'd get to save on rent even—but living on my own has nothing to do with rebelling against filial piety." I started chewing the edge of my thumbnail. "I just can't stay in a house filled with reminders."

Her eyes widened, maybe because of my subtle confession of grief.

She made a soft noise in the back of her throat. "Hey, what's that blinking light?"

I glanced over at the answering machine, which had a

new message on it. "Huh. Maybe it's Ba wondering how the food stall went?"

The recorded message didn't belong to my dad. Instead a voice from late last night resounded in the air. Detective Strauss spoke with a strong bass tone in his short message: "Miss Yee, can you give me a call back when you get this? I have some further questions for you."

I phoned the detective back straightaway.

"Miss Yee—"

"Please. Call me Yale. I'm not a schoolteacher." *Especially not* your *instructor.* I didn't think Detective Strauss could've been much more than a few years older than me.

"I understand that you were selling drinks at your food stall last night, Yale."

I gripped the phone tighter in my hand while Celine inched closer, no doubt in an effort to overhear the conversation. "Along with some food items."

He continued, "Do you remember handing out a glass in the shape of a light bulb?"

"Yes. My cousin had the idea to serve our drinks in special beverage containers."

A slight pause ensued. When he spoke again, the detective's voice seemed to rumble even lower. "Your cousin was there last night?"

"Yes. We ran the booth together."

"You didn't mention her before."

I glanced at where Celine stood hovering. Had I forgotten to talk about my cousin? I bet I hadn't even formed coherent sentences late last night.

The detective spoke. "Are you still there, Yale?"

"Sorry, I got lost in thought."

"Based on the contact info you gave me, the Eastwood Village Police Station isn't too far from your apartment. Would you and your cousin be available to drop by this afternoon?"

The detective had asked it like a question, but I knew

I didn't really have a choice, especially in the face of authority. Besides, I understood how death affected not just the person who died but the family around them, how people needed closure in their lives. I worried about the dead person's relatives.

My cousin shook her head and started to speak, but I cut her off.

"Celine and I would be more than happy to talk with you, Detective," I said.

FOUR

LIKE ALL THE PLACES IN EASTWOOD VILLAGE, THE police station was within walking distance of my apartment. The building had a sunny yellow exterior with plenty of windows that lent it a friendly vibe. Celine and I walked through the front doors into an open-space lobby with sleek linoleum flooring. To my right, I noticed a community room that looked like a nice space for important meetings. Directly in front of us lay a glass-partitioned booth. We went up to the officer on duty there, spoke through the intercom, and asked for Detective Strauss.

We didn't even need to sit in the waiting area with its row of hard-backed plastic chairs before the detective stepped through a side door and greeted us. Detective Strauss had close-cropped dark hair and piercing jade eyes. I definitely pegged him for being in his early thirties, around Celine's and my own age. He first glanced at me and then shifted his gaze to Celine.

She'd dressed up for the chat and looked very fashionable in her flowing lavender jumpsuit—she'd had to tell me the term for the one-piece ensemble—with a deep V-neck.

"You look familiar," he said to Celine. "Have I seen you somewhere before?"

Celine kept her gaze locked with his, a blush rising on her cheeks.

I interrupted their staring contest. "My cousin just flew in from Hong Kong. I doubt you've met her before."

Celine tossed her wavy hair. "But I do get mistaken for celebrities all the time."

"Right." The detective's jaw tightened, and he said, "Let's take you to one of our interview rooms."

As he walked us down a narrow corridor, I imagined someplace clinical: a tight space with hard metal chairs and a sturdy table. However, when he finally opened the door to the numbered room, I found myself feeling like I'd stepped into someone's living room.

A dove-gray suede love seat and two cushioned armchairs were positioned facing one another. In a corner, a small table with a mint green desk lamp resided. One of the walls even had an oil painting of a forest surrounded by mountains.

Celine dropped into the love seat and crossed her legs.

After a brief hesitation, I sat down next to her and said, "I didn't realize you guys had rooms like these."

The detective's green eyes seemed to darken. "This is our soft interview room . . . for when we talk to victims of sensitive crimes."

"Oh." I shifted in the love seat.

"Anyway, I thought this would be a nicer setting for you ladies. It's Yale and Celine, right?"

My cousin gave a brief nod, and the detective took his spot in one of the armchairs. He perched on its edge and pulled out a notepad. I liked him a little better for using paper and pencil to jot down information.

"I need to clear up a few points in this investigation," he said. "One is about the light bulb containers." He pointed the tip of his pencil at Celine. "Tell me about them."

"Sure." She crossed her legs the other way. "They're these neat glasses I found, and I thought we could make a marketing splash with them. Offer something beyond the usual cup for our drinks at Canai and Chai."

"That's the name of your food stall?"

Celine nodded, and the detective scribbled in his notepad.

"Did any other vendor have those glasses at the night market?" he asked.

"No. They were one of a kind. Which I'm pretty sure made us the place to be—or eat—at."

The detective continued writing and then asked, "What kind of drinks were you making?"

Celine swung her foot out in my direction. "That's Yale's specialty. She's the chef."

I counted the beverages on my hand. "We had black tea, green tea, and aloe vera juice."

"Did you add any special ingredients to those?" the detective asked.

"Well, condensed milk if the customers wanted their drinks creamy. Also, boba. We had three different flavors: regular, brown sugar, and lychee."

"Nothing else?" Detective Strauss hovered his pencil above his notepad.

I scratched the back of my neck and thought hard about last night's menu. "On some orders, I added grapefruit bits to the green tea to make it more refreshing."

"You wouldn't have put anything inedible in the beverages . . . ?"

What an odd question. I crossed my arms over my chest. "It's a food stall, Detective Strauss. Why would I serve something inedible or undrinkable to customers?"

"Aren't tapioca balls known to be choking hazards?" the detective asked.

"Not if you chew them properly." I frowned. "Why are you questioning us so much?"

"It's because"—the detective's eyes flicked between Celine and me—"we found your special light bulb, your unique glass, at the scene of the crime."

I remembered the forensics team recovering it as I'd left the fountain. "Maybe the customer wanted to keep it as a souvenir?"

Detective Strauss raised his eyebrow at me. "So you did know the victim? Because you didn't say that before."

"No, but if they had our glass, it seems logical that we'd served them."

He took out a phone, scrolled through it, and presented a picture to the both of us. "Recognize this woman?"

The shot was taken near the fountain, the body in the same curled position, but it was a close-up of the face. The clothes I'd thought of only as black in the dim lighting now were revealed as a ninja costume.

I replied with a stammer. "It was our first paying customer of the evening."

"Does the name Jordan Chang mean anything to you?" He carefully watched my reaction.

I shook my head.

"It's interesting to note," he said, "that not only did we find your unique glass near Miss Chang's body, but the medical examiner discovered something odd in her stomach contents. Gold metal flakes. Do you two know anything about that?"

Beside me, Celine gave a sharp inhale.

I looked at her in alarm.

Celine uncrossed her legs and stared at the detective. "I put the gold in the drink," she said.

"You did what?" I said.

"Placed some gold flakes into our first drink. You saw my foodie shot."

The Instagram picture she'd shown me during our beach lunch at Gladstones floated back to my mind. The drink I'd made had *glittered*. I thought it had been a trick of the light, but she'd actually infused my drink with shimmery metal.

I replayed the memory of last night in my head. Celine had poured the grapefruit green tea from my boring plastic cup to her more elegant light bulb glass. While her back had been turned to me, she must have added another ingredient to the tea.

"Those gold flakes were the only odd contents in her stomach," Detective Strauss said. "May I take a look at them?"

"I have the bottle back in my hotel room," Celine said, fluttering her gravity-defying lashes.

The detective fiddled with the tie around his neck. "I don't want to intrude on your private space. You can bring it back here."

My cousin smoothed out her jumpsuit. "Actually, I can't. I need to get ready for night market. This time I'll be in costume."

I gave Celine a pointed look, but she ignored me. Was she deliberately trying to not cooperate?

"I'll be at the event this evening trying to find witnesses," Detective Strauss said. "I'll go to your booth first thing tonight."

I swallowed hard.

After the detective left us in the lobby of the police station, I gripped Celine's arm.

"Why would you mess with my drink?" I whispered to Celine.

"It needed more razzle-dazzle, like those cupcakes with those harmless silver balls on them. People eat those all the time."

Those culinary decorations, called dragées, made baked goods more elegant looking. If they were allowed on cakes and cookies, maybe the detective's theory about a strange chemical reaction could be dismantled. I didn't want anything sullying the reputation of the food stall, and in turn, my dad's restaurant. "I'm going to walk to the library and do research on metals in food," I said.

"And I'm going shopping to get my costume, makeup, and accessories for tonight."

I wondered about Celine's priorities. Then again, I bet her parents' money often solved any difficulties that surfaced for her. For my family's sake, I sure hoped her name would be cleared tonight.

The Eastwood Village Public Library had high ceilings and soft beige carpet. Patrons sitting at wooden tables flipped pages, making a hushed paper whisper that calmed my nerves. I examined the 641 section of the Dewey decimal system and found a score of cookbooks, but nothing specific to the dangers or safety of metallic toppings in food or drinks. After an hour of searching various tomes, I approached the reference librarian and asked for his help. He sat at a quaint repurposed card catalog turned desk. The table was devoid of items on its well-worn surface aside from a desktop computer and a donation box for old spectacles.

With a clacking of his keyboard, the librarian accessed an online database of articles and showed me his findings. On the plus side, edible gold existed and was "inert," meaning it didn't interact with anything in the body. The negative, for Californians, was that a 2003 lawsuit existed where silver dragées were specifically banned from use due to potential toxicity. I bit at my thumbnail. Like the detective, I needed to examine that bottle of gold Celine had.

After the required food and drinks preparation, I showed up at the night market with my utility cart. I wanted to make sure I had everything ready before the event opened and that I had plenty of time to scrutinize the gold flakes and question Celine about her purchase. As it turned out, I must have arrived too early because my cousin was nowhere to be found.

Once I set up Canai and Chai food-and-drink-wise, I still had spare time and decided to venture out and meet the neighboring vendors. The first stall I went to had a huge banner draped over the counter advertising "La Pupusería de Reyes." A blown-up image of what looked like puffy tortillas decorated the sign.

I walked up to the counter, where a man in his late twenties stood, adjusting a placard that showed they accepted credit cards for payment. Behind him, I noticed a grandmotherly figure inspecting a portable griddle. A huge cooler sat near the cooking equipment.

Finally noticing me, the man said, "You're early to the market. Did you sneak in?"

"I would never—" Then I observed his wide smile and knew he'd been teasing. "I'm your next-door neighbor. At Canai and Chai. Currently, we serve cold appetizers and drinks. What's your specialty?"

"The huge photo didn't clue you in?" The man had dark hair, half-shaven on the sides. "We're all about *pupusas*."

"Those tortillas?" I pointed to the banner.

He put a hand against his heart in mock indignation. "They're nothing like tortillas. Maybe more like savory griddle cakes."

"I don't think I've ever had one."

"We'll need to remedy that. Plus, my grandmother makes the best pupusas in the entire world."

"That's a huge claim."

"You've never had her cooking," he said. "Since you're

working tonight, why don't you drop by tomorrow to our main restaurant? It'd be my pleasure to introduce a beautiful woman like you to your very first pupusa."

My mind snagged on the word "beautiful," and I felt heat radiate my cheeks.

"Here's a special offer just for you," he said, rolling up his shirtsleeves and flashing me the tattoos spiraling across his forearms. "We're located within walking distance of here. Ask for me by name. We open at ten tomorrow."

He handed me a business card with the line, "Good for one free pupusa—Blake." I pocketed it with halting thanks and stumbled away. Men had never paid much attention to me, although I'd had a few compliment me at Wing Fat when I waitressed there. I always thought they did so to get better service.

With my long hours helping out at the family restaurant, I'd never had a chance to date in high school. Then in community college, I'd focused hard on my studies, thinking I'd eventually transfer to a university after I finished my two years there.

I'd walked to the stall on the other side of Canai and Chai while lost in thought. It was called Ho's Small Eats. I balked at the name, recognizing it. It couldn't be the same Ho family, right?

Then again, the local Asian restaurant community was small and tight-knit. The interconnectedness often served as a communal grapevine of gossip. Restaurant owners would frequent each other's establishments, and the kids would get dragged along. I'd often found myself wedged between my parents sitting in a booth at Ho's on a Tuesday afternoon (the only day we closed the restaurant—our "slow" day). We enjoyed ordering their Taiwanese lunch specials. I'd gone to school with the owners' son, Nik Ho, my childhood academic rival. But I hadn't seen or wanted to contact him after high school graduation.

I could spot Nik's bedhead even from this distance and bypassed the stall, scurrying toward a silver food truck instead. It had a cute window to order from and a foldout counter. Below Freezing sounded like a great place to get dessert. Stamped on the food truck were several icons for social media and a hashtag for their business: #Below-FreezingIceCream.

I wandered over to their window and checked their menu to see if I could find my favorite flavor.

"Can I help you?" A woman in her forties wearing a white lab coat popped up from below the window.

I shuffled a few steps backward. "I'm sorry. I didn't see you there."

"I was below the frame, going over our inventory of spoons and cups."

"Right," I said. "Do you happen to serve mango ice cream?"

"Yes, and it's one of my absolute favorites. Would you like a scoop?"

"I can't now, but maybe later." Jerking my thumb toward the left, I said, "I'm selling at the food stall over there, Canai and Chai."

"Sounds like an excellent combo."

I hesitated before responding. "Well, we're still working on our menu."

A hand clamped down on my shoulder, and I jumped.

"It's only me," Celine said. "It took longer than I thought to get ready, but I made it."

I turned around and observed my cousin in her full costumed self. She wore a clingy one-piece ensemble in orange with stripes running across it. A fuzzy tiger's tail was clipped to the back of it. She also wore knee-high black leather boots. "Going for the wildcat look, I see."

"Hear me roar." She made clawing motions with her hands.

"How about I hear you explain something instead," I

said, marching her to the privacy of our booth. "Show me that bottle of gold flakes before the detective arrives." I quickly explained to Celine about my library research and how even those "harmless" silver balls she'd talked about were considered dangerous and banned in California.

She dug into the cardboard box she'd deposited in the back of the booth and pulled out a clear bottle. There wasn't much printed on the label beyond the two words: "Gold Flakes."

I rotated the bottle, which revealed nothing beyond the thin gold pieces inside. Then I tilted it upside down and spied a barcode sticker on the bottom. Besides the jumble of numbers, in tiny fine print it read, "For decorative purposes."

"Uh-oh," I said.

"What's wrong?" a male voice asked. I looked up to find Detective Strauss staring at me as I held the incriminating bottle in my hands.

FIVE

"MAY I?" DETECTIVE STRAUSS ASKED, BUT HE didn't wait for an answer before coming over to where I stood.

I handed him the bottle with reluctance.

In less than a minute, the detective had spotted the fine print on the bottom. "I'll have to take this into evidence," he said.

"Okay," Celine said. "Do you also need the receipt?"

"This should do. Thanks for your cooperation." He turned to my cousin, and his eyes widened slightly. "That's some costume."

I detected a hint of admiration in his tone. Celine did wear it well. If I'd donned the same outfit, I would have looked like Tigger. Celine looked like a powerful tigress, especially with those distinctive amber eyes of hers.

My cousin, placing her priorities on fashion, still probably didn't realize how much trouble those gold flakes could get us in. I started imagining judges, trials, jail, the whole nine yards. "It could've been something else that caused Jordan's death, right?" I asked Detective Strauss.

He looked at me, not with unkind eyes, but said, "The medical examiner found puncture wounds in her stomach. Metal can do that."

"But little flakes of gold?"

"The other stomach contents seemed typical. Tapioca balls, fruit . . . Plus, there's that light bulb container near her body."

The evidence really was stacking up against us. I felt my breath quicken. "Could you get a second opinion?"

"Tell you what, Yale. I'll turn this in to the lab and see what they say about the gold."

"And in the meantime, you said you'll be looking for eyewitnesses from last night?" My hope for some wild alternative for Jordan Chang's demise must have been evident.

"Of course. I have a picture of Miss Chang with me and will be asking around. I'll do my due diligence," he said.

Once Detective Strauss left, I motioned for my cousin to come closer. Lowering my voice, I said, "Show me that receipt ASAP."

She rummaged through her slouchy leather bag and retrieved a crumpled piece of paper. I was surprised she'd even kept the receipt, given the lack of organization apparent in her purse.

I smoothed it out, hoping to find that she'd purchased the metallic decorations at, say, a bakery. Unfortunately, she'd gotten the gold flakes at Crafts City. "You bought this at a hobby store?"

"What?" She stood with her arms akimbo and faced me. "It's a catchall store. Don't give me that look. I bought the gold in the cooking section."

I didn't think Detective Strauss would care much about

the aisle where my cousin had located the lethal bottle. "Can I keep this?"

"Sure." She fiddled with her hair until an even amount of wavy strands bounced against each shoulder. "But put it away quickly because here comes a customer."

I turned around to find a young Asian woman approaching our food stall. Her long dark hair was parted down the center, and she wore thick-framed black glasses. Her eyes seemed to study my cousin and me more than our whiteboard menu.

"We have appetizers of spicy cold cucumbers and soy sauce eggs," I said. "Also, there's a wide variety of drinks to choose from."

The woman pushed her glasses against the bridge of her nose and sniffled. "This might have been one of the last places where she ate or drank at."

"Excuse me?" I tamped down my growing unease.

"I'm Jacey, and my sister is Jordan Chang. She was here at the night market yesterday at your stall." From behind me, I heard a tiny gasp from Celine, and I bit down hard on my tongue to keep from reacting in a like manner.

Jacey continued, "She was dressed as a ninja. Black from head to toe."

I focused on Jacey's top, a simple teal blouse, and murmured, "Yes, and she had amazing violet eyes, right?"

"That was her." Jacey took time reading through our menu and said, "I'd like green tea with fresh grapefruit and black tapioca pearls." She pulled out a pretty silk coin purse.

After hearing the drink order, I noticed Celine shifting the contents around in a box. She lifted out a light bulb glass, and I took it from her.

"I'll fill this one," I said. "Why don't you ring her up?"

I provided a gold-free refreshing beverage to Jacey. She gripped it with her right hand, as she examined the glass and its contents with care. While she studied our drink, I noticed two silver rings printed with "Big sister" and "Little sister" stacked together on her thumb.

"Enjoy!" My cousin practically chirped the word out, and it seemed too cheery in light of the recent death of Jacey's sister.

I watched Jacey scrutinize the names of the other food stalls with a frown on her face. It didn't seem like she thought we were the ones responsible for Jordan's death, or at least, not yet. If it'd been an accidental death due to Celine's impetuous addition, that would be tragic. I shuddered to think of the alternative, though. Detective Strauss had mentioned puncture wounds in Jordan's stomach—those sounded devastating and hinted at malicious intent.

The detective had seemed forthcoming with us about wanting to ensure "due diligence" while handling this case. I wondered if after more thorough investigating, he'd clear my cousin of any suspicion. I knew firsthand that sometimes one thing masked another.

When my mom's old car had experienced a glitch in its electronics system, Ba had blamed the manufacturer for causing her death. Investigation had uncovered that the vehicle had malfunctioned, making her stall on the road. Thankfully, she'd been on a small residential street, and nobody had crashed into her while she was stuck in the middle of the road. The traumatic shock, though, had triggered something fatal in her body. Eventually, we learned that it had been her own faulty organ, an enlarged heart, that had caused her life to shut down.

An orange tail swished in my face and interrupted my morbid thoughts.

"Earth to Yale," my cousin said. "Maybe you should be wearing a spacesuit costume . . . Anyway, I don't know why business is super slow tonight compared to yesterday. Do you mind if I walk around and do some foodstagramming?"

I waved her off. At least one of us could still enjoy the festive night.

Celine wandered around for about an hour. In that time span, I could count on one hand how many customers showed up at Canai and Chai.

When she returned, Celine said, "Look what I got. A free meal and a dessert."

My cousin placed two scoops of ice cream in a cup on the counter before me. Then she plunged her hand into her purse, felt around its contours, and slapped a familiar-looking business card down. It appeared that Blake had also invited my cousin for a free pupusa sample for the following day. It made me feel duped.

"Dig in," Celine said, offering me a small plastic spoon for the ice cream.

I scooped up the sweet cold dessert. Despite it not being my favorite mango flavor but Thai tea instead, I ate spoonful after spoonful, reveling at the spices on my tongue, especially the kick of the tangy tamarind. Eating the dessert also helped to physically numb my senses. It kept me from thinking about our slow business and the implications of an open murder case.

Celine nudged my shoulder. "The way you eat, I'd think you were born in the Year of the Pig."

"Very funny," I said, but I slowed down my scooping and diverted my attention to watch the attendees passing by our booth. One of them, dressed as Pippi Longstocking, with her bright red braided hair, held a light bulb glass drink in her hand. However, it wasn't any of my teas in the container, but a purple beverage swishing around in the glass.

"Our cup," I said, darting out from the food stall and chasing down the woman. I managed to catch up and tap her on the shoulder. It wasn't that hard because she'd paused to watch pachinko, which looked kind of like vertical pinball.

She stopped observing the rubber ball bouncing down a tunnel of needles and turned to face me. "Yes?"

I pointed at her beverage. "That's a neat light bulb glass. Where'd you get it?" For a moment, I wondered if she'd come last night to our stall, but I didn't recognize her freckled Pippi face.

Then she said, "From the Taiwanese place. It's an off-shoot of Ho's, located in Westwood. I got the taro milk tea. Highly recommended." She lifted her glass up to me and swished it around.

"Thanks," I said before squaring my shoulders and marching over to interrogate Nik Ho. I didn't realize that Ho's Small Eats had been serving their drinks in light bulb glasses, too. If that was the case, maybe the empty drink container I'd seen last night didn't belong to our stall but to our food-serving neighbor.

I had to wait for a few customers to disperse before attracting Nik's attention. He didn't seem surprised to see me loitering at Ho's Small Eats.

I disliked the bedhead hair that Nik had styled for himself. He'd swapped his preppy-boy haircut from middle school, grew it long, and spiked it up in various directions using copious amounts of gel, starting from ninth grade. His messy hairdo now also had streaks of bleached strands in it. Nik's round face remained the same as before, except he sported a full goatee to make him seem more mature, I supposed.

Using my dim sum personality test, I'd long assigned him the dish of steamed red bean bun. I'd been fooled more than once trying to grab a barbecue pork bun, only to end up with bean in my mouth. The red filling was called *dow sah*, which meant "bean sand." That's how disappointed I felt when being tricked to eat one of those buns when I'd expected sweet pork instead. I also always felt a little sandy after interacting with Nik.

I spoke up over the sound of the deep-fryer unit in the

background, where Ai Ho, Nik's mother, was cooking something tantalizing. Without preamble, I said, "You're using the same light bulb glasses as us."

Even his facial hair couldn't hide his smirk when he answered back. "You mean, you're using light bulb glasses like *us*."

"Did you have those yesterday?" I asked.

"Yep. Not as original as you thought, huh?" He pointed to the Canai and Chai banner. "What a way to fake out the customers. Hiding the real name won't work, though. The food map still lists your stand as 'Yee Snacks,' so everyone knows who's really behind that food stall. Can't believe your dad let you run it."

I straightened up to my full five-five frame. "He believes in me. Always has."

"Don't see a crowd around your stall," Nik said. "Could it be your cooking?"

"Very funny. What are you doing in Los Angeles anyway? The last I heard you were enjoying life in Sacramento." Nik had gone to school near the state capital and had majored in food science. Before I'd stopped working at Wing Fat, he'd still been up north, but then again, I hadn't listened to the restaurant owner grapevine in years.

The oil stopped sizzling in the fryer, and Nik's mother glanced my way. She placed a stack of popcorn chicken, spiced with chili powder and topped with basil, on a plastic plate and came our way.

"Nikola, your snack is ready," she said, putting the full plate on the counter, along with a few long wooden skewers to stab and pick up the bite-sized fried chicken pieces.

"Um, thanks, Ma," Nik said, his face turning a deep red.

He hated being called by his official first name. Although I'd been named after a university, he'd been given the full weight of inventor Nikola Tesla's acclaim and history to shoulder. Also, he hated being coddled by his mother, especially in front of me.

"Hello, Mrs. Ho," I said.

Nik's mother, now with more lines around her eyes than I remembered, blinked at me. "Yale Yee?" she said, and I nodded.

She continued, "I know Ah Sing applied for a food stall here." She'd used Ba's nickname to refer to him. "Is your father around?"

"No, Auntie. He decided to pass the food duties to me for this weekend."

"Capable hands, I'm sure," she said. "You're such a good daughter, letting him rest. We all need that as we get older."

"You look as energetic as ever, Auntie."

She stretched out her wrists and grimaced. "I wish I were about a decade younger." That was probably around the last time she'd seen me in her restaurant, before Ba had altered our schedule to a full seven days a week of work after Mom had passed away.

"Good thing you have Nicky here to help out." He hated that moniker and flinched when I said it.

"Nikola." Mrs. Ho shook her head in slow motion. "Even after his fancy food science degree, I still have to do the cooking."

"It's because you won't let me—" Nik broke off his sentence as his mother's mouth flattened into a thin and disapproving line. For offspring to say something disparaging about a parent meant a violation of the unsaid rule of respecting elders.

"You know, there's more than enough to share," Nik's mother told me, gesturing to the popcorn chicken. She'd always shown me care. Given her first name of Ai, meaning "Love," it was quite appropriate.

"No, thank you, Auntie. I'd better get back to work and help my cousin."

"Your cousin?" Mrs. Ho asked, surprised.

"Yes, my only one," I said. "You might remember seeing her years ago. Celine."

"How old is she again?"

"Three years older than me."

Her eyes seemed to shine with hope. It'd been clear ages ago that Nik and I would never get along, despite some subtle messages from Mrs. Ho, like having us share plates of food. A cousin in town, though, meant a new marriage prospect for her to mine.

I left Nik's mother dreaming away while Nik gobbled the snack he'd been lovingly given. Returning to Celine's side, I said, "Ho's Small Eats has been siphoning off our customers by using the same light bulb glass drinks."

"Really?" Celine almost growled the word out, her tigress attitude matching her costume. "I thought we were the only ones."

"Guess not, but that might be a plus," I said as I watched a tired Detective Strauss approach our food stall.

Perhaps now in a foul mood by my telling her we weren't the first to use the unique glass, Celine occupied herself with cleaning up. Of course, she could've been acting practical. It was only half an hour until the event's official closing time.

I wondered if Detective Strauss had spent his entire time canvassing the night market and asking questions to both attendees and vendors. "How'd it go?" I said as I slid him a soy sauce egg on a paper plate, along with a pair of disposable wooden chopsticks. "On the house. I can spot a hungry man a mile away."

He glanced at the dark brown egg but didn't reach for it.

"Go ahead. It's just a hard-boiled egg—with more flavor."

Detective Strauss used the chopsticks to split apart the

egg. He placed a piece into his mouth and chewed. "Tasty."

"My dad's handiwork," I said. "He's a genius in the kitchen. He runs Wing Fat, the local dim sum restaurant."

The detective's green eyes seemed to glitter. "That restaurant always has a line snaking out the door."

"There's a reason for that." I waited until he finished the entire egg before asking, "Did you find any new leads?" More promising ones than my cousin, I wanted to add.

"Can't say that I did." He dabbed at his mouth with a paper napkin. Having some food in his stomach seemed to make him less reserved. "I can't believe the number of people walking around here."

I glanced at the crowd, noting revelers dressed as zombies, gangsters, and magicians. "Well, I found out something very intriguing while you were gone. Ho's Small Eats next door also uses light bulb containers."

"Are you sure about that?"

I pointed over to where Nik was serving a customer and giving him a glass filled with bubble milk tea.

The detective balled up his napkin, adding it to his empty plate. He dumped the trash into the nearest receptacle and strode toward Ho's Small Eats with determination.

I watched him start asking Nik a flurry of questions. At first, Nik looked nervous. He patted down his puffy bedhead hair once or twice.

Then he noticed me staring at them. Nik crossed his arms and seemed to give terse replies to Detective Strauss.

In the end, Nik nestled a glass light bulb container inside a brown paper bag and handed it over to the detective. I turned to my cousin and said, "Mission accomplished."

"Maybe. Maybe not." Her eyes focused on something over my shoulder.

I whipped around as Detective Strauss dropped by our booth and held up the bag.

"You got the evidence," I said.

"What I have is an empty glass. It's interesting that you both were selling drinks in similar containers." He drummed his fingers in a soft dance against the serving counter. "When all is said and done, though, we're still more interested in the things the victim ate than the container they came in."

The detective left after dropping the heavy-handed hint. Everything came back to Jordan Chang's eating habits. What could she have eaten to cause such damage to her stomach and result in her subsequent death? Could it have been the gold flakes my cousin had added to the tea? I certainly hoped it'd been something unlinked to our family, even if it meant that Jordan had enemies.

I jammed my hands in my pockets in frustration. The edge of something hard bit into my palm. Wincing, I pulled out the offending object, the business card that advertised La Pupusería de Reyes.

Celine spied it in my hands. "Oh, I thought I'd left that on the counter. Anyway, I told Blake I'd be there at ten for sure. You should come along. I'm sure he won't mind."

I couldn't believe she thought she'd been the only person invited. I *would* come along, if only to see the precious reaction of Blake and my cousin when I showed up to their "private" encounter.

SIX

IN THE MORNING, CELINE AND I MET UP AT LA PU-
pusería de Reyes. She parked her royal blue Boxster in
the empty customer parking lot. Maybe people didn't get
a pupusa craving this early in the morning.

My cousin had put some effort into her appearance. I
could tell by how her hair bounced against her shoulders.
She'd also contoured her cheeks somehow and outlined
her bow lips with a rich red lipstick. I felt the same wanting as I had during childhood and could smell a ghost
whiff of Dr Pepper in the air. In contrast to her primping,
I'd barely splashed some cold water over my face before
leaving my apartment.

The outside walls of the restaurant were painted a
blinding white, and a sign done in blue block letters hung
above the doorway. We walked inside to find tiled flooring and compact tables. There were no decorations on the
walls except for a flag of El Salvador pinned to one of
them.

The same grandmotherly woman from the food stall shuffled toward us and held up her fingers. "Two?"

"Yes." My cousin smiled at her. "I'm also looking for Blake. Can you tell him I'm here? My name is Celine."

The woman nodded and disappeared through the door to the kitchen.

We sat below the flag at a wooden table meant for four and waited for Blake's arrival. He came stepping out of the kitchen within minutes.

"Celine," he said, "how nice of you to come."

He hovered at our table and blinked at me, as though I were a mirage he was trying to make disappear from sight.

"Surprise, Blake," I said.

Celine's mouth dropped open.

"You two ladies know each other?" Blake asked.

Neither Celine nor I answered him.

My cousin whispered to me, "How did you meet Blake?"

I pulled the restaurant's business card out of my pocket and flicked it on the table, like a blackjack dealer. "You weren't the only one who got invited, Celine."

Blake ran his hand across one of the shaved sides of his head. "Huh. I didn't know you knew each other. Also, I figured you two wouldn't come at the exact same time."

"How could you, Blake?" I laced my voice with mock indignation. "I thought I was special."

Blake took a step backward and glanced over his shoulder. I wondered if he thought he could make a run for the kitchen and hide in there until we left.

Celine shifted in her chair and spoke up. "Very funny, Yale."

Blake held his hands up, palms out, and backed away another step. "Uh, I don't want any trouble."

I dropped the act. Did he think we would actually fight over him? What an ego. Men didn't mean that much to me . . . unless Mr. Darcy himself ended up tumbling out of the pages of Austen's novel. "Please," I said. "I'm just here for the free pupusa. I was playing with you."

Celine added, "But I'm single. Not looking for anything too serious at this point."

Blake angled his body toward Celine, and his face seemed to open up. "Same here, but one of the women I went out with didn't get that. She wanted to be exclusive with me right away. Even issued me an ultimatum, but that's not how I roll."

"Did you lure this lucky lady in with your pupusa talk?" I asked, with a hint of sarcasm.

"No," he said with a straight face. "She was really taken by my *ensaladas*."

All this talk about salads and pupusas made me quite hungry. "Our free pupusas, Blake."

He glanced between the both of us. "Neither of you are vegan or vegetarian, right?"

When we answered in the negative, he said he'd be back with chicken and cheese pupusas.

They came off the griddle piping hot. I blew on mine only once or twice before taking a bite into the most delicious stuffed tortilla (could I still call it that?) I'd ever tasted.

Meanwhile, Celine pulled out her camera and started taking multiple shots of her untouched pupusa from various angles. She even stood up on her chair to snap one of the pictures.

"Oh, you're one of those," Blake said, crossing his arms, and pushing up his sleeves. This time around I got a better look at his tattoos, which were images of snakes crisscrossing around his arms.

My cousin paused in her picture taking. "A skilled photographer?" she said.

"A foodie-grammer. That girl I dated, Jordan, she does that, too."

I didn't realize Jordan was such a popular female name.

Celine's face seemed to glow from within. "Ooh, maybe I know her. What's her handle?"

"It's long. Let me spell it out for you." He took the business card on the table, flipped it to the blank side, and wrote it down: ma_jor_hankering.

Celine's lipsticked mouth dropped open, looking like a miniature cave for a moment. "I recognize that account," she said. "But I thought it was a guy. The foodstagrammer goes by the name of Chang."

"That's her last name," Blake said.

I put the two names together. The previously tantalizing pupusa no longer appealed to me. I pushed it away, even though I'd only taken a few bites. "Oh my gosh," I said. "The woman you dated was Jordan Chang."

"You know her?" He squinted his dark eyes at me. "She graduated just last year from UCLA. Are you also an alumna?"

I snatched the business card from the table and took my merry time placing it into my pocket to tamp down a sudden sense of shame at my not having graduated from any university.

In a light tone, Celine said, "Jordan came by our booth the other night and got one of our signature drinks. That's how we met her."

I didn't correct or elaborate on Celine's abbreviated version of our knowledge of Jordan Chang. Blake didn't need to know any more, like how I'd stumbled onto her body late at night. I wondered if he even knew that Jordan had died. He'd referred to her using the present tense, and they'd only gone out a few times, after all. Had Detective Strauss talked to him yet? Did I need to break the horrible news to him? No, I wasn't prepared to be the messenger of bad tidings.

Blake must have felt my growing unease because he

soon left us alone. It seemed to take a long time for Celine to finish her pupusa as I counted out the minutes. When she was finally done, I made sure to slip ten dollars on the table for Blake even though I couldn't really afford it.

As soon as we'd left the restaurant, Celine said, "You know, even fifteen percent of free is zero. Why'd you leave him a tip? That's essentially like us having treated him instead of the other way around."

"I felt bad for the guy. It didn't seem right that I knowingly didn't tell him about the death of someone he'd dated."

My cousin looked over her shoulder back at the restaurant. "He didn't seem too serious about her."

"Yeah, makes me wonder if the love I read about in books really exists."

"Men in real life are way more interesting," Celine said, with a smack of her lips, before sliding into the driver's seat. "Where to next, Yale?"

"By the way, thanks for driving." The fact that Celine had a rental car made it easy for me to squeeze in multiple errands before I had to show up for duty at The Literary Narnia. I took in a deep breath to calm myself, still not ready for the reality of my last working day at my favorite bookstore.

Celine started the car, bringing me out of my reverie.

"It's time to go to Crafts City," I said.

The arts and crafts store was located right off the 405, making it easy to spot from the freeway. It had stylized signage with an outline of a skyscape along with the words "Crafts City."

Inside, the store had strong fluorescent lighting, which made everything feel clinical. Signs with dark lettering hung down from the ceiling like a verbal road map.

The "Cooking and Baking Supplies" section consisted

of three rows of tools and decorations. Celine showed me the shelf where she'd found the gold flakes.

"That's a relief to see that they're next to the rainbow sprinkles and sugar pearls," I said.

My cousin whipped out her phone. "Let me take a quick pic." I could see the value of a phone for its rapid camera capabilities. Detective Strauss couldn't deny that the gold flakes had been surrounded by edible decorations.

I picked up the same brand and bottle that Celine had purchased. Then we strode toward the registers and the long line.

When our turn came, I let a customer go in front of us in order to end up at the register with a middle-aged (and hopefully knowledgeable) woman behind it.

"Hi," I said. "My cousin bought this same type of gold flakes here before." After I'd placed the bottle down with care, I pulled out the old receipt and laid it on the counter.

I continued, "We wanted to make sure that the gold can not only be used for decoration but is also edible."

The woman examined the bottle. "We sell those here all the time, but I'm not sure if you can eat them or not. Let me double-check the item description."

She scanned the SKU code and looked at her screen. "These are pure gold, twenty-three karat to be exact, which should be okay to consume."

I turned to Celine, and we grinned at each other.

"Just to be sure," I said, tapping at the receipt, "these were the kind we purchased."

The woman scanned the item code and the bottle. "It's a match," she said.

"Perfect," I said, purchasing the gold flakes.

Celine and I thanked the woman for her time before almost skipping out of the store.

"Glad we're in the clear. I've already had enough scandal in my life," Celine said as we got back into the car. "Time to restore my name." She sped through the intersections, even through two yellow lights, to cut our travel time.

Celine took charge at the Eastwood Village Police Station and marched straight up to the reception desk and asked to meet with Detective Strauss through the glass partition.

The cop picked up her phone and dialed the detective's extension. After a moment, she told us, "He's occupied right now. He'll be with you in about ten minutes. Please have a seat."

Celine and I planted ourselves at the edges of the hard-backed plastic chairs. I perched for comfort's sake, and I suspected my cousin did the same, but it could've also been a desire to not sully her clothes.

I tracked every movement out of the side door where we'd previously seen the detective emerge from. After a few minutes of waiting, I noticed a uniformed officer escorting a familiar-looking Asian woman out the door connected to the interior hallway. She wore thick-framed black glasses.

"Jacey," I called out.

She turned toward me and squinted.

"It's Yale Yee," I said. "We met at the night market. My cousin and I run the Canai and Chai booth. You ordered my grapefruit green tea."

She gave me a tight smile. "That was . . . an enlightening . . . drink," she said.

Jacey moved toward the exit, but I stood up and blocked her. Finally, someone who appreciated my cooking. "I'm glad you enjoyed it," I said. "That means a lot to me."

At that very moment, though, I noticed that Jacey had a frown on her face. She also had used the adjective "enlightening," which wasn't a true compliment. The word reminded me of light bulbs. I realized then that Jacey had gotten the exact drink as her sister. Since they were family, they could have ordered the same beverage out of similar tastes, but it seemed like a huge coincidence.

Jacey noticed me watching her and stared back at me with a piercing gaze.

Finally, I asked, "How did you know Jordan had come by our booth and her exact order?"

"Easy. She highlighted everything she ate and drank that night on Insta." I wondered if Jacey had told the detective about that insight.

As if by thinking of him, I'd mentally called out to the man, Detective Strauss came strolling into the lobby.

"This is the second time you ladies have stopped by," he said before noticing that instead of a duo, our group consisted of three people. He paused a few feet away from us.

Jacey blinked at Celine and me through her glasses. "What are you two doing at the station anyway?"

I started biting at my thumb instead of answering. Celine, however, said in an unwavering voice, "We're here to share a lead in the investigation with the detective."

"Is that right?" Jacey said. "Because I now know that my sister must have drunk something suspicious that night to cause her death."

I shuddered at her barbed words.

Detective Strauss took a few steps forward and stood between us. "Miss Chang," he said, "I will be the first to inform you when we have sufficient evidence to press charges."

"See that you do it sooner rather than later," Jacey said, before leaving the station. The air in the lobby suddenly felt frigid, and I rubbed at the hairs rising up on my arms.

"Are you really here about a lead?" Detective Strauss asked us.

"Of course," Celine said, her chin jutting forward. "But it's more about removing a lead from your case."

"Let's talk in a more private setting," Detective Strauss said.

I figured we'd be brought over to the cozy sitting area we'd experienced before, but Detective Strauss led us down the corridor past the previous room and over to a different door. When we opened it, I almost didn't want to enter.

This chamber—I couldn't think of a better word to describe it—looked to be about a third of the living room set we'd previously enjoyed. It didn't have any amenities like the dove-gray suede love seat and cushioned armchairs. No artwork adorned the bare walls. The furniture in the room was made of unforgiving metal. A few folding chairs were shoved up against a thick table. The floor was hard concrete.

Detective Strauss urged us forward and then closed the door. It shut with a clang. Celine and I rearranged two of the chairs, scraping them against the floor in the process, and sat down next to each other. I noticed that the metallic surface of the nearby table bore scratch marks of an unknown origin.

The detective took another chair and faced us. He pulled out his notepad and pencil. "Go ahead and tell me."

I looked up at the upper corners of the room and noticed a mounted camera. No doubt the detective would be recording everything Celine and I said.

I nudged her shoulder and whispered, "I think this is on record."

Celine placed her hands palms up on the metal table and said, "I have nothing to hide. You heard what the Crafts City lady said."

I took out the receipt and positioned it in front of the detective.

Celine pulled up the image on her phone of the gold flakes shelved next to the rainbow sprinkles and said,

"See where the gold flakes are kept? Everything on this shelf is edible."

"Are you sure about that?" the detective said.

"Of course I am." Celine added, "The cashier said that everyone she knows buys these flakes to put in their food."

I felt my face turning red. That was not exactly what the cashier had told us.

Detective Strauss leaned back in his chair, maybe to create physical and emotional distance from our testimony.

I hurried to correct Celine's exaggeration. "Maybe she didn't say *everyone*, but they do sell a lot of these bottles." I turned to my cousin. "Her exact words were—wait, didn't you record her with your phone?"

"Um, no. You didn't tell me to do that."

"Strange that you didn't record this important conversation but relied on your memory," the detective said. "What other ways could you be misremembering things, Celine?"

Did he think my cousin was a liar? Celine looked affronted, and I turned to Detective Strauss. "My cousin is telling the truth. The cashier scanned the item number and said the gold flakes are edible. Pure twenty-three karat. I even bought an extra bottle, which you can take a look at."

The detective crossed his arms over his chest. "We already have the gold flakes in evidence, and we're interested in that specific bottle, which may very well have been tampered with. Besides, after talking with her sister, I found out that Jordan Chang was allergic to nickel."

"I'm not following you," I said. "Why do her allergies matter?"

"As someone allergic to nickel," the detective said, "Miss Chang could have adverse reactions to any type of metal in her system."

Oh. I felt a wave of dizziness assault me, and I wobbled

in my chair. I'd thought we were in the clear until this sudden turn of events.

"Plus, I'm not going to just take your word that the flakes are unadulterated pure gold. I'll need to get them tested."

Had my cousin actually killed someone, even if by accident? I felt the bile rise up in my throat and made a few strangled noises.

"Uh, you don't look so good. You look like you might—" The detective hurried to open the door, and the rush of wind from the adjoining corridor refreshed me.

"Sorry, I was feeling queasy," I said. "It must have been the shock."

"Right," Detective Strauss said. "Er, let's get you outside just in case you're not all the way better." He escorted Celine and me back to the lobby.

Once he'd walked away from us, Celine bunched up her hands into fists and said, "I bet he's lying. Just trying to pin this on me because I'm an easy scapegoat."

"I don't know, Celine." I believed Detective Strauss when he'd revealed the info about the nickel allergy. I'd seen with my own two eyes the jewelry on Jacey Chang's thumb. She'd worn stacking rings saying "Big sister" and "Little sister." I'd originally thought Jacey retrieved the ring from her sister's belongings for sentimental reasons as she grieved, but what if that was how she usually wore them? Maybe Jacey had both rings on her thumb all the time because her sister had never been able to tolerate the jewelry.

I closed my eyes. "Can you take me to the bookstore now?" I asked Celine. I needed to return to my sanctuary of books.

SEVEN

THE LITERARY NARNIA HAD JUST OPENED WHEN WE walked into the empty bookstore. Its operating hours were a relaxed schedule from noon to six in the evening.

After I introduced my cousin to Dawn and Kelly Tanaka, I took my final employee walk around the store. I lingered at the worn shelves, brushing my fingertips against the colorful spines. I even pulled out a paperback book and patted the uneven deckle edges.

When I'd completed a loop around the store, I ended once again before the Tanaka sisters. Celine had retreated to a corner of the store where the nonfiction books were shelved. I didn't remember her being a big reader, but she did seem quite interested in the volume she held. Its title alluded to taking "Gram-worthy" pictures.

Dawn took one look at me, pulled me into a hug, and said, "I can't believe it's your last day."

I patted her back, in what I hoped was a soothing motion, until she let go of me and sniffed.

Dawn retrieved a handkerchief from the pocket of her

cardigan and blew her nose on it. Then she excused herself.

Kelly shook her head as her sister escaped to the back room. Her coiffed bushy silver hair didn't budge in the slightest. "Dawn's a softie."

"I really will miss this place," I said, smiling at the ordered bookshelves and even the spinning rack near the register.

"At least you have the restaurant to go back to." Kelly adjusted her wire-rimmed glasses and stared out the front door.

I knew the two sisters had invested their life savings to open the store and keep it running. They would lose a lot more than an employee if business continued to suffer. "Everybody who comes into The Literary Narnia loves it," I said. "We just need more people to show up."

"From your mouth to their ears," Kelly said.

The door sprang open at just that moment, depositing a haggard-looking college student on the threshold. From the bear on her sweatshirt, along with the blue and gold school colors, I could tell she was from UCLA.

"All yours," Kelly said. "It may be the last book customer you serve."

I walked over to the student, who looked like she might have recently rolled out of bed. She'd pulled her hair up into a greasy ponytail. Her sweatshirt had telltale swipe marks of powdered orange (Doritos, or possibly Cheetos).

"I need these books," she said, pulling out a crumpled sheet of college-ruled paper and handing it over to me.

I scanned the list. They looked like scholarly books, plus a literary novel thrown in for a mandatory English course. "Should be able to locate these quickly."

"Great." She tugged at her ponytail. "Because I need them fast. Finals are just around the corner."

College students often arrived at The Literary Narnia in a harried state, looking for books. The prepared ones came at the beginning of the quarter. Lackadaisical students showed up right around now, soon after the add/ drop classes deadline had passed, so they could load up on required, or even supplemental, texts.

I took the student around the store, piling up the books in my hands. This dance of finding the right volumes in record time gave me a sense of accomplishment. In the end, I located all five books on her list. "There. Done," I said.

"You're a lifesaver." The student bustled over to the cash register, and Kelly proceeded to ring up her purchases.

"How'd you hear about us?" Kelly asked.

"You guys give a student discount. Word gets around."

A smile stretched across Kelly's face because the incentive had been her brainchild. We had seen an increase of college-aged customers ever since then, but it remained to be seen whether the extra sales outbalanced the costs that the bookstore, or rather the sisters, had to cover.

Kelly started placing the books in a single plastic bag but soon realized she would need more to hold all the purchases. "Thanks for getting your books here. You know, we offer even more coupons if you agree to be on our mailing list." She swiveled toward the clunky desktop computer.

"Nah, but thanks anyway," the student said. She paid for the books with a credit card and then shuffled off with her load.

After she left, I heard a sharp cry from the corner of the room where Celine had hidden herself. The book on social media lay by the wayside, and she seemed to be furiously texting and scowling at the screen in her hand. Then she stopped and must've dialed somebody because she started half yelling into her phone. "You can't do that to me."

Horrified, I felt my cheeks heating up, but I stood rooted to the spot. How might I approach my cousin and tell her to lower her voice and stop embarrassing both her and me?

"I'll take care of this," Kelly said. "Let Celine know there's a more private area in the back to have this sort of discussion."

Kelly managed to corral my cousin, and they edged toward the back room. Meanwhile, I kept my eye on the front door, in case a customer—perhaps another student— showed up.

Thoughts about college led me back to Blake and how he'd asked if I'd known Jordan Chang from UCLA.

The university. I wondered if Jordan had ever signed up for the mailing list.

I snuck over to the desktop computer at the front counter. We kept a database of our customers on it.

My head whipped toward the back room. I didn't see a shadow of movement from there, and I could still very well hear my cousin shouting. Her voice rose up and down in decibel. On this last day, I was still an official employee of The Literary Narnia. Surely I had the authority to peruse the customer database.

I held my breath as I typed in "Jordan Chang" in the search parameters. It yielded one result. She *had* ordered academic books from the store last year, and it appeared that she lived off Gayley Avenue. Could she have remained in the same apartment? I searched around the counter, grabbed a spare scrap of paper, and jotted down the address before I could regret my actions. Then I refreshed the screen.

My heart felt like it was hammering so much it echoed in the air around me. I calmed my breathing and listened again. In contrast to my frenzied personal state, an unsettling quiet now pervaded the bookstore.

I inched around the counter, and leaned my body toward the back room. Maybe I sensed the stillness better because I could no longer hear the frustrated tone of Celine's chatter. I crept over to the back room and looked inside the open doorway. I found the Tanaka sisters there, but Celine had disappeared.

"Where did my cousin go?" I asked.

"Celine ran out the back door before I could stop her," Dawn said.

"I'd take off, too," Kelly said. "Clear my head after an explosive argument like that."

"Do you know who she was speaking with?" I said.

"She mentioned 'Ma Mi' and 'De Di,'" Dawn said. Both accented words were derived from the English parallels of "Mommy" and "Daddy."

"Her parents?" I stared at the closed back door as though it had shut out not only my cousin but also her secrets. Did her dear-daughter status get compromised somehow?

"You can leave early today," Kelly said. "I'm sure we can handle this rush of customers." She jutted her jaw toward the empty front room.

Dawn nodded. "Go, Yale. Family is one of the most important things in life." She looked at her sister, and they exchanged some secret signal that made their eyes sparkle.

"If you're certain . . ." I said.

They walked me to the front of the shop. Dawn waved to me, and Kelly said, "Don't be a stranger after this. We still expect you to come in here and buy up all the books."

"Deal," I said. "Once I land a paying job."

Outside on the pavement, I peeked at the empty parking lot, even knowing that Celine had long left the premises. I looked left and right, as though I could see the ghost of a trail she had left.

Where could she have gone? I doubted she'd be in a

mood to take in the sights if she were so enraged. Plus, the only people she knew here were Ba and me.

Wing Fat. I bet she'd gone to the restaurant. If anyone could mediate between Celine and her parents, it had to be my dad. Or, if all else failed, he could stuff her full of dim sum comfort food.

When I showed up at the restaurant, a short bus ride away from the bookstore, I bypassed the hostess on duty and barged into the sectioned-off banquet room. I breathed out a sigh of relief as I spotted Celine sitting next to my dad at a table. She had a half-eaten basket of steamed *siu mai* dumplings before her.

"What's going on?" I asked my cousin, but she stayed silent, her gaze centered on the tablecloth.

Ba spoke up. "The bad news is that Celine needs to stay longer in the States but can't remain at her fancy hotel." He took a red platter with a geometric pattern and presented it to me with a flourish. "Sponge cake?"

I salivated at the thought of tasting my favorite steamed dessert.

"Please take a piece," Ba said. "This *ma lai goh* is solely for you, Yale."

I grabbed a piece and took a big bite of the puffy vanilla cake. Mmm.

"And the good news," Ba said, "is that you have a new roommate."

I swallowed the chunk of cake and coughed.

"It's settled, then," Ba said. "You have an extra room, and Celine needs to use it."

I couldn't really argue with his statement. I'd set up the spare room for visitors, and Celine met that qualification.

"Fine," I said and took another huge bite of the cake. I really did enjoy the angel food cake texture of it.

Celine glanced up at that point, and I studied her face. Her eyes appeared red, like she'd been crying.

I saw my cousin pick up her phone, and I looked in

alarm at the platter. "Oops. Did you want to take a pic of that?"

"Oh no," my cousin said, her mouth dropping open. "I didn't even get a chance to . . ."

"I can put it back." Once I glanced at the half-eaten piece in my hand, though, I knew I'd already destroyed any chance of a "Gram-worthy" shot. "Or maybe not."

"JK," she said, a little sparkle coming back to her eyes. "Of course I already staged and photographed everything. That's the *second* sponge cake Uncle made."

"Hmph." I pulled the platter closer to me, guarding its treasure. "Guess who's not sharing this cake with their new roomie tonight."

I stood up from the table and went to the lacquered cabinet at the side of the room. After tugging on the brass ring handle to open it, I retrieved a white foam takeout container to place my precious sponge cake in.

"Do you want anything else to go?" Ba asked. "We still have some extra food in the kitchen I can give you."

Without waiting for my answer, he dashed away. I already had leftovers in the fridge. Did I really need the extra food?

All of a sudden, I had a better idea on how to use the dim sum dishes Ba was giving to us to their full advantage. A bonus was that it'd take Celine's mind off her troubles, too. I touched the slip of paper with Jordan Chang's address on it, like a kind of paper talisman, and asked Celine, "Care for a joyride?"

⊂▭▭▭▭▭⊃

Gayley Avenue curved around the west side of the UCLA campus. After studying the GPS navigation system on the rental car, I realized that people who lived there could take a brisk walk east and hit the main thoroughfare of the campus called Westwood Plaza.

As we drove along, looking at the addresses on the avenue, I noticed both vehicles and fearless pedestrians on the road. We passed by a line of fraternity houses before locating the apartment building, a towering beige stucco complex. An underground parking lot existed for its residents, but its locked gated entrance seemed to discourage visitors. Celine drove about a block down before finding a spot to parallel park.

At the apartment building's glass door entrance, I noticed a metal intercom box. I scrolled through the names on the screen, pressing the arrow buttons until I landed on "Chang, J." I hoped that it was the right person. I hit the call button and waited.

Soon, a raspy but fuzzy voice answered, "Yes? Can I help you?"

It didn't sound like Jacey's voice, but I couldn't discern the tones very well through the speaker. If Jordan's sister opened the door to us, I bet we'd get reported right away to the detective and be in big trouble. Perhaps I should have thought through this spontaneous plan better.

I scratched at the back of my neck. "Is this the unit for Jordan Chang?" I asked.

"Who's this?"

Celine budged me out of the way and spoke into the intercom. "Food delivery," she said. "From Wing Fat. It's already paid for."

I heard two more voices debating this tidbit of news and leaned into the intercom. Did any of those voices belong to Jacey?

I heard a voice almost squeal in excitement. "Ooh, I love that place!"

Another individual, in a quieter tone, said, "But we didn't put in an order from there. Was it Jordan's sister?"

"Too bad she's not here to ask."

A sense of relief flooded through me. We must have

the right apartment, and Jacey wasn't lurking inside, ready to report us to the police once she recognized our faces.

The roommates or friends debated the merits of receiving free food versus a random botched delivery.

The original voice finally said, "Come on up."

We got buzzed in. As we took the creaky elevator to the fourth floor, Celine said, "Let me do the talking. I'm way better at improvising."

I found myself holding the takeout bag while Celine knocked a staccato beat on the door to the apartment.

It swung open with a groan to reveal a young woman with luscious Shakira-esque curly brown hair and thick smoky eye makeup. "This is from Wing Fat?" she asked in a raspy voice.

"Yes. Just look at the logo on the bag," Celine said.

I held the bag in front of the woman's face, but she didn't take it.

Another woman, with auburn hair, darted forward and grabbed the food. "I can't wait to see what we got," she said. "Their egg rolls are the yummiest."

Behind the other two stood an Asian woman. She had her black hair pulled up, which showed off her freckled face. Behind clear-framed glasses, her dark brown eyes scrutinized the takeout bag. "Seems legit," she said.

The roommate with the bag cradled it in her arms. "You heard what Sierra said, Genesis. We're keeping the food. And guess what? Everything is still warm."

In a quiet voice that carried across to where we stood, Sierra said, "Too bad Jordan isn't here to take her amazing foodie pics."

The woman with the curly hair—Genesis, according to her roommate—blocked the doorframe with her body. "Why did you two mention Jordan's name in the beginning?"

I squeezed behind my cousin. Celine said she could improvise, and I hoped it wasn't empty boasting.

In an even voice, my cousin said, "Because this food was sent from Blake, and he mentioned her name."

"Blake Westby Reyes?" Genesis's raspy voice went up in pitch. Her eyes took on a moony look.

The woman holding the food said, "I thought Jordan dumped him a week ago after she found out—"

"That jerk," Sierra said. "Give back the food, Reagan."

Reagan rebelled against the order by nestling the bag closer to her body. "Maybe he's not so bad. If Blake ordered the food, he must be thinking of us during this time."

Genesis played with her curly hair. "Okay, majority rules. Let's keep the food."

Reagan did a shimmy with her hips in excitement while Sierra threw her hands up in the air.

"You can set the table without me," Genesis said. "I'm going downstairs with Jordan's old stuff. Be back in five."

Genesis picked up a small cardboard box from behind the door, and we walked over to the elevator together. Once we were trapped inside, she asked, "So, I'm curious. Did Blake say the food was to be delivered to Jordan? Or in remembrance of her?"

My eyes widened at her audacious question, but she must have taken my reaction as shock about Jordan's death.

"Sorry to spring that on you," Genesis said.

"Yeah," I mumbled, "I heard your roommate mention she wasn't around to take photos anymore."

"Jordan passed away very recently," Genesis said with a hitch in her voice. "I was wondering if Blake knew . . ."

The elevator doors slid open, and we filed out into the lobby.

"Er, we're just deliverers from Wing Fat," Celine said.

"Oh, of course." Genesis dropped the cardboard box on the floor.

I nudged it with the toe of my shoe. "What do you want done with that?"

"Whatever. I don't care. It's just some junk from Jordan's room. Even her own sister didn't want it."

Without another word, Genesis turned on her heel, headed to the elevator, and jabbed at the button on the control panel.

EIGHT

AFTER THE ELEVATOR SPIRITED GENESIS AWAY from us, I picked up the box at my feet with Jordan's old belongings. "Free" was scrawled across one side in black marker.

"I wonder what's in there," Celine said.

Was she thinking about searching for potential clues?

My cousin continued, "Do you think there are any clothes in my size? Or fun accessories?"

I spluttered. "Don't you have the money to buy new stuff instead of practically robbing the dead?"

"Hey, I'm just saving the earth," she said.

I really didn't understand how my cousin's mind worked. Out of curiosity, though, I peeked inside the box. I could see the bottom with a single glance. "Not much in here, I'm afraid."

"No wonder they wanted to toss it. Let's go," Celine said. "I called the hotel and had to beg and pay extra for a super-late checkout time. Usually, I'd need to leave by at most two, but I managed to convince them to extend the time until five."

"Wait a moment," I said as I carried the box and followed her outside to the street. I placed Jordan's old belongings down with care. Pulling the objects out, I studied each one at length.

The unwanted items from Jordan's room were: a yin-yang poster, a mini water fountain, and an old eyeglasses case. Taking a guess at the dimensions, I thought the artwork measured approximately eight by ten inches. One corner was ripped off the poster, which disturbed the mystical feel of the circle with its S-shaped line down the middle and its black and white halves.

Half the decorative pebbles in the mini water feature were missing. I didn't see any stones at the bottom of the cardboard box. The plug trailing from the side of the fountain appeared cracked, and a wire jutted out from the rubber casing.

The eyeglasses case, a soft-shell version, seemed warped, maybe by moisture. I tried closing it, but the button no longer lined up with the clasp and wouldn't lock.

"All rubbish," Celine said after I'd taken out each item in turn and put it back.

Indeed, all the objects were broken in some way. I'd hoped for more of a clue in the tossed items. I made sure to position the cardboard box away from the entry, with the "Free" side facing out, and close enough for curious pedestrians to access from the sidewalk. As we headed to the parked car, I looked back once at the cardboard box and wondered if I'd missed something.

Then we arrived at the Boxster, and I buckled my seat belt. Celine eased away from the curb and headed down Gayley Ave. The wind blowing through my hair made me grip the edges of my seat as we traveled toward the hotel she'd stayed in.

Everything about the Four Seasons Hotel Los Angeles

at Beverly Hills conveyed elegance—and intimidation—
to me. The valet parking, the suited doormen, and the
fancy chandeliers all made me feel surrounded by luxury
and out of my element.

Even Celine's room seemed larger than life. It looked
more like an apartment to me, with its separate living area
and the accompanying sleek television set. It even included an exercise bike and yoga equipment in the modern and bright space. I took a peek at the marble bathroom
and darted out after spying the high-end collection of
European bath amenities.

Eventually, I stepped out through the French doors
onto the balcony to take a breather. The jaw-dropping
view of the distinctive Los Angeles skyline reminded me
of the fancy hotel's prime location.

By this time, Celine had gathered all her belongings
and organized her three purple suitcases to her satisfac-
tion. I'd glimpsed some of the contents as she scurried
around the room. She seemed to possess an endless array
of clothes, scarves, and pairs of shoes.

Celine checked out with ease, and I silently celebrated
leaving behind the uncomfortable setting. Besides, the car
ride to my apartment also meant I could broach a difficult
subject with her.

"Celine," I said, staring at her profile in the driver's
seat, where she had one hand resting comfortably on the
wheel, "what's going on with your parents?"

She put her other hand up to steady her driving.

"From what I heard at the bookstore, it sounded pretty
intense," I said.

"I don't want to talk about it." She turned on the air-
conditioning full blast even though the wind still whipped
my hair. "What's going on with *your* work situation, huh?
Dawn Tanaka was bawling her eyes out."

"A temporary break. Everything will turn out okay and
go back to normal."

"Wishful thinking. It's not my problem, Yale, but it might become your dad's if he has to bail you out." She pinched her lips tight after that and concentrated on driving.

It took us an excruciating half hour more of slow-going traffic to reach Fountain Vista.

My stomach started grumbling as soon as we entered the apartment. While Celine unloaded her belongings into the spare room, I scrounged around in the pantry and the refrigerator for leftovers. Soy sauce eggs with ramen could be a dinner possibility.

"Done," Celine said with a chirp to her voice as she joined me in the kitchen. "Too bad the closet's so small. I really had to stuff things in."

I didn't think it was the size of the closet that was the issue.

"What's for dinner?" she asked.

"Want ramen with egg?"

"Bleh." She stuck her tongue out in a juvenile gesture. "Come on, Yale. Think bigger. And don't worry, I'll cover the food."

With her budget, the dining options could be endless. I wondered whether she'd offered out of kindness, or to increase her collection of foodie posts.

I then remembered Jacey Chang mentioning following her sister's social media feed. "I think I have an idea. Can you log on to your Instagram?"

"Sure," she said. Celine opened the app on her phone. "Look at my latest." She zoomed in on her photo, a close-up of a fluffy dome of sponge cake from Wing Fat.

"Nice shot," I said, almost wanting to dart over to the refrigerator to eat it instead of a more nutritious dinner. "Can you check on Jordan's posts from the night market?"

"Just a moment." She selected the "following" tab and found Jordan's profile. It pulled up a grid of her most recent pics. I saw posed shots of a scoop of ice cream against a smoky background, a yellow drink with chunks of bobbing fruit, a mountain of shaved ice with strawberries on top, and my own green tea bubble drink with the sparkling addition by Celine.

"Are you done yet?" my cousin said, holding her hand out for her phone.

I gripped tighter. "Not quite. Where'd she get the shaved ice from?" I asked, a suspicion forming in my mind.

"It doesn't really say." Celine proceeded to read off the caption: "'Indulging in this snow mountain topped with vanilla ice cream and strawberries.' Hashtagged with 'foodie,' 'yummy,' 'Eastwood Village Night Market,' and many others. No food stall name, though."

I bent my head over my cousin's phone. At the very edge of Jordan's snow mountain photo, I could see the telltale golden crisp of popcorn chicken. She must have gotten the dessert at Ho's Small Eats.

"I know just the place to have dinner," I said.

"Let's do it." Celine put her phone away, and we headed out.

Ho's used to be the location of a small retro diner. Even after the change of hands, Nik's parents had kept the checkerboard flooring and red vinyl booths. They even left the swivel barstools running down the length of the long counter.

Nobody else was inside when we entered the restaurant besides Nik, who stood bored behind the counter, wiping it in lazy circles with a wet rag. If anything, he looked even more dismayed as he spotted us, his newest and only customers.

The extra facial hair he'd grown since high school didn't manage to hide his scowl. "Why are you here,

Yee?" he said. Nik used my last name when he wanted to rile me up.

"What's with the third degree? We're here to eat dinner obviously. This is a restaurant. I'd ask you to find us a table"—I made an exaggerated motion of looking around the empty room—"but I guess every spot is available right now."

I led Celine over to the booth closest to the kitchen door. Even though I didn't cook much anymore, I still liked smelling the alluring fragrances and spices floating in the air. Every restaurant and kitchen had its own distinctive culinary perfume.

Once we sat down, Nik trudged our way. He deposited worn menus on our table. As I touched one, I figured they must have been the stickiest he could find. A few crumbs decorated the edge of mine.

"What do ya want?" he said.

"Better service," I said with a sweet smile.

Celine arched an eyebrow at me and slid her manicured finger down the page. "I'd love a bowl of your spicy beef noodle soup. And an Apple Sidra."

"And for Your Highness?" Nik said with a mock bow to me.

"Yes, that's a much better tableside manner," I said. "I'll have the pork chop rice."

He narrowed his mud brown eyes at me. "You're not here to play another prank, are you?"

"I don't know what you're talking about," I said. "We're not going to do a runner on you if that's what you're thinking. We'll be paying for our meal fair and square."

Nik plucked the menus up, holding them by their edges, maybe to keep the gunk away from his hands. "I know you sent that fake detective to my booth last night to interrogate our food practices and figure out if we were the original stall handing out light bulb drinks. But his bad Halloween disguise with the dark suit and flimsy badge didn't fool me for one minute."

"You've got it all wrong, Nik—"

He held up the menus like plastic shields against my words. "Time to put your orders in."

Shoving the menus back into some dark corner behind the counter, he speed-walked into the kitchen. I could hear a snippet of his mother's cheery greeting to him before the door shut behind Nik.

"We should probably tell him the truth," Celine said. "That he met an actual detective."

"I don't think he'd listen to a thing coming out of my mouth."

"Yeah, you two bicker like schoolkids secretly crushing on each other."

I crossed my arms over my chest. "Ha. Very funny." It did feel like entering a time warp whenever I spoke with Nik, though.

"Okay, I'll be the adult in the room and tell him," my cousin said right before Nik returned to our table with the canned apple soda for Celine.

"Nik," she said, "maybe Yale here gave you the wrong impression. And I don't know the history between you guys, but that detective was for real. He's investigating a death that happened at the plaza where the night market was held."

Nik rubbed his goatee. "I thought I saw some headline about that. Someone died near the plaza. But I don't have time to pay attention to the news beyond major headlines. Too busy."

"The victim was a young woman named Jordan Chang," I said. "Did you see her around your booth? She was wearing a ninja costume, all in black, but with a small opening for her to see out of. Her eyes were unique, violet colored."

He hesitated before saying his next words, maybe uncertain if I was still trying to play a trick on him. "If I did see someone like that, she might have ordered an *authentic* green tea bubble drink from our booth."

"As opposed to a pretend boba beverage?" I said.

"Well, it *is* a Taiwanese drink, not a Cantonese one. And definitely not served alongside dim sum." His face seemed to darken along with his mood.

"Are you saying something about the drink I made? That it's not good enough?"

"Well, did she die after drinking it?" Nik said.

Celine gasped, although it was half-covered by a faint *ding* that came from the kitchen.

I stayed silent, unwilling to say anything that could implicate my cousin.

"Who knows?" Nik said. "Maybe it was your tapioca balls. So hard she choked on them."

The kitchen door burst open with a whoosh. Nik's mother rushed out, balancing a bowl and a plate in her arms. "Nikola, I rang the bell, and you didn't answer."

Mrs. Ho hovered near our table with the dishes. I could discern the tantalizing five-spice powder she'd used in the batter to fry up the meat.

"The pork is mine," I said. "By the way, smells divine, Mrs. Ho."

She slid the plate over to me, the pork chop flanked by a small mound of rice and stir-fried green cabbage.

"This noodle soup must be yours, then," Mrs. Ho said, setting the bowl down before Celine. She paused, wiping her hands against her apron, and said, "I don't think we've met. You must be Yale's cousin."

Celine offered Mrs. Ho a friendly smile. "Yes, Auntie. Lovely to meet you."

Nik's mother focused on my cousin. "Do you happen to live nearby?"

In my peripheral vision, I noticed Nik place his palm over his eyes.

"I live in Hong Kong," Celine said, "but I'll be here in the area, um, for a while."

How long did Celine, or perhaps her parents, want the stay to last?

"Did you hear that, Nikola?" His mother's voice sang out in triumph.

Nik covered his face with both of his hands.

"Hmm, I wonder why Ah Sing didn't tell me," Mrs. Ho said, her body angling toward me. "Could it be because . . ."

Nik's mother turned to me and placed a sun-spotted, or perhaps oil-spotted, hand on my arm. "Tell your father that we are still friends. Even with all those rumors."

I wanted to ask her what she meant, but she seemed strained even after referring to this gossip peripherally. In typical dutiful mode to an elder's request, I answered, "Yes, Auntie."

After she shuffled back to the kitchen, with one hand bracing her back, I tried to question Nik about her comment. "What are these rumors flying around?"

"As if you don't know," he said before retreating into the kitchen, either to escape from us or to check on his mother.

"That was strange," Celine said, while popping the tab of her soda and taking a sip.

"Indeed."

We lapsed into silence as we finally ate dinner. I wondered if I could get Ba to be more forthcoming about the matter.

When we returned to the apartment, I knew it'd still be several hours before my dad would finish tidying up and closing down the restaurant. If he decided to go over the finances, it'd take even longer for him to return home.

Celine popped into her room to "change into something more comfortable." She came back out in a cinched silk robe, dangling a toiletry bag by her fingers. "Yale," she said, "the light's flashing on the answering machine."

For a brief moment, I thought maybe my dad had taken the initiative and called me tonight, but that didn't make much sense when I assessed the timing. He'd be busy cooking—unless it happened to be an urgent matter. My mind flashed back to college when I'd received the dreaded phone call from my dad about my mom's breathing troubles.

I rushed into the spare room and pressed the playback button. At first, I felt relief upon hearing a different male voice speaking to me from the answering machine. Then I wondered why Detective Strauss would be contacting me again. I rewound the message to hear the few words I'd missed at the beginning because of my sheer panic: "We have a problem, Yale," he said. "Call me back anytime tonight."

Did that mean he'd moved forward in the investigation? I located his business card and dialed the number printed on it.

He answered on the first ring. "Thanks for returning my call."

"Sorry, I was eating dinner and—"

"Is your cousin still around?"

"Yes." I stared at the three suitcases, stacked together in a neat bundle, in the corner of the room. "In fact, she's staying with me now instead of at the hotel."

"Great," he said. "Make sure she doesn't leave your sight."

"Uh, sure. Is there something I need to know, Detective Strauss?"

"It's late tonight, and I really should've clocked off earlier. I'll tell you both tomorrow."

"What do you mean?"

"I'll be in the neighborhood, going over the crime

scene again." He cleared his throat. "From my notes, I see that you live in Fountain Vista. How about I meet you two in front of the fountain at The Shops at Eastwood Village at nine o'clock tomorrow morning?"

Folding in the face of his authority, I said, "Okay, I guess."

After I hung up, I wondered what I'd done. When my cousin slipped into the room, I said, "There's something I need to tell you . . ."

NINE

AS AGREED UPON, IN THE MORNING CELINE AND I directed our steps toward the fountain at the nearby shopping plaza. My cousin strolled the short distance, busy checking her phone even as she walked, while I took bumbling steps toward the water feature, uncertain of how the detective would receive us.

Detective Strauss was waiting for us and faced our direction as we approached. He gave a subtle head nod in acknowledgment. "Thanks for coming on time. I thought we'd meet here to jog your memory."

I didn't want any memories resurfacing. I'd prefer erasing the night I'd stumbled over Jordan Chang's body. If only it hadn't been so dark, perhaps someone else would have found her, and I wouldn't be entangled in this mess.

As I underwent an internal debate, Celine sat down on the large lip on the fountain. Her sitting position pulled me out of my deep thoughts. Usually, the spray of the water prevented people from pausing for more than a moment, forcing them to admire from a safe distance.

Glancing at the center of the stone fountain, I realized that its water source had been shut off. Without that playful arc, it seemed too quiet in this spot, almost sinister.

Celine didn't seem to care because she crossed her leg over her knee, tucked a long strand of honeyed hair behind one ear, and said, "What's up, Strauss?"

My cousin had opted to sit down in the same area where I'd discovered Jordan. Suppressing a little shiver, I moved about half a foot away from her and leaned my leg against the overhang in solidarity. Detective Strauss continued to stand and stare at us with his piercing jade-green eyes.

"I wanted to tell you about something that cropped up. It took a while to access the victim's social media since we had no phone. Plus, the usual expectation of privacy." He focused on my cousin. "Celine, would you call Jordan Chang a foodstagram friend?"

My cousin jiggled her foot before responding. "Nothing close to that. I actually thought she was a *he* until very recently. Goes to show how much I knew."

The detective took measured steps to decrease the distance between them, right into her comfort zone. Celine scooted back an inch.

"She sent you a direct message," Detective Strauss said.

"I get a lot of those," Celine said. "If you go to my account, there's a queue of men in uniform starving to meet me." Her lips curved into a mock smile.

"You had a whole conversation with Jordan Chang," Detective Strauss said.

My cousin planted both feet flat on the pavement.

"Do you need me to remind you of the exact words exchanged?" Detective Strauss dug out his notepad and read. "Miss Chang messaged, 'I know about your slip-up. Wait 'til I spread the word.' You responded with, 'Don't tell a soul.' And the last message from Jordan Chang to you? 'Who's gonna stop me?' It was sent the day before she died."

Celine's face turned the pale white of a radish cake, but she recovered her voice in a moment and said, with a flip of her hand, "That was just trash-talking. Harmless."

"It's also a possible motive," the detective said. "I find it mighty interesting that you showed up in the States this same tragic weekend. And I should tell you, I'm not a man who believes in coincidences."

I walked over to intervene, inserting my body in between them as a physical, maybe even an emotional, shield. "Detective Strauss," I said, "if Celine had anything to do with the unfortunate death, she wouldn't still be around, right? She'd have flown back to Hong Kong right away."

He extracted a pencil from his pocket. "Maybe. Maybe not. A sudden escape might have roused more suspicion. Sticking around would be the smarter move."

I wracked my brain for a way to take the suspicion off my cousin as a prime suspect. "What about Jordan's other contacts? Have you looked into them? A graduate of UCLA living near the campus probably has a lot of connections in the local area."

He turned toward me and raised his eyebrows. "How do you know all that?"

"Um . . ." I latched onto a fact that I could provide the detective. "She often ordered food from my dad's Chinese restaurant."

He snorted, as if in disbelief, but I noticed he scribbled something down in his notepad. I'd just linked our respected family name even more to this sordid affair. I tugged at a hangnail on my pinky finger and winced.

Detective Strauss cleared his throat and said, "She does have a lot of friends, either in person or through on-line gaming. Lucky for me, Miss Chang only has a small network of acquaintances who actually attended the event at the same time as her."

I observed the night market space. Everything had been cleaned from the ground. No garbage in sight. All traces of the Eastwood Village Night Market had disappeared. It almost seemed like it'd been a dream, or perhaps more accurately, a living nightmare.

Detective Strauss spoke again. "All I want is the truth from you Yee cousins. I'll be sure to stay in touch with you both."

Celine and I watched the detective stash his notepad and pencil. When he left, his quick and confident footsteps rang out in a drumming pattern.

"We need to talk," I told Celine. My cousin started rubbing her arms as though goose bumps lined her flesh.

Checking our surroundings, I didn't notice any cameras in the area. Plus, many of the stores didn't open until later, so nobody walked around in the plaza. Still, I felt more comfortable talking in the privacy of my own home. "Back in the apartment," I said.

She nodded and followed a few steps behind me as we slogged back to Fountain Vista.

I didn't have any type of truth serum in my kitchen, so a fresh-brewed batch of tea would have to do. After I placed the kettle on the stove, I scooped out the osmanthus oolong leaves from a shiny metal canister, dumping them into a sea green teapot with delicate pink cherry blossoms painted on the side.

From the corner of my eye, I noticed Celine pacing back and forth in the living room.

"Go and sit down. At the dining table," I said.

To my surprise, she obeyed my command. Celine slid out one of the high-back chairs with scrollwork upholstery and settled there. She waited for me, her hands clasped against the delicate lace tablecloth.

Once the kettle issued a piercing cry, I poured the boiling water over the tea. Of course I threw out that first batch of water, only meant to wash the leaves. Then I added in more, letting it steep. The small petals and rolled leaves soon unfurled and danced in the teapot.

I brought over the pot and placed it at the center of the table. Only after I'd poured the oolong for us both did I look her in the eye. "Did you do it?" I asked.

She reared back as though I'd scalded her with the tea. "*What?* Kill Jordan Chang? Don't be ridiculous."

I studied my cousin while sipping my tea, and she didn't flinch at my prolonged stare. We'd lost touch for many years. What did I really know about her, aside from one distant childhood memory? On the other hand, I didn't think there were any murderous skeletons in the Yee closet.

"I didn't do it," she said in an even tone.

"Really?" I said. "Then why didn't you tell me about the direct messages?"

"Honestly, I'd forgotten all about the harmless banter by the time I landed in the States."

I wanted to believe her. The trendy girl I remembered from my Disneyland trip had morphed into an even more glamorous one, but she seemed more fixated on *dressing* to kill than in any actual murderous intent.

I leaned back in my chair and relaxed my shoulders.

She must have seen the shift in my posture and drank from her teacup.

"So, why the escape from Hong Kong?" I asked.

She fanned her face, and I knew it wasn't from the heat of the beverage. "Let's just call it fashion drama."

I remembered that Celine's mother—her English name was Cher—participated in all sorts of charity galas. Her parents were sometimes photographed at celebrity-studded activities. Had Celine somehow embarrassed herself at one of those prestigious events?

My cousin traced the outline of a cherry blossom on her cup with the tip of her index finger. "Anyway, I'm waiting for it to blow over."

"Speaking of 'blow over,' I'm not so sure this case is going to go away on its own. The detective keeps finding more and more things stacked against you."

Celine swigged her tea. "Well, *I* didn't kill Jordan Chang. So who did? We can find out together." Her amber eyes seemed to light up from within.

I stared into my tea, hoping that disaster wouldn't be spelled out in the leaves at the bottom of the cup at the mention of my cousin's dangerous idea.

"Come on," Celine said. "Now that you're unemployed, you've got extra time on your hands."

I wanted to say, "I'm hoping not for long," but before I could respond, Celine spoke again.

"It'll be a sisterly bonding activity," she said.

A warm glow infused me. After decades of waiting, she'd recognized us as sisters. Even though I felt nauseated at diving into a murder case, I also longed to accept her invitation.

"Nothing illegal," I said.

"Wouldn't dream of it," she said and winked at me. "Thank goodness we live in an age of instant information. Let's see, who would know if Jordan had any enemies?"

"Her sister, Jacey? Or maybe one of the roommates?"

Celine pulled out her cell phone, tapped away on it, and started searching. She bit the bottom of her lip as she scanned the results. "Apparently, Jacey Chang is a pretty common name. What about the roomies?"

I pinched the scalloped edge of the lace tablecloth with my thumb and forefinger. "Their names were . . . Genesis, Reagan, and Sierra. Genesis met us at the door, Reagan grabbed the food bag, and Sierra lurked in the background."

"You have a great memory," she said. "Too bad those are only first names. Not much to go on."

I pointed to her shiny screen. "What about on Instagram with all those 'followers' and 'following'? Can you find out Jordan's contacts from that?"

"Kind of. We'd have to sift through strangers versus friends. But there is a search function."

After culling through the names, we'd gotten a hit only for Genesis. Even from the beautified headshot with soft romantic lighting, I recognized her signature curly brown hair and smoky eyes. She had a profile, which listed her full name as Genesis Aldana and described her as the lead singer in a local band called Tresillo Trio.

"Anything interesting?" I asked.

"Mostly song lyrics quotes and pics of her bandmates. But she does have an Instagram Story." Celine clicked on the glowing ring around Genesis's profile.

It displayed a banner advertising her band, which would be playing tonight at a local restaurant.

"I feel like eating out this evening," Celine said. "How about you?"

"Definitely. But for now, let's grab something quick at Wing Fat."

"Leaves and flowers don't fill you up?" Celine said, tilting the empty cherry blossom cup at me.

"Not when I'm hungry for information." I'd forgotten to call Ba last night after the surprise message from the detective. Then earlier today, my attention and energy had been channeled toward the meeting at the fountain. With this break now in the late morning, I could talk to my dad about the rumors Nik's mother had mentioned.

A fter we'd parked at Wing Fat, I stopped Celine from entering through the front and motioned for her to go around to the back. Nobody but employees walked through the smaller entrance found in the alley. The door was usually left open, covered only by a screen, in order to air out the constant cooking heat from inside.

I pulled it open and gestured for Celine to go in first. No one noticed us entering, perhaps because an old Sam Hui song blasted from a retro CD boom box housed on a shelf.

In the open-space kitchen, I spotted a prep person peeling carrots, an extra cook plating some stir-fried vegetables, and the dishwasher loading the industrial machine with dirty glasses. The staff often came and went in transitory Los Angeles, and I couldn't keep track of their names. Although, truth be told, it'd been five years since I'd stepped foot inside the kitchen because of the heartbreaking tie to my mom, so they could've been long-term employees for all I knew.

I spied my dad at the range, where he stood by a wok, and bustled over. "Hi, Ba."

He smiled, the happy lines near his eyes springing to life. "Yale," he said. "Nice of you to visit."

"Hello, Uncle," Celine said, standing several feet away, perhaps to avoid getting splashed with the steaming water I now noticed in the wok.

My dad swirled around the hot water with a metal ladle, cleaning off the various bits of food stuck at the bottom of the wok. "Celine," he said. "I'm so glad you and Yale are spending more time together."

If only you knew how. "Ba, I don't want to bother you too long. I had a quick question—"

He waved one hand at a nearby tray of glazed honey golden buns. "Plenty of *guk bao* for you and your cousin to take a few."

Despite my rumbling stomach, I said, "I'm not here for food. Celine and I went by Ho's yesterday, and Nik's mother wanted me to pass on a message. She said you're still friends despite the rumors."

Ba carried the heavy wok with one hand and, with a mighty heave, dumped the dirty water down the drain. "Those false claims floating around the restaurant grapevine. I hope she understands I'm not actually trying to take over her business."

"What? Why would people think that?"

He dried the wok with a clean towel using a slow circular motion, like some sort of Zen ritual. "I think it's because there are only a few of us authentic Asian restaurants in the local area."

It was true. Numerous eateries existed in the San Gabriel Valley. However, in West Los Angeles, where we lived and worked, there seemed to be less of a customer base. People either wanted to eat fusion-style food or trekked a little bit farther out to find a variety of restaurants that could provide a certain specialization, like tongue-numbing Szechuan cuisine or the perfect Hainan chicken rice dish.

"But Nik and his mother are Taiwanese," I said. "Totally different type of food." Even as I said that, though, I remembered that I'd offered bubble tea at the Canai and Chai stand. Could Nik be mad that I was taking away Ho's customers?

"Ai and I have known each other a long time," Ba said, depositing the wok back on top of the range. "We must stick together as business owners, not attack one another. As elders, we know that, but the next generation may think differently and assume we follow their competitive philosophy."

A waitress hurried in, asking for an order of crispy pan-fried noodles, so I left my dad alone.

"Don't forget about the guk bao," he said, with his back turned as he oiled up the wok.

"Already done," Celine said in a bright voice. She lifted a porcelain platter filled with a mound of the golden buns, baked and filled with sweet *char siu* barbecued pork.

We stood by the screen door, near the wooden peg rack holding spare clean aprons for the kitchen staff, and ate every delicious bun until the platter was empty.

Then I dodged the kitchen staff to get to the enormous dishwashing machine. A half-filled beige plastic tray stood ready for more dirty dishes, and I added the platter to the mix. Since the machine was already in washing mode, steam billowed from it, increasing the temperature in the kitchen.

Celine and I shouted above the noise of Ba's cooking and waved goodbye to my dad. Outside, in the cool autumn air, I pulled the collar of my shirt away from my body to find relief.

"It's like an oven in there," my cousin said.

"You don't realize it when you're caught up in the flow of spices and sizzling."

"Spoken like a true chef. Why'd you stop cooking anyway?"

I edged in front of her, even though she knew the way back to the parking lot. She couldn't continue the conversation with my back turned to her.

When we got into the Boxster, Celine's fingers hovered over the navigation system. "You seemed hot back there. What do you think about getting a scoop of ice cream?"

"Baked *char siu bao* and ice cream, the lunch of champions," I said.

"Maybe a lunch for champion detectives," she said. "We'll see at least one of Jordan's roommates tonight. Maybe even more. But there are other people who we can question."

"There were tons of people at the night market," I said. "How would we even—"

Celine dropped her phone in my lap, the screen unlocked. "Her IG feed. We foodstagrammers always hang around where the eating action is. Do you remember the name of that ice cream truck?"

"Below Freezing," I said.

"Can you find its location?"

After fumbling around with her phone, I figured out how to access the internet and discovered Below Freezing's truck schedule. "It's in Palms, where I grew up. You won't need the GPS. I can tell you how to get there."

"Wow. You really do try not to use any tech." She glanced in the rearview mirror and then reversed out of the spot with ease. "Not that I blame you. I heard from my father that the car's electronic system shut down that day."

I closed my eyes and tried not to remember my mom's body, so still, like her broken car. Somehow the two blurred in my mind, as though her heart's functioning had been tied to the car's electrical system failure. A logical assessment of the situation meant I knew there wasn't any connection beyond the metaphorical, but I still associated the two. I also understood that Ma wouldn't have been on the road at all if it hadn't been for me.

"Yale, where should I turn?" Celine asked in a loud voice. I surfaced from my memories and returned to the present.

I avoided all other thoughts and concentrated on providing turn-by-turn instructions to the location of the food truck. We found it stopped at a local park, where it lured both children and adults who anticipated its frozen delights.

TEN

THE SILVER FOOD TRUCK GLEAMED IN THE LOS AN-
geles sunshine, and the palm tree behind it served as
an iconic backdrop for Below Freezing. Celine and I
waited until the line dispersed before making our move.

My cousin sidled up to the order window. "Remember
me from the Eastwood Village Night Market?" she said.

The same woman I'd seen before, still wearing a crisp
white lab coat, said, "Of course. I'm good with faces and
details. You ordered the Thai iced tea flavor. Want more
of the same?"

Celine tilted her head to study the extensive menu. "I'll
have the matcha this time around."

"What about you, honey?" the woman said, staring at
me. "Oh, wait." Her blue eyes twinkled. "You want the
mango."

"Yes, please," I said, delighted she'd remembered me
and my favorite ice cream flavor.

She proceeded to pour cream into a stainless steel
bowl, added in green matcha powder, and whisked it.

Humming, she placed the bowl under a nozzle and pressed a lever. Without any warning, a cloud of puffy white smoke blasted the bowl.

"What was that?" I said, darting in front of Celine to get a better view.

"First time having nitrogen ice cream?" the woman said, mixing the ingredients with a metal spatula.

"Uh-huh," I said. "It's like watching a magic show."

"Good thing you stopped here. I'm the best in the business." She scooped the matcha ice cream into a cup, sliding the container to my cousin.

"Take one of my business cards," she said, pointing her ice cream scooper at a stack on the counter.

I grabbed one and read it aloud: "'Lindsey Caine, Owner of Below Freezing.'"

"At your service," she said, spraying more nitrogen into the air until it resembled a cloud of wonder.

She handed the still smoking cup of mango ice cream to me. I could feel the wisps of chill against my face.

"Astounding," I said out loud, remembering Jordan Chang's ice cream photo. "I thought her Instagram shot had special effects done to it."

Celine circled around me and took the lead in the conversation. "Did you see that pic from the Eastwood Village Night Market? Chang, a foodstagrammer, took it."

"Nope." Lindsey played with the top button on her lab coat. "Can't say the name rings a bell."

My cousin provided her with Jordan's profile name, a play on words of "major hankering."

Lindsey shook her head, a wisp of blond hair threatening to pop out of her mesh hairnet. "Still nothing. Then again, I don't follow amateur critics." She pointed to the amount displayed on the cash register and said, "If you don't mind."

Celine handed her a twenty-dollar bill. "Keep the change," she said.

Lindsey retrieved two plastic spoons and passed them over to us. "Thanks for the business."

"Let's eat our ice cream in the park," my cousin said to me. "I don't want to pay cleaning fees for the rental car."

We skirted around the food truck to stroll along a defined dirt pathway. A few power walkers maneuvered past us with ease.

I spooned the ice cream into my mouth, relishing the fresh mango taste for a moment before saying, "Did Lindsey seem kind of rude at the end? Like she wanted us to leave?"

"Yeah. She made us pay quickly even though nobody else was standing in line."

"It was right after we asked about Jordan Chang," I said.

Celine plunged her spoon into her ice cream. "She put my community down. Foodstagrammers aren't 'amateur critics.'"

"Why would she say that about someone she'd never heard of?"

"That is strange." Celine paused and leaned against the gnarled trunk of an oak tree. "Hold this," she said, handing over her cup of matcha ice cream. She'd eaten almost three-quarters of it.

My cousin checked her phone and said, "Huh. Jordan hashtagged Below Freezing in her post."

I glanced back at the truck. Although from this distance, I couldn't see the side, I remembered all the social media logos and the "#BelowFreezingIceCream" painted on it. "Wouldn't that mean Lindsey was aware of the post?"

"Most likely," Celine said. "Jordan even tagged Below Freezing, which should've alerted Lindsey to the picture."

I balanced the two cups of cold treats and peered over Celine's shoulder to read her screen. "What does Jordan's description mean? She says, 'Talk about brain freeze. So dangerously cold I want to tell EHD about it.' Who's EHD?"

Celine put her phone away and finished off the rest of her ice cream as we continued our stroll. I scraped at the bottom of my own cup as I tried to go through the people in Jordan Chang's life with those same initials.

By the time we'd circled back to the front of the park, the Below Freezing truck was gone. And any connection from Jordan to someone named EHD had similarly escaped me.

We spent the rest of that afternoon trying on clothes for the upcoming dinner, where Tresillo Trio would be performing. Celine seemed to have stuffed a whole department store's worth of attire into her three suitcases. She finally selected an off-the-shoulder silk minidress "in champagne." For me, we'd gone through more than a dozen combinations, with me hoping for a high-collared Victorian-style dress to no avail. We ended up compromising on a simple olive-green wrap dress—with pockets.

Celine also decided to give me a makeover so I could "go incognito." I think she wanted to dress me up like a living Asian Barbie doll, not that anyone could live up to that impossible hourglass-figure standard. By the time she'd finished with my makeup, I couldn't even recognize myself in the mirror. She'd explained everything as she worked on my face, applying contouring, a cat eye, and false lashes, to transform my typical dull self into a shinier version.

She made sure not to lower the convertible car top when we drove on the freeway because she didn't want to destroy her "hair art": my now long glossy waterfall of strands, created with highlighted extensions. Soon, we arrived at the restaurant with its unpronounceable (to me) French name, where she opted for valet service instead of self-parking.

Inside, the space was dark despite the soft light emanating from the paper lanterns dangling off exposed wooden beams. The mysterious ambience was heightened by the presence of black cloth draped over tables surrounded by ebony velvet chairs. The alabaster plates at the place settings seemed stark white by contrast.

A raised stage in the back of the long room already held sound equipment, a drum set, and an electronic keyboard on a stand, but I didn't see Genesis or her bandmates up there.

My eyes hadn't quite adjusted to the dim interior, but Celine whispered, "Genesis and her roommates are sitting together, at a table to the left of the stage."

I turned my head to locate the group and found them nestled at a four-seater, their chairs already turned toward the stage to watch the performance.

The hostess maneuvered behind us and said, "Please feel free to sit wherever you'd like, and your waiter will be with you in a minute."

Celine and I chose a cozy table for two behind the roommates, so we could better listen in on their conversation without them noticing. After we sat down, I craned my neck to check out the surface of their table. It appeared laden with appetizers and half-empty cocktail glasses. They must have shown up in advance for the Happy Hour deals.

When I perused the menu, I held back my inner gasp. Perhaps it would've been wise of us to also have come earlier, given the prices of the meals.

Plus, I couldn't understand some of the dishes anyway, which were labeled "New American" and seemed a combination of different cuisines. "You can choose for me," I told my cousin.

While Celine scrutinized the entrée options, I leaned toward the table in front of us and eavesdropped.

Sierra touched Genesis on the shoulder. "Too bad your relatives couldn't come see you tonight," she said. "They're only here for a couple more days, right?"

Genesis patted her hair, which seemed especially curly tonight, probably done up for her musical performance. "It's okay. I know they're not here to listen to my music. They want to spend time with family."

Reagan took a sip of her drink, a pretty red beverage with an umbrella floating in it. "I still can't believe your parents don't mind having so many people in their condo. Seven is a lot for a two-bedroom."

Genesis flipped her hand up. "Like I told Jordan"—her voice quivered—"it's not a big deal. They're family. My folks want them around."

"You're right, of course." Reagan toasted Genesis and finished her drink.

"Okay, I've got to set up now," Genesis said, standing up with a jerk of her shoulders. "See you afterward."

The waiter came by our table, so I missed the extra whispering between Reagan and Sierra. With authority, Celine ordered "seared wild salmon with strawberry demi-glace sauce" for herself and "steak and truffle frites with aioli" for me. After the waiter disappeared, I focused back on the roommates' table—and found it empty.

I bolted up from my seat and strained to see in the near darkness. Two figures traveled down a lit hallway, its archway labeled "Les Toilettes" in a cursive script.

"Be right back. Going to powder my nose with the ladies," I said as I scurried to catch up with Reagan and Sierra.

They'd already entered the restroom before I made it to the door. I hurried inside and found it empty. Nobody stood near the marble washing stations with their stacked cloth towels. The stalls themselves had full-length black doors that left only a gap at the bottom. All of them were closed, but I heard rustling behind the doors.

Should I pretend to use the facilities and continue to eavesdrop, sifting through random discussion points, or could I somehow direct the conversation myself? Near the entrance, I noticed a lounge area with a cushioned couch and a large bronze mirror.

Studying my reflection, I hoped I might pass as a stranger to the ladies. It could work. My new hair reached past my shoulders, and I wore heavy makeup. I played around with my hairdo, using the long strands to partially hide my face.

How would I strike up a conversation with them? I pulled out the fresh tube of lipstick Celine had supplied me with as a prop. When they came out of their respective stalls, I studied the women in the mirror.

They'd finished washing their hands and started walking toward the exit when I interrupted them.

"Wow," I said, turning around to face them. "I love your matching outfits." Indeed, they'd both opted to wear lilac chiffon blouses and dark jeans. Although their faces contrasted completely. Sierra wore no makeup whatsoever, showing off her fresh freckled face. On the other hand, Reagan had gone for a fun look to match her personality, using electric blue eyeshadow and sparkling face glitter.

"Thanks," Reagan said. "Us roomies like dressing the same whenever we can."

"Must be fun," I said. "Especially for Halloween. Did you wear anything special this year?"

"We were all ninjas," she said. "Dressed from head to toe in black."

The same outfit Jordan Chang had worn. I uncapped the metallic tube of lipstick. "Oh. Too bad you didn't get to attend the Eastwood Village Night Market."

Reagan's face paled. I wondered if she was thinking about Jordan—and missing her.

To change the direction of her thoughts, I said, "The night market had discounts for dressing up."

Reagan recovered and pasted a smile on her face. "Yes, we went and took advantage of that deal."

"I was there, too, over the weekend," I said. "The whole thing seemed successful, super crowded."

"Yeah, that's why we used rideshare even though I wanted to drive. We didn't want to be stuck getting in or out of the parking lot." Reagan jerked her thumb at Sierra. "Actually, that one bailed on us. Said she couldn't stay up all night because of her job. She works at a dermatologist's office, open seven days a week."

Sierra rubbed her palms against her dark jeans. "Couldn't help it. They wanted me to come in early the next morning to cover the front desk. And you know I need the cash. I'm already late with rent this month."

Reagan chuckled. "You mean, the last few months."

"Not everybody has a rich family willing to pay for their singing career," Sierra muttered.

"Should've been born an Aldana instead of a Tang," Reagan said.

Sierra didn't reply, and they headed for the door as I started swiping lipstick on.

A moment later, Reagan stepped back in.

I froze. Had I done something to tip her off to my true identity?

"Sorry, thought I left my phone in here." She checked around the room but soon gave up. "Must have left it back at the table."

I continued putting on the lipstick.

"By the way," she said, "I'm not sure about that color on you. Try a cooler tone."

"Oh, do you work in the beauty industry?"

"No, I'm at Maximal Games, except Jordan—never mind. Anyway, I've helped style my friends for elaborate events."

She stuck around, and I felt compelled to wipe off all my lipstick under her watch. Then Reagan pushed the door open and held it for me as I bustled out of the washroom into the corridor.

Sierra peered at my face in the brighter light of the hallway. "Huh," she said but then turned to Reagan. "What took so long?"

"Just some lipstick correction," Reagan said as she caught up with her roommate.

Sierra said, "We'd better hurry, Reagan. The music has started."

They scampered off as the strains of a jazzy melody reached my ears.

When I returned to my seat next to Celine, the trio onstage seemed to be in the middle of a set. The pianist played a trill on the keys while the drummer tapped out a soft rhythm in the background. Genesis took the spotlight in the center as she crooned the lyrics in her raspy voice.

The music drowned out all chances of overhearing any more comments between the roommates, so Celine and I concentrated on eating our food. I admitted that I admired both the taste and the presentation of the dish, but it seemed like a steep financial investment. With the same amount of money, I could have ordered a mountain of delectable dim sum dishes at Wing Fat.

When we'd finished our meal, the Tresillo Trio announced they were taking a quick break. Genesis spoke into the microphone and said, "We have a donation box here onstage for those who'd like to support us."

Celine stood and moved with grace up to the stage. She dropped something into the donation box and then returned to my side.

"They're pretty good," I said. "You like jazz?"

"I enjoy all forms of artistry. Besides a generous tip, I also dropped off an extra goodie."

"Which was?"

She flicked her fingertips toward Genesis. "A promise for a free pupusa from a certain someone. Seemed like there was a love triangle happening in that apartment."

I nodded at my cousin's ingenuity, remembering Genesis getting moony over the mention of Blake's name. She'd be delighted upon receiving the business card from La Pupusería de Reyes. "I bet she'll show up there tomorrow."

"I even circled the opening time for her. And added 'XOXO' next to his signature."

"Guess we're having morning pupusas," I said.

"You betcha." Celine lowered her voice and tilted her head toward the table in front of us. "I hope that trip to powder your nose was worthwhile."

"Yeah, I picked up a few things," I said.

"Great." Celine signaled for the waiter and paid the bill.

After we retrieved the Porsche from the valet and Celine started driving, I filled her in with the information I'd gleaned. I let Celine know that Reagan worked at a place called Maximal Games, and I also told my cousin how the roommates dressed alike on special occasions, including Halloween. I ended with the most important tidbit I'd discovered that evening: "Jordan Chang wasn't alone at the night market. Reagan and Genesis were also there."

Celine steered with one hand and snuck glances at my reaction while barraging me with questions: "What happened to Reagan and Genesis that night? Did they get separated? Why was Jordan all alone when you found her?"

The more flustered my cousin got, the more she pressed down on the gas pedal. Beyond my window, the streetlights blurred as we sped by.

"I really don't know," I said, "but hopefully we'll find some answers from Genesis tomorrow morning."

ELEVEN

At ten in the morning, we parked in the lot of La Pupusería de Reyes and waited for Genesis to show up. She arrived five minutes late, triple-checked herself in the rearview mirror, and then waltzed through the door of the restaurant. We counted to twenty before slipping inside. No bell chimed above the door, and we sneaked into the back of the eatery undetected.

Genesis already stood at the counter, babbling away, and Blake faced her, a crease forming between his thick eyebrows.

"Anyway, thanks for watching me play," Genesis said. "I wasn't sure because I thought you might still have feelings for—"

"I don't know what you're going on about, Gen."

She shifted from one foot to the other and said, "I saw you at your booth in the night market, busy chatting with Jordan. I wondered if maybe she'd changed her mind, and that the two of you got back together."

"She was just doing her usual foodie thing." Blake

rubbed at his chin, and his voice sounded rougher when he spoke again. "Um, I heard the news about Jordan."

"The food you sent," Genesis mumbled.

I knew she must've been referring to the special Wing Fat delivery that "Blake" had ordered for the roommates. They both exchanged stilted condolences.

Blake stared at her for a moment before saying, "Right. What would you like to order?"

"You said something about a free pupusa?" Genesis rummaged in her crocheted bag and yanked out a crinkled business card with the added "XOXO" to show him.

"Where did you get that from?"

"Didn't you drop it off at my performance last night?"

Blake blinked at Genesis, and Celine used the awkward moment to stride forward. "Don't forget about my cousin and me over here."

Blake and Genesis turned toward us, and recognition dawned on both their faces.

"Go get her pupusa. Put it on my tab if you need to," Celine said. She studied the menu. "Yale and I will take a catering tray to go. Let me see what we'd like . . ."

Celine turned her head in my direction. "In the meantime, Yale, why don't you chat with Genesis?"

I escorted a very confused Genesis to a table far away from the counter, and once we sat down, she said, "I thought you two didn't know Blake? That you were just deliverers."

To not outright lie, I said, "I met him at the Eastwood Village Night Market. We worked in adjacent food booths."

"I still don't get why the two of you are here."

By this time, Celine had paid for the food and sidled up to our table. She leaned over and whispered, "Isn't it obvious? I was trying to hook you up."

"What?" Genesis fluttered her fingers against the tabletop.

"Call me a romantic sap," Celine said, "but I could tell

you really liked the guy. And maybe he did, too, because he ordered the food delivery to your place, right?"

Genesis let that sink in, and her hands stilled on the table as she considered the scenario my cousin had painted.

Celine continued, "But maybe you felt shy around him? You didn't go up to his booth at the night market, I'm guessing."

She looked away from my cousin, focusing on the flag of El Salvador on the wall. "I couldn't. Not after seeing the two of them together again. I left the whole thing pretty soon after. Made my excuses to Jordan and texted Reagan that I felt sick."

Celine said, "Well, Blake was giving out these free pupusa discounts there. I hadn't used mine yet, so I thought I'd give you two the opportunity to connect by dropping the card in your donation box last night."

Genesis startled. "You tracked me to my gig?"

"No." My cousin flipped her hair. "Yale was just taking me around town, showing me the hot spots. When I saw you performing, I was inspired to play Cupid."

Genesis glanced toward the kitchen door, and a blush colored her cheeks crimson. "It's that obvious, huh? All the roommates think badly of him. Jordan even labeled him 'a player,' but she had such a strict sense of propriety, like a . . . what's that phrase again?"

"Goody Two-shoes?" I said. I'd heard the term applied once or twice to me, maybe because of my bent toward respecting authority.

"That's it. But Jordan did it to the extreme," Genesis said. "She was like a cop."

The harshness in her tone gave me pause. I'd unearthed a vein of anger in her. I wondered if Jordan had elicited those same sorts of dangerous feelings from others around her. Perhaps someone had acted on those frustrations, which had led to Jordan's untimely death.

Blake rushed out of the kitchen carrying an aluminum foil tray. "Your pupusas to go, ladies. Gen," he said, "I'll come back with yours soon."

As he left again, Celine got up and winked at Genesis. "That's our cue to leave you two alone. Some advice? Act confident, like how you owned the stage last night."

Genesis shook out her hair and straightened her shoulders as we marched out the door with the catering tray.

"Why'd we order so much food?" I asked Celine in the car.

"We're doing a little visit. To Maximal Games."

Celine googled the company and found a hit right away. The office was actually a quaint house located on Hilgard Avenue.

When we got there, the goldenrod stucco building looked friendly. Sculpted green bushes flanked the few steps up to the front door.

Although I noticed a doorbell, Celine used the brass knocker to announce our arrival. After a few minutes of waiting, a strawberry blonde opened the door. She wore a bright orange shirt that featured a cartoon cell phone with a smiley face.

She glanced at our huge tray. "I'm not expecting a delivery. Is that for a neighboring house?"

"Nope. Our friend asked us to deliver these to Maximal Games." Celine paused. "Is this the right place? It's what was listed on the internet."

"That's us, and this is our company shirt." The blonde puffed out her chest. "I'm Elodia Jones, head of Maximal. But all my employees are WFH now. Who did you say ordered this?"

"The pupusas are from Reagan," my cousin said.

I could tell Celine was holding her breath, hoping she wouldn't have to supply the last name.

Elodia bit her plump bottom lip. "Oh. Reagan Wood.

She doesn't let up, even though I told her she's no longer welcome here."

"Why's that?" I asked, but Elodia wouldn't bite. She offered me no further information.

Instead, she grabbed the tray of pupusas from Celine and said, "I'll take the food, but my mind won't be so easily changed."

When the door closed in our faces, Celine said, "Gee. She seemed upset."

"Sounds like Reagan isn't a valued employee at Maximal at the moment," I said.

We returned to the car, but before Celine could start the engine, her phone rang. She listened for a few minutes before saying, "We'll be right there, Uncle."

"Was that Ba?" I said, buckling in on the passenger's side.

"Yeah. Nik's at Wing Fat making a big fuss, and your father is hoping to get him out of there before the dim sum rush."

W e found Nik in the empty banquet room at Wing Fat. Someone had closed the sliding door to the area to give him privacy as he paced around.

He greeted us by saying, "You two are always making trouble for me."

"Did something happen?" I asked. "Let's sit down and talk it through."

He sulked but sat down at a table holding a single glass of water.

"Would you like something to eat?" I said.

"Nope. And your father already asked." Nik stuffed his hands into the pockets of his jeans. "I'm not going to get caught eating anything from here."

"I'm just trying to be hospitable," I said.

"I think we're past manners," he said. "This Jacey chick came into Ho's today, asking me what I had served her sister at the night market."

"You did give Jordan Chang something, a 'more authentic' green bubble tea than mine."

"Of course I didn't tell *her* that."

Celine moved in on Nik. "I bet Jacey wouldn't have appreciated the fact that you served it in a light bulb glass, like the kind found next to her sister's body."

"It was a regular plastic cup. Never mind." He pulled his hands out of his pockets and grabbed the water glass in a chokehold.

"You didn't serve light bulb glasses that first night?" I said.

He raked his hand through the bleached strands at the top of his head. "I only said that to mess with you. I wanted to take away your thunder by saying we'd handed them out early on."

Nik had changed his tune about being the first at the night market to serve beverages in unique light bulb containers. While growing up together, he'd always been my rival and tried to outdo me. But was he telling the truth now or lying because of the crime scene evidence?

"If you're innocent, why are you so riled up?" I said.

Nik said, "Jacey was going out of control in the restaurant, searching high and low. She even made it a few steps into the kitchen before I kicked her out."

"I wonder what she was looking for," I said.

"Who knows? When I asked her to leave, she started calling someone on her phone. Probably that detective you sicced on me."

"What'd the cop say?" Celine asked.

"He must not have answered because she hung up. Anyway, she didn't find a single clue at Ho's."

"I don't get it," I said. "Why are you here, Nik? Unless you're trying to just vent."

He pointed a trembling finger at me. "It's all your fault, Yale. You started that detective hot on my trail. Out of spite, I bet. Then Jacey makes trouble at the restaurant, almost giving Ma a heart attack."

I reared back.

"Sorry," he said, his gaze dropping down to the table. "Scratch that last part."

I *had* informed Detective Strauss about the similar light bulb containers, but that didn't mean I was responsible for Jacey's actions, right? In no way did I want Nik's mother to suffer because of my simple observation.

"What do you want me to do?" I asked in a gentle tone.

"I don't know," he said. "But Jacey left muttering about going to the library and doing research on poisons, of all things."

"When did she leave Ho's?"

He checked his watch, a solid Timex piece with a leather strap. "Twenty minutes ago."

"Okay, Nik." I scratched the bridge of my nose. "I'll think of something."

"You'd better," Nik said. "Because if you don't, I'm going to use the restaurant network and spread rumors that someone died from *your* cooking. And it'd be even better if not only your name suffered, but also the attached rep of Wing Fat."

"But your mother and Ba are friends," I said. "She told me so herself. Auntie wouldn't let you do that."

"Ma wouldn't need to know that I was involved with the rumor," he said. "You have forty-eight hours, Yale. Make them count."

Nik marched out of the banquet room with a new swagger to his step.

"You went to school with that guy?" Celine said.

"Yeah, and I thought college might change him. I was wrong. He's a clear example of *once a jerk, always a jerk*."

"Are you really going to help him?"

"The sooner we figure out what really happened to Jordan Chang, the better. We have forty-eight hours. And I think I know where to start."

"Then let's get moving."

As we passed behind the hostess stand in the restaurant, we noticed a commotion. A young woman with black hair gestured with vigor, throwing her hands out in a wide motion that almost knocked me over. I edged around to her side. Even from her profile, I recognized Sierra.

"They showed up on my doorstep with a wrong delivery." She wrung her hands. "I just want to make sure it was legit. There were two of them, and the taller girl had wavy hair with these huge eyes, amber colored."

I halted at Sierra's words. It was obvious she was talking about Celine and me.

"I'm sorry," the hostess said, "but we don't even offer delivery, and I really have to take care of these customers." She scrambled over to a waiting family with a bawling toddler to hand them a ticket.

Sierra turned around, perhaps to leave, and spotted me standing there frozen. "You're here," she said. "Who are you exactly? Wing Fat doesn't deliver, so why'd you bring over food?"

Celine stepped beside me, and we both faced Sierra.

"Let's take this outside," Celine said in a cool voice.

Sierra stood her ground. The freckles across her face seemed more prominent up close. "No, thanks."

As customers started giving each other uneasy looks, I crept over to Sierra and whispered, "We visited your place because of Jordan Chang."

Sierra's body seemed to sag at the mention of her roommate's name, and I convinced her to move to a quieter spot in the restaurant.

"They think my cousin is involved," I said, darting a quick glance at Celine.

"But why?" Sierra said.

"Because Jordan bought a unique drink from our food stand at the night market."

Celine hung her head. "I added a special ingredient to the tea."

"Like what? Metal spikes?"

"Not funny." Celine pulled herself to her full height. "They were actually edible gold flakes."

Sierra trained her dark brown eyes on Celine. "You've got nothing to worry about, then. Nobody's gonna alert the CDPH or EHD."

"Those initials again," I said. "What do they stand for?" EHD matched the mysterious person Jordan had mentioned on Instagram.

"California Department of Public Health. And the Environmental Health Department. They're responsible for checking on consumer complaints."

EHD. Jordan Chang had mentioned the initials in conjunction with the Below Freezing food truck. I needed to look at that IG post again and examine the wording in light of this new revelation.

Celine chimed in and said, "Glad you're on my side, Sierra. If only the homicide detective saw it the same way."

"Law enforcement," Sierra said. "They're not always the brightest bulbs. But the next time you two want to pull a Nancy Drew, don't be so weird about it. Just talk to me straight up."

"We should have. I apologize for our stunt. You've given us a lot to think about." I glanced over at the clock above the hostess stand, the one with numerals written in Chinese characters, and translated the time in my head. "Sorry to dash, Sierra, but we've got a lead to follow."

TWELVE

SINCE THE EASTWOOD VILLAGE PUBLIC LIBRARY was the closest branch to Ho's, I bet Jacey had chosen it after confronting Nik. Celine and I entered the hushed environment, hopeful.

While Celine examined the patrons in the open area, heads bent over their books, I approached the reference librarian, the same one who'd talked to me about metallic food decorations. If Jacey was anything like me, she'd be thorough in her research and ask him for help.

He sat behind the repurposed card catalog and said, "How can I assist you?"

I made a pretense of looking around the room. "I'm searching for someone. I was supposed to meet my friend Jacey here, but I can't seem to find her." I described Jacey's height, her long black hair, and her thick glasses.

The librarian scratched his head for a moment. "We get so many people who come in . . ."

"She also wears stacking rings on her thumb. They say 'Big sister' and 'Little sister' on them," I said.

His eyes brightened in recognition. "Yes, I noticed the rings when she donated her glasses."

I peeked over at the nearby box of donations. A few pairs of glasses lay in the container. One of them didn't have a case around it. Jordan's old pair, I deduced. It would explain the warped eyeglasses holder I'd seen in the discards box back at her old apartment.

"Is Jacey still around?" I asked.

"I think she might be in one of the study rooms in the back," he said. "I printed out some stuff for her. She must be a foodie because she was looking at articles about restaurants around town."

I bet she'd been ready to jump on those newspaper reports, perhaps to tie Nik or any of us food vendors to Jordan's demise. After I rounded up my cousin, we snuck over to the study rooms.

The three rooms in the back were arranged in a row, but all featured clear glass to look through and see the participants inside. Any library patron could ask for the privilege of entering the quiet domain if it hadn't already been reserved. One room held two high school students, with graph paper and protractors scattered across the shared desk. Another lay empty. The third held Jacey, her attention fixated on some paper printouts before her, which she scribbled away on. She also had a towering stack of books on the wooden desk.

Celine and I tiptoed into the room, and then my cousin stood with her back against the door, essentially blocking it.

Sensing our presence, Jacey looked up. The pen flew out of her hand. "Yale Yee," she said, pushing her glasses up the bridge of her pert nose. "I've been reading about you and your *lou dao*'s business."

The informal phrase she'd used for "father" sounded like an insult. She'd called him an "old bean," or more generically, an "old man." It might have been acceptable if we were buddies and shooting the breeze, but we were strangers. For sure, she'd said it to rile me up, but I wouldn't take the bait.

"Ba runs a respectable business," I said. "It's been thriving for years."

"Who's your bestie over there?" She retrieved the multicolor ballpoint she'd been using and pointed its tip toward the entryway.

"I'm Celine," my cousin piped up. "I don't think I ever told you my name."

"Right. You were at the police station, and I remember you both from the night market," Jacey said.

"You must have seen Nik at the event, too," I said. "He was next to us in the Taiwanese food booth. I heard you paid him a visit today."

She rolled the ballpoint pen between her palms. "How'd you find that out? Are you and Nik friends?"

"Frenemies," I said. "He blamed me for somehow making you barge into Ho's."

"He's high on my list of suspects, although I haven't crossed you two off yet. Besides, Detective Strauss seems particularly keen on tracking your movements that night."

Celine groaned and sagged against the doorknob. "This was supposed to be a fun trip to the U.S., not a hands-on lesson in Crime 101."

Jacey's sharp voice sliced through the air. "Show some respect. That's my sister who died."

"Sorry," Celine said, her face turning splotchy and red. "Really, I am."

"Me too," I said, my voice shaking. "I know what it's like to have a loved one die unexpectedly."

Jacey's dark brown eyes seemed to perceive my inner sorrow. "I think you do," she said. "Tell me why you've hunted me down to the library. You know that these walls are see-through, so you can't harm a hair on my head without any eyewitnesses."

"That's not why we're here. We also want to figure out what happened to your sister," I said.

"Yeah." Celine jutted her chin out. "Especially since that detective dislikes me so much."

"Why is *Nik* so high on your list?" I asked as I edged closer to her desk.

She retrieved a yellow legal pad that had been hidden behind the towering stack of books. "Read this."

I moved over to stand next to her. Names and associated food stalls were scribbled onto the page: Nikola Ho and Ho's Small Eats, Blake Westby Reyes and La Pupusería de Reyes, Lindsey Caine and Below Freezing. The Canai and Chai food stall also made the cut.

"I still don't get it," I said. "Why did you confront Nik?"

Jacey jabbed at the fine print next to Nik's name. I read, *Nikola Ho. The only stand missing a foodstagram. Why?*

"I'm not sure what that means," I said.

"Did your friend Nik tell you that he served my sister?" Jacey asked.

I dug back into my memory. "Yeah. He gave her a green tea."

"There was no pic of it on Jordan's IG account."

Celine rushed forward. "That's weird. I take a shot of everything I eat and drink. Every foodstagrammer does."

Jacey circled Nik's name on the paper. "I think he must have got hold of her phone and deleted the post to erase evidence of his involvement."

"Can't you just check her camera roll?" my cousin asked. "Even if he purged it from Instagram, there should be a backup shot."

"The police never found her phone," Jacey said.

"Let me get this straight," I said. "You think Nik was somehow involved in Jordan's death and tried to cover his tracks by stealing her phone and deleting her Instagram picture."

"And then he must have destroyed the phone," Jacey said. "There's no signal for it now."

I stared at the Ho surname on the paper. "But why Nik? He doesn't even know Jordan. What motive could he have had?"

"I don't know." Jacey gathered her long hair into an updo and stuck the pen in it to secure the messy bun. "But Jordan had excessive *yeung* energy. She got peeved by people's mistakes, and her temper ran hot."

I remembered her roommate describing her in a similar way. "Huh. You know, Genesis said something about Jordan being a kind of extreme Goody Two-shoes."

Jacey snorted. "It's no wonder. All of Jordan's roommates had their problems. My sister just called them on their crap."

"Like what?" I said.

"Genesis had relatives defying the housing code, Sierra was a freeloader, and Reagan was irresponsible at work."

Celine joined us at the desk. "Your sister had the dirt on everyone in the apartment."

"We were raised to follow the rules by our parents," Jacey said. "That's how we grew up levelheaded. And Jordan was very observant."

"Or nosy," Celine mumbled.

I flashed my cousin a warning look, but Jacey didn't appear to have heard Celine's negative comment. She seemed focused on the yellow sheet of paper.

Jacey whipped her head up and glared at me. "Why would Nikola want to poison her? You know the guy. Is he aboveboard?"

"Nik's arrogant," I said. "Thinks his restaurant has the best Taiwanese food around and is the only place for authentic bubble tea. But I don't know how his cockiness could have translated to murder."

Jacey looked between Celine and me. "What about you

two? Did you do something off the cuff that evening with your food?"

Celine and I exchanged a glance. It probably wouldn't be a good time to ask Jacey if her sister had been allergic to gold as well as to nickel.

Jacey continued, "My sister ate or drank something fatal that night, and I intend to find out who and what was the cause of her death." She gave us a penetrating stare. "I'm going to cross off these names one by one until I find the killer or killers. Be sure of that."

My cousin nodded while I said, "Good luck."

We backed out of the room with care. Although we'd started out thinking we'd trapped Jacey inside to gather information from her, it felt like we'd inadvertently locked ourselves in with a ferocious lion ready to pounce.

"That was intense," Celine said when we exited the library. She took a moment to roll out some kinks in her neck.

"Agreed, but Jacey wasn't wrong to be suspicious," I said. "We need to look at the vendors and everything Jordan ordered that night, including that super-cold ice cream."

"From Below Freezing?"

"Yes. Do you remember what Sierra told us at Wing Fat? EHD stands for the Environmental Health Department, the place to make food complaints. What if the ice cream served by Lindsey Caine had been fatal somehow?"

Celine checked her phone to verify Below Freezing's current location. "It isn't too far from here. Let's take a closer look at their food practices."

◁▭▭▭▭▭▷

We stalked the ice cream truck from down the street. Below Freezing was parked, along with other food trucks, at the intersection of two major streets in Eastwood Village.

Celine and I stood in the shade of a large palm tree, and I hoped the shadow, along with the distance, would disguise our features if Lindsey happened to lean out the window to check for potential customers.

"She seems to be doing everything right," I said. Lindsey would take the order and go through the motions of freezing the cream, putting in the flavors, and mixing the batches. "How could she mess that up?"

Celine pulled out her phone and accessed Instagram. "Jordan mentioned something about a brain freeze. She called it 'dangerously cold.' But people get brain freezes all the time and don't die from them."

I peeked again at the shot of the ice cream with swirls of smoke framing it. "Could the ice cream have been too cold to eat?" I remembered Lindsey operating the liquid nitrogen and making our ice cream scoops. "Maybe she pumped too much into Jordan's batch. How cold does liquid nitrogen get?"

My cousin tapped at her phone. "Negative three hundred and twenty degrees Fahrenheit." She waved her phone in the air. "Info right at your fingertips. You should think about getting one."

"Meh. How many times will I need to search up something like that?"

"You'd be surprised." She looked me in the eye. "Technology makes your life so much easier."

"For all you know, tech might have been what got Jordan in trouble in the first place. Let me see that Instagram post again."

I reread Jordan's entry about Below Freezing and her mention about wanting to tell EHD about it. "Do you think Lindsey could've taken that as a threat?"

"Maybe," Celine said, squinting at the woman doling out ice cream. "You think she tried to literally freeze Jordan from the inside out?"

"Negative three hundred–plus sounds mighty cold to me."

"But it's tempered with ice cream. Besides, we both ate it, and we're fine."

"We didn't threaten her livelihood," I said.

Celine clicked back on Jordan's account, and I spied the grid-like array of photos.

"Can you run through the shots from the night market again?"

"Sure thing." She scrolled through the foods and beverages displayed. Beyond the boba from our stall, I spotted ice cream, a yellow drink, and shaved ice.

"Something's missing," I said.

"Yeah. Nik's drink."

"Besides that. What about anything from the pupusa place?" I rubbed my forehead with my fingertips. Blake had said Jordan liked to order . . . what? I massaged my temple some more. *Ensaladas.* "She liked salads from there, but I don't see a photo of anything green."

"Also, like Jacey said, it *is* weird that the police didn't find the phone," Celine said.

"I have to agree with her theory. The killer must have taken it. Maybe because of the incriminating photos."

"Or texts," Celine said.

"Can't the police retrieve messages from the phone provider?" I asked.

"Not if they're through an app." Celine pointed to the various icons on her phone. "WhatsApp, Messenger, et cetera. These all send messages that aren't recorded with the company."

"I wish I'd written everything down like Jacey to keep track of all this info instead of constantly repeating it in my head."

"Your wish is my command," Celine said. "You can either do a voice memo or type it in."

"I like writing stuff down."

She opened up some sort of notepad program on her phone and handed it over. "Try it, but don't lose my phone."

"Why? Where are you going?"

She gestured over to a nearby Vietnamese sandwich food truck. "To get us some lunch, Nancy Drew."

"Good idea." Even though we'd gone to the pupusería and Ba's restaurant today, we hadn't bothered to get any food. If we alleviated our hunger pangs, we'd be able to think more clearly.

Using the notepad app that she'd opened up, I started listing the food vendors first. They'd been on-site and had the means to slip something dangerous into Jordan's food or drink.

Nik Ho could have laced her shaved ice mountain, or more likely, slipped something into her green tea, since Jordan no longer had an incriminating picture of the drink. Blake Westby Reyes could've doctored her salad, another missing item. Lindsey Caine might've added more than the fair amount of liquid nitrogen needed to chill the ice cream to frozen deliciousness.

Speaking of food, Celine showed up right then with the bánh mì. I loved the crusty bread of the sandwiches, along with the fillings inside, which included pickled radishes, thin carrot shreds, and sprigs of fresh cilantro.

As we ate, I continued to make notes on the phone. It took some maneuvering to use one hand to type and the other to eat, but I managed to balance both tasks.

I took a swallow and said, "So, I have the vendors down and the foods or drinks they served Jordan. They definitely have the means to poison Jordan somehow, but what about the motive?"

"The roommates also might not have been too happy with Jordan nosing around their business," Celine said. "We heard that straight from Jacey."

I typed the names of the roommates: Genesis Aldana, Sierra Tang, and Reagan Wood. "Jacey made it sound like

Jordan had a tense relationship with all of her roomies. Could things have gone sideways with one of them? Let's go over her issues with them and see if we can discover more."

"With Genesis," Celine said, "I know it had to do with her relatives."

I took another bite of the scrumptious golden bread of the sandwich and mulled over the snippet of conversation I'd overheard at the French fusion restaurant. "Reagan mentioned something about Genesis's family having too many relatives staying in a small condo. I wonder what that was about."

"And according to her sister, Jordan didn't like Sierra's freeloading ways," Celine said before digging into her bánh mì.

"Jordan also had something on Reagan and her work-place."

Celine wiped some crumbs off her mouth with a paper napkin. "The big question is who was around Jordan during the night market?"

I looked over my list of suspects. "We could potentially cross out Genesis and Sierra. Genesis slipped out early when she mistakenly thought Jordan and Blake were trying to patch up their relationship, and Sierra was home during that time."

Celine peeked at the screen. "Let's keep Genesis on the list. Then we also have Nik, Blake, Lindsey, and Reagan. That's five people for us to investigate."

"Yeah. We've got our work cut out for us."

I closed down the app, and we finished our sandwiches in silence.

<hr/>

We continued to remain quiet in the car, lost in thought. About halfway back to the apartment, the Boxster started wobbling. I felt like I was tilting on a carnival ride. A loud noise rumbled from below us.

"What's wrong with the car?" I said, checking the gauges on the dashboard.

"Strange." Celine slowed down and leaned her head to the side to listen.

"Is it trying to kill us?" I asked.

"Cars aren't sentient," Celine said, pulling over to the side of the road.

Once parked, she walked all around the car. Finally, she crouched down and examined the wheel on the front passenger's side. "It's flat."

I glanced at it. The front tire was deflated.

"Probably hit some road debris," my cousin said. "L.A. has street improvement projects going on all the time."

I didn't remember driving through a construction zone.

"Anyway, don't worry." She flashed her cell phone at me. "Because tech for the win."

Roadside assistance arrived within twenty minutes. The mechanic checked out the tire and whistled. "If there had been any more damage, I wouldn't have been able to patch it."

He went to work fixing the tire.

"Can I see the nail or whatever poked it?" Celine asked.

"No," he said. "I can't find anything."

"Well, what could have possibly made the puncture?" I asked, staring at the patched spot.

The mechanic packed away his tools. "Don't know. And, oddly, it was more of a slash than a hole."

I glanced at Celine. Could someone have targeted our car? The shiny blue rental Boxster was easily recognizable.

Celine frowned and turned her attention to the mechanic. "When do you think the wheel got damaged?"

"Hard to say," he said. "It's so small it might have been leaking air for a while without you even noticing."

We thanked the mechanic for the repair and buckled back into the car.

"It's safe to drive now, right?" I said.

"Absolutely." Celine started up the engine, but she didn't put the car into gear. "You think the flat tire is a coincidence, right?"

I hesitated. "Or it could be a warning from someone wanting us to stop snooping."

THIRTEEN

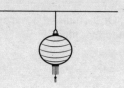

BACK AT FOUNTAIN VISTA, WE FOUND ANOTHER unexpected interruption to our day in the form of an unwelcome guest in the lobby. Detective Strauss sat in an overstuffed chair near a flickering gas fireplace. He homed in on every person entering the premises. The security guard seemed unfazed by his presence, so he must already have introduced himself and flashed his badge at the front desk.

When he spotted us, he waved us over to the mock library area where he sat. An entire side wall was dedicated to a nook of pretend books. It looked like an antique bookcase filled with classics, but every tome was a hollowed-out replica placed on the towering shelves.

"Yale," he said, "have a seat."

Why me? I perched on the chair opposite him while Celine stood behind me, her hands resting on the curved back of the furniture.

Detective Strauss swept his hand in the air to encompass the surroundings. "Do you know what I love about Eastwood Village?"

The serene atmosphere? The luxurious amenities? I settled for something relevant to his line of work. "The low crime rate?"

From behind me, I heard Celine murmur, "Except for this past weekend."

"You're right, Yale," the detective said. "I appreciate the upstanding citizens here and how people respect the law. It helps that there are incentives to do so." He tilted his head and stared up.

I followed his line of sight to the surveillance equipment installed at the corner of the lobby's ceiling.

"Cameras," he continued, "capture people coming and going, which helps shed light in our cases."

"Okay," I said, "so you appreciate having video records."

He leaned forward, placing his elbows on his knees and clasping his hands together. "Tell me, Yale, why did you need to reenter this apartment building before alerting the police about the victim's body?"

"I live here. And I needed to come in so I could make that crucial call to report the crime."

"What about your cell phone?"

Celine piped up from behind me. "She doesn't have one. Sad but true."

A muscle twitched near his jaw.

"She's right," I said, standing up for a moment. I turned my pockets inside out to show him their meager contents: my apartment key and a small credit card holder. Then I lowered myself back down.

Detective Strauss unclasped his hands and scooted back in his chair. He aimed his gaze above my head to where Celine stood. "And where was your cousin during that time? Why wasn't she with you?"

"She'd left for her hotel already."

His green eyes focused back on my face. "And the other vendors?"

"Everyone had gone or were on their way to go."

He shifted his suit jacket with one hand, and I could see the glimmer of his badge. "That's interesting that you took some time between finding the body and then placing the call. And it's convenient how your cousin had already left the night market."

"Are you trying to imply something, Detective Strauss?"

He held his hands up in the air in mock surrender. "I'm making an observation that there was a lot of time elapsed between when you left the body, made the call, and when the first officer arrived. Someone could have tampered with the crime scene during that gap."

"I ran right away to make that call and report the death," I said.

The detective scanned the mock library and selected a thick book. "Do you know the term 'obstruction of justice'?" he said. "And 'accessory to murder'?"

I crossed my arms over my chest and hugged myself. "Those phrases don't apply to my cousin or to me."

His mouth drew into a grim line. "I sure hope they don't. For your sakes."

"Maybe you should look at some other leads." I turned my head and signaled my cousin. "Show him our list, Celine."

Celine stalked toward him, her phone held away from her body to show him the screen. It seemed like she wanted to remain as far from him as possible.

He skimmed the list in a few seconds. "I have all those names down already."

I said, "What about Nik from Ho's Small Eats? Didn't they also give out light bulb glasses at the night market?" I still wasn't sure which version of Nik's story was correct. He'd either been lying about serving their beverages in light bulb containers before us, or he'd tried to cover his tracks by mentioning that he'd used plastic cups on the very first night.

Detective Strauss flipped the hollow book in his hand a few times before answering. "It doesn't really matter if they did or not."

"Why's that?" Celine pocketed her phone.

"Because the glass we found at the scene of the crime didn't match the one I confiscated from Ho's Small Eats."

"But they look exactly the same," I said.

"They were very similar, but the thickness of the glass differed."

"Oh," I said.

Celine shuffled over to me and patted my shoulder.

Detective Strauss rose to his feet. "There's a backlog at the lab, so I'm still waiting on the results about the bottle of gold flakes and what specific metals were found in Jordan Chang's system. In the meantime, feel free to call me if you want to get anything off your chest." He laid the book down on the middle of the chair cushion and strode off.

"He could've at least put that away," I said.

"Maybe that's why his investigation has turned out so messy," Celine said.

I picked up the tome, and only then did I notice the title printed in faux gold lettering across the spine: *The Murder of Roger Ackroyd.* Did he think of my cousin or me as an unreliable narrator? I shoved the empty tome back on the shelf.

In the apartment, I discussed the detective's revelation about the light bulb glass with Celine. "If Nik wasn't using the same type of material, isn't he off the hook?"

"With Detective Strauss maybe," my cousin said as she lay down on my settee upholstered in a chocolate twill material. She took up the entire length of the couch. "But Jacey is still hot on Nik's trail."

"And we have forty-eight hours, until Friday, to decisively clear his name before Nik starts spreading vicious rumors about us."

"Yes, and gossip is hard to kill," Celine said. "Trust me on that."

I still hadn't figured out the exact disgrace Celine had suffered overseas. "What happened in Hong Kong?" I asked. "It can't be worse than getting accused of murder."

"Let's do a swap of secrets," my cousin said. "Tell me why you feel responsible for your mother's accident, and I'll spill."

I'd never told anyone why I still felt guilty, not even my dad, the person I was closest to. I curled my toes around the fringe of the patterned rug on the floor and felt the soft fibers tickle my feet.

"Or you can wait," Celine said in a carefree tone. "If you're going to be locked up with me, we'll have plenty of time to share our stories behind bars."

"Not funny," I said, moving a round ottoman in a matching brown shade over to the settee. I sat down across from my reclining cousin. "Fine. Let's share, but you go first."

"Okay. My parents bribed everyone to take down mentions of an unfortunate incident, but there are still a few cached websites to scrub clean."

"What incident? Somebody talked about it on the internet?" I said.

"A lot of *somebodies*. Reporters, bloggers. It was a splashy headline. Everybody loves a good wardrobe malfunction story."

"Oh no."

"Oh yes. Let me find a shot they haven't erased yet. It's like whack-a-mole with the media. That's why Ma Mi and De Di haven't been able to stop the gossiping and the reason they don't want me back yet." Celine scrolled through her phone and then handed it over to me.

I'd been expecting to see Celine with some sort of

wardrobe mishap, but the shot focused on a celebrity pop star's spaghetti strap sliding off her bony shoulder, revealing more than she'd bargained for. "What's this have to do with you?"

"I caused the literal slip-up, or slip-off," my cousin said. "It was at this huge charity dinner my parents attended. The paparazzi were there to snap photos of us saying hello. After I greeted her with air-kisses, I noticed the plates of fabulous entrées on the table. The perfect foodgasm shot."

"People use that adjective?"

"It's an Insta hashtag. Anyway, keep up with the story," Celine said. "I leaned over to take the pic, and somehow snagged her purse and yanked it down. Unfortunately, when the bag slipped, so did her dress strap. In the end, I didn't even get the shot because she elbowed me out of the way in order to fix her dress and cover up."

"Sounds like quite the eventful gala."

Celine flung one arm across her face. "You should've seen the horrible headlines. The story blew up, and each article published was worse than the previous. Soon, my parents didn't even want to talk to me, just asked me to locate my passport. Before I knew it, I was basically shipped to L.A. to hide out. That's my tale of woe. Now it's your turn."

I found it helpful that Celine wasn't looking at me as I spoke. Closing my eyes, I remembered the night my mom had gone driving, and shuddered. "She didn't have to go out. Wasn't supposed to be on the road, but my mom drove as a favor to me."

"What do you mean?" Celine said.

I punched at the puffy fabric of the ottoman. "It was some stupid idea I had. I wanted to add fresh chives to this recipe I was experimenting with, and we didn't have any in the walk-in fridge. The restaurant had run out."

Celine uncovered her eyes, but she focused on the ceiling above her instead of turning toward me. "There wasn't a collision, only the car stalling because of an electrical system problem," my cousin said. "And even if there had been a crash, that wouldn't have been your fault either."

"But she went out that night because of me."

"Your mother could've had a heart attack anywhere."

"But the car broke down"—I gripped the edges of the ottoman and squeezed—"and that's what aggravated her heart condition."

"You don't know that," Celine said.

My eyes felt raw and itchy, but I willed myself not to cry. I'd held it in all these years, and I forced myself to remain strong.

"It's not your fault, Yale."

I wasn't sure if I believed my cousin, but I felt lighter at having shared my thoughts.

Celine sat up, brushed at her sleeves, and gave me a lopsided grin. "Anyway, it's not like what happened with me and that celebrity. Totally my fault. That was cause and effect, pure physics."

I reached over and gave her a half hug. "Thanks for listening, Celine. To be fair, though, I don't think anyone could've predicted *your* mishap."

"Except for Newton." She sprawled back across the settee. "Ugh. I need a nap."

The home phone rang then, and I hurried to pick up the call.

"Yale," my dad said, "I'm glad I caught you."

"Do you need something?" Maybe one of the waitresses had gotten sick and bailed on him.

"There's going to be a quick meeting tonight for any available Eastwood Village Night Market participants. At eight. Will you and your cousin be able to attend?"

"Sure." I tightened my grip on the phone. "Is there a reason for the sudden gathering?" If it was to analyze the attendance and popularity from the weekend's event, I doubted it would've been organized so last minute.

Worry laced my dad's voice. "The police got in touch with Ai Jeh about potential ramifications from the death of Jordan Chang."

"I see." Could the detective have been issuing a veiled threat to the night market organizers?

"If you could swing by Wing Fat this evening around seven, I'll be sure to make something to share with everyone tonight. Also, you and Celine can eat dinner here."

"That sounds good, Ba. Where's this meeting going to be held?"

"At the community room in the police department," he said.

The phone felt slippery. "Ah." I switched hands to wipe my sweaty palm against the side of my pants. "See you soon, Ba."

The hostess who greeted us at Wing Fat that evening was the same one we'd seen all week long. At nighttime, Ba's restaurant didn't have as many customers waiting around as during the hectic dim sum hours. I saw the hostess playing on her phone, half-hidden inside the podium, before she noticed us waiting at the entrance.

"Oh, sorry," she said. "Didn't see you there. The latest release from Maximal is too addictive."

"No problem," I said. "Wait, are you talking about Maximal Games?"

"Yeah." She made a sad puppy-dog face. "Their new one almost didn't get made. Read all about it on Discord."

"Why? What happened?"

She shook her head, and I marveled at how her elegant bun—pinned up with Maximal Games–logoed chopsticks—didn't unravel.

Celine leaned against the podium and dropped a twenty-dollar bill on it. "What happened at Maximal Games?"

I thought the hostess would've enjoyed gossiping to us without the extra incentive, but she still took the money. "There was a rumor that the events coordinator overshot their budget by a lot. Naturally, the employee doesn't work there anymore."

That sounded awfully familiar. "Wow," I said. "What a story."

My cousin pointed to a table in the dining area about ten feet away from where we stood. "Keep on playing your game. We can find our own seats."

I followed her as she sauntered over to the table for two. "You can't just throw your money around like that."

"Can't I?" she said. "My parents will float me."

"Money doesn't solve everything."

"Don't I know it," Celine said, a wistful tinge to her voice. "But it can smooth over things."

Although I'd opened up my heart to Celine back at the apartment, I realized again how different we were in our personalities and the way we operated. Instead of sitting, I made a detour to the kitchen to get a quick break from her.

I popped my head through the swinging door. "Hi, Ba. We're here."

Everybody in the kitchen looked my way: the assistant, the dishwasher, the other cook, and my dad.

Ba paused in his cooking and seemed to straighten to his full height when he said, "You all remember my daughter, Yale, right?"

They waved and greeted me with a warm welcome. I'd forgotten how working in close quarters on a daily basis could create a tight-knit community.

"I'll have someone bring your dinner out in a few minutes. Where are you sitting?"

"Table two," I said without thinking. Despite the gap in years, I still remembered the numbering system of the tables in the dining room.

When I returned to my cousin's side, I felt calmer and ready to discuss the murder case. "Jacey mentioned her sister knew Reagan was an irresponsible worker," I said.

"Yep," Celine said. "And didn't Elodia tell us Reagan was no longer welcome at the company?"

A waitress came by and deposited porcelain platters of food before us. Ba had cooked up a simple meal of white rice, steamed whole fish, and stir-fried pea sprouts.

I maneuvered the chopsticks with sure strokes and deboned the fish. Then I took the mealtime to expound on a new theory. "Could Jordan have accidentally gotten poisoned?"

"That's kinda hard to do," Celine said, between bites. "How do you not know what you put into your mouth?"

"Or maybe," I said, "Reagan dared Jordan to a challenge."

"Mm, that sounds off to me," Celine said. "A person like Jordan, who followed all the rules, wouldn't eat something toxic on purpose. Especially since there were warnings issued by a national safety commission."

We finished up our meal, and Celine checked the time.

"Let's get the goodies and head over to the police station," my cousin said.

Ba had made an entire catering tray's worth of sesame balls, or *jin deui*. In Cantonese, it meant a "fried pile." With its *golden* exterior dotted with sesame seeds and its hollow interior filled with *rich* red bean paste, the name carried a positive symbolization of wealth. It meant my dad hoped the meeting would go well.

Maybe he wished to sweeten the atmosphere? I wanted the same thing. Celine and I hadn't experienced much good news from the police recently, and we'd be walking straight into Detective Strauss's domain.

FOURTEEN

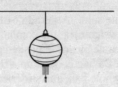

THE COMMUNITY ROOM AT THE EASTWOOD VIL-
lage Police Station seemed like a welcoming setting,
with its rows of long gleaming cherrywood tables and
ergonomic, padded chairs. However, the man in a suit
standing near the large whiteboard gave me shivers. I
hadn't expected to see Detective Strauss twice in one day,
especially after his warning remarks to us.

The detective examined each individual as they trailed
into the community room. My foodie vendor neighbors
had all shown up, as had a number of arts and crafts people. Even the breakdancer and the hula dancer, who'd
twirled fire, had decided to come.

Celine and I made sure to select a position in the back
corner of the room, away from the door and the farthest
distance from the detective. The aluminum tray in front
of us also half-blocked our bodies and served as a physical partition from him.

Detective Strauss waited until five minutes after the

hour before issuing his opening remarks. All chatter stopped once he spoke.

"The Eastwood Village Police are glad to host this meeting," he said. "We wanted to officially inform you about an incident that happened around two in the morning on Sunday."

Nobody moved a muscle, and even my cousin beside me seemed to hold her breath.

He continued, "The body of Jordan Chang was found near the fountain at the north side of the plaza. The culprit remains at large."

I heard a tiny gasp from somewhere in the room but couldn't pinpoint the person who'd reacted.

"However," Detective Strauss said, "we do have a very promising lead." His head pivoted in our direction. I hoped that hadn't been deliberate.

I tried to slouch down in my chair in order to hide from his view.

"The victim," Detective Strauss said, "was a young woman in her early twenties, who had a promising future before her. Jordan Chang graduated from UCLA and worked in HR at a local company. She wore a black ninja costume that night. Although her garb covered most of her features, she had distinctive violet eyes."

He didn't have a megaphone, but his voice boomed across the room. "This is a terrible tragedy, so you'll understand that I would appreciate any information you could provide. I've already interviewed many of you, but perhaps you now remember something new or know of another eyewitness who might step forward."

Picking up a dry-erase marker, he scribbled his contact information on the whiteboard. "Feel free to call or email me if you think of anything. I'll also remain in the building until nine this evening. Ask for Detective Greyson Strauss. Now, I'll leave you to the business side of your meeting."

He strolled off toward the exit but paused at the end of our table. Neither Celine nor I reacted to his lingering presence, and after a stretched-out moment, he continued on his way.

Ai Ho took over the spot that the detective had vacated. My dad had referred to Ai *Jeh* when he'd called me, but I hadn't realized the "Sister Ai" he'd referred to had been a respectful term for Nik's mother.

"As you know," she said, "I'm the organizer of the Eastwood Village Night Market. I personally contacted all the vendors, made sure to get the required permits, pursued marketing opportunities, and even set up the booths along with the volunteers."

Hearty applause sounded throughout the room.

Mrs. Ho continued, "Permission was granted for us to run the night market this previous weekend on a trial basis. I'd hoped that it would be a time to showcase our local artists and natural talent"—she gestured toward the breakdancer as an example.

He whipped the black beanie off his head and took a bow.

"And to introduce people to a few of the great eateries around here, including mine. Couldn't we all use a few more customers?" Mrs. Ho said.

At a table diagonal from us, I noticed Nik shift in his chair.

His mother continued, "I talked up our night market event to the owner of The Shops at Eastwood Village, saying that the tie to Halloween would bring in a large crowd. We also had been slated to run another night market around Thanksgiving to capitalize on that holiday. Depending on the success of the night market, instead of being a seasonal offering, the owner said he might be able to continue it on a weekly schedule." She held her hands out, palms up, like weighted scales. "Would you like to hear the good news or the bad news first?"

Blake, in the front row, raised a steel thermos in the air and said, "Good news."

"Okay." Mrs. Ho turned to the whiteboard and wrote down a few sums. She circled the larger number. "As you can see, the income generated from the night market exceeded our expenditures."

People clapped.

"I hope that means some of you also made a profit," Nik's mother said.

I turned to Celine, leaned in toward her, and whispered, "We actually did pretty well, especially since we didn't need much equipment or a lot of ingredients for the cold dishes and drinks."

"What's the bad news?" a woman asked. It sounded like Lindsey, and I recognized her profile seated the next row over.

"Our holding another night market is now contingent on getting this investigation cleared. There's also talk of adding more security in the future, if there will even be a repeat event."

Mrs. Ho wrote Jordan Chang's name in large letters on the whiteboard. "In light of this, I urge you to think really hard about Saturday night. Did you see or notice anything strange? Remember, this was a recent college student. And from what Detective Strauss told me privately, she'd worked really hard to get into university. Her parents couldn't help with expenses, so she had to save up before applying and getting into UCLA."

Nik's mother wrapped up the meeting by asking if people had any questions or comments.

I put my hand up like a schoolgirl and waited, while others blurted out their statements.

Lindsey raised her voice and said, "Jordan came by my booth, and I can tell you she was fit as a fiddle when she left."

The hula dancer sprang out of his chair and said, "Why

should we be punished for an incident that we couldn't control? She was surrounded by her friends the last time I saw her. Must have been peer pressure, and she partied too hard."

I waved my hand to get Mrs. Ho's attention, the last to get called on. When she finally spotted me in the back and called my name, I said, "My dad, Sing Yee, owner of Wing Fat Restaurant, wants to extend his well wishes to the community. He's provided me with a tray of sesame balls to share with everybody."

"Please give him our thanks," Mrs. Ho said. "Since there are no further questions, you're officially dismissed."

People soon clamored to get in line and surrounded Celine and me. From the attendees we heard variations of "It's a shame" and "What a tragedy."

Before long, Blake stood before us. "After all of your patronage at the pupusería, the tables have now turned. I finally get to try some of your goods. What are they called again?"

From next to me, Celine said in a curt tone, "Do you have issues with your short-term memory? Yale said they're sesame balls." Maybe she was still miffed about his past comment on foodstagrammers.

"What are they called in Chinese?" he asked, angling toward me, perhaps in hopes that I might answer with less rancor than my cousin.

"Jin deui," I said. "They're made with glutinous rice and have sweet red bean paste inside them."

He lifted his thermos in a salute. "They'll go well with my ensalada."

"You brought a salad?" I said.

"No." He unscrewed the lid of his tumbler, tilting the container toward me, and I spied a familiar-looking yellow beverage. "This is a *refresco de ensalada*. It's like a drinkable fruit salad."

I'd seen that drink featured on Jordan's Instagram feed. It seemed like Blake's concoction hadn't been missing from her photos, like I'd assumed. I snuck a glance at Celine, who looked flabbergasted.

While Blake selected a jin deui from the tray, I asked, "Can you stick around for ten minutes? My cousin and I would like to ask you a few questions."

"Sure. I'll be enjoying this sesame ball over there." He loped back to his original sitting spot.

Celine and I established a rhythm of doling out napkins and sesame balls to the remaining people. The last person we served was the hula dancer.

"Did you say you noticed Jordan with her friends that night?" I asked him.

The man nodded. "I noticed them watching me from near the stage."

"It was a breathtaking performance," Celine said.

"The ladies all appreciate my fire," he said.

My cousin fanned herself. "I bet."

The man did a subtle flex of his biceps as he reached for a sesame ball.

"How many friends were there?" I asked, wondering if Jordan had been watching the performance with her roommates.

"About half a dozen," he said.

That didn't make sense. There were only four roommates.

"Mahalo," the hula dancer said, picking up a sesame ball and strolling out the door.

After he left, only a handful of people lingered in the room, chatting. Nik and his mother were in that huddled group.

I figured we could stay a few more minutes. Besides, Detective Strauss hadn't barged back in and demanded us to leave yet.

With Celine following, I carried the empty foil tray

over to Blake's spot. A wadded-up paper napkin lay before him.

"How was the sesame ball?" I asked.

"Pretty good." He patted his stomach. "What did you want to talk about, ladies? Pull up a chair."

Celine and I sat down, deciding to trap him on either side through our seating arrangement.

"Can we see your ensalada drink?" I said.

He raised his eyebrows, but uncapped it and showed us the contents. In the bright lighting of the room, I definitely recognized the yellow drink with its fruit bits.

Celine searched her phone for Jordan's Instagram pic and showed it to him. "Is this the same thing?"

"Yeah," he said. "It's a popular drink in El Salvador, and Jordan lapped it up."

"Jordan called it a fruit drink," my cousin said. "And she didn't tag you in the post either."

"She was probably still ticked off at me," he said. "Didn't want to waste her precious influencer power on highlighting my family's restaurant."

Jordan had posted the photo, though. If her phone had been stolen, whoever had taken it hadn't bothered to erase that shot. It didn't totally absolve Blake of guilt because he still could have acted out against his ex. Given their troubled history, I wasn't sure I trusted his words about Jordan, but I knew I'd be able to pry some solid information about her roommates from him.

"How long did you and Jordan hang out?" I said.

"For a few months," he said, snatching the paper napkin wad and tossing it like a mini basketball into the empty aluminum tray.

"I bet you met her roommates a few times, right?" I said.

"Here and there, and she used to jabber about them all the time to me."

Celine placed an elbow on the table and rested her chin

on her palm. "Genesis for one seemed to react to your name. She practically drooled when I mentioned you."

His lip curled up. "She has a bit of a crush on me."

"Yeah," my cousin said. "How did that pupusa date go?"

"When you left Gen with me at the restaurant?" He scratched his jaw. "I had to let her down easy. She reminds me too much of my little sister."

"A shame," Celine said. "She's a nice girl."

"I know," he said. "That's why I even stood up to Jordan for her. Jordan was going off about how Gen's relatives were visiting, how'd they break the housing code—that it'd be a fire hazard. I told Jordan to chill. She didn't like that."

He swigged his drink.

"Jordan sounds intense," Celine said.

"Sometimes I'm glad she decided to break things off with me," Blake said. "Jordan was definitely high maintenance."

"That's interesting that she was so catty about her roommates," I said. "I thought they were really close. After all, they even dressed alike."

"That was Reagan's idea," Blake said. He drank all the liquid in the thermos and nibbled on a pineapple piece. "She thought of the four of them as sisters. That's why Reagan was really hurt when Jordan fired her."

"What? *Jordan* did that?"

"Kind of. The decree came from on high, but Jordan was the HR person." It clicked then. Jordan had told her sister that Reagan was irresponsible at work because Jordan had inside knowledge. According to the hostess at Wing Fat, Reagan had overshot the company budget, almost causing the newest video game to not get released.

"Interesting," I said. "And what'd you think about Sierra?"

"The nervous type," Blake said. "Jordan said Sierra was always stressing about bills and making ends meet."

"There's a bunch of mixed personalities in that household," I said. "Have they been friends long?"

"Jordan and Reagan longer. They knew each other at college, though Reagan's a year older." Blake emptied the remaining fruit into his mouth and chewed. "The rest are newer. They've been together since last year."

"How'd Jordan and Reagan connect with the other two?" I asked.

"Some sort of virtual community bulletin board. Lots of people are looking to share housing. Living in Westwood is expensive."

"I hope they catch Jordan's killer soon," I said, observing his face with care.

"Me too." He took his thermos and left us with a jaunty wave.

"What do you think?" I asked Celine. "Guilty or not?"

"Seems too full of himself to be bothered about someone breaking up with him," my cousin said. "Probably plenty of other women lining up for his version of tall, dark, and handsome. Including Genesis."

"We should rank the suspects," I said. "Let's move him farther down on our list."

"On it," Celine said, tapping away at her phone.

A shadow loomed over us. "Any breakthroughs yet?" a male voice asked. "Because time's running short."

FIFTEEN

NIK HO BRACED HIMSELF AT THE EDGE OF OUR table and faced Celine and me. "Remember, you have two days to clear my name."

"Relax," I said. "I heard it from the detective himself that he dismissed your light bulb glasses as having anything to do with the case. They were of a different material . . . because you ordered them after ours."

"That's right," he mumbled and then caught himself. "I mean, we originated the light bulb glass idea."

"Come on, Nik," I said. "You just admitted that we were first."

He straightened up and tugged at his goatee. "Anyway, I'm still giving you a Friday deadline. I didn't realize we'd need an emergency meeting because of this fiasco, and now my mom's reputation is on the line. The local night market was her idea. If it fails, it will tarnish the Ho name and might even permanently ruin our business."

Celine tossed her hair with a flip of her hand. "If you're so keen on helping solve this case, maybe you can tell us more about Jordan. When she came by your booth and what she ordered."

"There's not much to tell," he said. "She enjoyed the *authentic* food and drinks at Ho's Small Eats." Nik's constant questioning about the authenticity or tastiness of my food revived the competitive spirit that I'd thought I'd laid to rest long ago.

"I'm no stranger to customer love myself," I said and held the empty catering tray up. Loose sesame seeds dotted the bottom of it. "I heard everyone praise our jin deui tonight. Every single one of them is gone."

He puffed out his chest. "Well, she relished our food. I've never seen anyone shovel shaved ice into her mouth so fast. I even warned her about brain freeze, but she waved away my concern. It must have been the best she'd ever eaten."

"Jordan came to our booth, too," I said. "She posted a pic on Instagram with my bubble tea."

"Which was obviously a terrible choice," Nik said, "because she's *dead* now."

I rose from the chair to glare at him right in the eye, but Nik stood a good six inches taller than me; I still had to tilt my head. "Are you accusing me of killing Jordan Chang?"

"If the shoe fits," he said. "Maybe you would stoop to murder, if it meant also destroying the restaurant competition. You could have planned this all beforehand, knowing you could bring shame to the event and destroy Ho's in one fell swoop."

"What are you talking about?" My voice rose an octave, matching my spiraling anger. "I didn't even know Auntie Ai coordinated the Eastwood Village Night Market until this evening."

"Did I hear my name being called?" Mrs. Ho shuffled into our line of sight, and Nik moved down the table to make room for her.

For her sake, I corralled my emotions. In a calmer voice, I said, "Hello, Mrs. Ho."

Celine echoed my greeting.

"Would you like to sit down?" I asked.

"Yes. Too much standing," she said, propping a hand behind her back to support it. Nik's mother sat next to Celine, and I pulled a chair over to them to make a mini circle.

"I'm really sorry about the uncertainty of the night market," I said. "It seems like you did a lot of work to organize everything, so it must be stressful not knowing if it's going to continue."

"There's no need to apologize," Mrs. Ho said. "I'm more worried about Nikola. He's so gloomy these days. Maybe he needs more friends to come by and cheer him up." She spoke these last words to Celine.

My cousin pretended not to notice the sharp gaze on her.

"Celine," Mrs. Ho said, "you should stay in the U.S. longer to better appreciate this country."

"Yes, Auntie," my cousin said. It sounded like an automatic response.

"You may eventually find that it's a nice place to live and settle down."

A groan escaped from Nik. His face went crimson, and he mumbled some excuse before scrambling over to the other side of the room.

I gestured toward him. "Nik was just telling us about how Jordan Chang enjoyed the food at your booth."

"Yes, I heard she came by twice," Nik's mother said. She smiled wide and showed off a crooked incisor.

"You weren't there the whole time?"

"I had to run out for a minute to direct some volunteers, but Nik was fine. He served her a bowl of shaved ice, which doesn't require any cooking."

"What about the second time?" I asked. Jordan had come by the food stall to order a shaved ice and later a green tea, according to Nik. In that time span, she might have already been feeling the effects of poison or whatever had damaged her stomach. "Did you notice anything strange? She look ill or weak then?"

Mrs. Ho took a moment to think over my question. "I couldn't see much because I was at the deep fryer, but her posture was straight as she ordered from Nikola. Too bad she's so tall, not a good fit for him. My husband and I, he was a full foot taller than me." She held her hands apart to indicate the distance. "That's a nice amount. A husband must be taller than his wife. Helps him feel more important."

Nik's mother had been widowed about seven years now. They'd run Ho's together before that time, she as the cook and he as the general manager. From personal experience, I knew it was hard to run a family business after a loved one had gone.

Mrs. Ho seemed at a loss for words for a moment, perhaps drawn into a bout of grief. I decided to pay her a compliment to improve her mood.

"For what it's worth," I said, "I think Ho's makes the best Taiwanese food around. *Jin ho ja.*" I added the last line about "very delicious" in Taiwanese as an icing to my praise.

"Thank you," she said. "But my life is not all about business. I worry about my son. I know I can't take care of him forever."

Did Ba feel that way about me? I wondered how a daughter who'd left her studies, the family restaurant, and a bookstore looked like to him. Before I could mull more about my dependency on my dad and his perception of it, a knocking sounded on the closed door of the community room.

The door swung open and revealed Detective Strauss. "Time's up," he said.

Everyone left in an orderly single file, perhaps because of his authoritative attitude. Celine and I brought up the rear of the queue since I didn't want to knock into anyone with the catering tray we'd brought to the meeting.

"Have a good night," he said to us as we drew level with him at the doorway.

Celine halted. "You know what would really make this day better for me, Detective? If you had a new prime suspect. Have you thought about Lindsey Caine as the culprit?"

"The ice cream truck owner?" Detective Strauss said.

"Uh-huh." Celine placed a hand on her hip and jutted it out. "She had the opportunity when she served Jordan her ice cream. And she's got a motive, too."

"That's a heavy accusation," the detective said and waved us on to proceed through the doorway.

We filed out.

"I've got proof," Celine said as she searched her social media for the incriminating words. "Look at what Jordan said about Below Freezing."

"What?" the detective asked, but he didn't bother to peek at Celine's phone. He focused on closing the door to the community room and locking it tight.

"Jordan said that the ice cream was too cold and talked about possibly mentioning it to EHD. That's a veiled threat to report Lindsey's food truck to the Environmental Health Department, who could shut down her business."

"I see where you're going with this," the detective said as he turned to face us. "But the two of them were strangers. I'm sure people often make negative comments about the food they eat."

"You could at least give it some thought," Celine said. I added, "And while you're at it, maybe you should look again at the roommates. According to Jacey Chang and Blake Westby Reyes, all three of them might have their own reasons to dislike Jordan."

His green eyes narrowed. "Been playing the sleuth, have you? For your information, those roommates have alibis. Sierra vouches for Genesis coming home early, and Reagan has the support of some work colleagues."

"What about the time when Genesis wasn't at home yet? Or when Reagan wasn't with the others? Something might have been slipped into Jordan's food or drink then."

He strode over to the entrance of the police station, his footsteps ringing out against the hard floor. "It was really crowded at the night market, and I talked to a lot of people who attended. Nobody noticed anything strange. Now, if you two will move along . . ." Detective Strauss held the front door open. Celine left in a huff, but I dragged my feet over the threshold.

Eastwood Village Night Market had been a crowded event. More people meant an increased amount of eyewitnesses for the detective to question. However, I doubted he'd asked everybody who'd attended, and even if he had, crowds also meant extra people who could block others' line of sight and obscure shady happenings.

On our drive back to Fountain Vista, Celine asked me, "Do you think Detective Strauss is going to follow up on my tip?"

"I sure hope he will." I leaned against the headrest and welcomed the cool breeze blowing through the open top of the convertible. "Can you hand me your phone?"

"Trusting technology more now?" Celine said.

"I want to go over the list again, and it's been such a long day that I can't keep everything straight in my head."

She plucked her phone out of her bag and handed it over.

It took me a moment to find the notepad app. I read

through the suspects again. "I'm going to write some comments on this to keep us organized. On the food vendor side, I think Lindsey's our best bet."

"Agreed." Celine placed two hands on the steering wheel and tightened her grip. "Like I said, Blake doesn't seem to care enough about losing one of his many admirers. And, Nik, well, you'd know more about him . . ."

I added a minus sign beside Blake's name.

"Nik could be a contender," I said, "but the only reason he'd do it would be to shift the blame onto us Yees. He's definitely worried about his mother's restaurant, but if something bad happened during the night market, it could blow up in his face. It'd have a negative repercussion on Auntie Ai, which is what's happening now. It's just such a roundabout way for him to be vindictive to Ba and me."

On Nik's line, I added a question mark.

"Then we have Lindsey," Celine said. "She was hashtagged and alerted to Jordan's comment about Below Freezing and EHD. Plus, there's that liquid nitrogen tank she had at the ready."

I put a plus sign next to Lindsey's name on the list.

"What about the roommates?" I said. "They could have plotted beforehand and decided the crowded night market would be a great opportunity for them to exact revenge."

"But they all have alibis." Celine made a hard left turn, and I gripped my seat.

"That's only what the detective said. How solid are their alibis, though? Sierra could've been just looking out for Genesis, and Reagan's innocence depends on a bunch of work associates who might not even have noticed if she'd slipped out of their midst."

Celine pulled the car into a parking spot near the apartment building. "Maybe we should separate them from each other and check out their alibis individually."

"Who should we start with?" I asked.

"Someone willing to chat," my cousin said. "Bonus points if she has some sort of Achilles' heel."

"Well, I know one of them has a weakness for Wing Fat egg rolls," I said.

"Excellent," Celine said. "I think we'll have to do another food drop-off tomorrow."

SIXTEEN

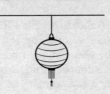

W E STOOD BEFORE THE BEIGE STUCCO APART-
ment building on Gayley Avenue, and I pressed the
button on the intercom.

"Who is it?" Reagan answered.

"Food delivery," I said, hoping she couldn't recognize
my voice through the static-filled transmission.

"You must have the wrong unit," she said.

"It's an order of egg rolls," I said.

"Come on up."

At the apartment, Celine rapped on the door, while I
stood at the ready with the bag before me like a peace
offering.

Reagan opened the door, which groaned on its rusted
hinges. In contrast, she looked very fresh this morning
with her glossy auburn hair brushed to a shine. At first,
she lurched forward to reach for the bag, but then she
stepped back.

Her eyes widened as recognition set in. "What are you
two doing here again?"

"Another wrong delivery?" Celine said.

"Yeah, right." Reagan tucked her hair behind one ear. "Sierra told us about your snooping, trying to weasel out information with your food bribes."

"Sorry," I said. "We're just trying to understand what really happened."

"That's for the police to do. But I'll keep the egg rolls," Reagan said, snatching at the bag.

She gripped the side of it, but I held on.

"Could we ask a couple harmless questions?" I said.

"It'll only take a few minutes of your time," Celine added.

"Can't. Sorry," Reagan said.

"The sooner you answer, the quicker you'll get to bite into an egg roll." I gestured to the bag like a game show hostess.

Reagan hesitated.

What else could I use for motivation to convince her? In a desperate ploy, I said, "We also have a message for you from Elodia Jones."

"You know Elodia?" Reagan said.

"I saw her just the other day when we delivered a tray of food, and she mentioned you."

Reagan glanced behind her, back into the apartment. "Okay, you can come in, but only for a moment. Let's go to the kitchen." She moved aside from the doorway to let us pass.

We walked by a shoe bench and wall rack near the front door. It didn't take us long to reach the kitchen, which appeared a few feet from the entrance on the right-hand side. An archway framed the cozy cooking area.

"Go ahead and place the egg rolls on the counter," Reagan said.

I put the takeout bag on the tiled countertop near a cereal bowl with a speckled design, a blue Bruins mug with raised lettering, and a stainless steel lunch container with a Post-it saying "Do Not Touch."

Celine stood close to me on the other side of the white porcelain sink while Reagan took a spot near a humming refrigerator plastered with flyers and scraps of paper.

"You have two minutes," Reagan said.

"It's so quiet here," Celine said. "Where are your roommates?"

"Genesis is in a jam session down the block." Reagan tugged at her earlobe. "You can probably hear her from outside. And Sierra's doing her side gig. Anyway, you're lucky they aren't around. I bet the others would never have even buzzed you up."

"Can you walk us through the timeline of your night market visit on Saturday evening? It seems like you all went together, what with your matching ninja costumes. How did you get separated?" I asked.

Reagan leaned against the refrigerator and seemed lost in thought. Then she said, "We took a Lyft, but then split up because we wanted to explore different areas. Genesis was interested in the arts and crafts, and Jordan headed straight for the food section. I decided to stay near the main stage, so they could find me easier, and the break-dancer guy was really good."

"When did they meet back up with you?" I asked.

She played with the edge of a flyer stuck to the refrigerator's surface with an apple magnet. The paper advertised Sierra's tutoring services held at a local coffee shop. "It took a while for Jordan to come back. She arrived near the end of the breakdancing, but before the hula guy."

"What about Genesis?" I asked.

"She never showed up but texted me that she felt sick and went home early."

Yes, that had been Genesis's story to Detective Strauss as well. "How did Jordan end up alone later in the night?"

I asked. Like when I'd found her lying at the base of the fountain.

Reagan said, "Jordan had this cute light bulb drink during the show, but it was almost empty. She said she wanted a refill." This must have been right before she went to Ho's Small Eats to order her second round of tea.

She continued, "After Jordan left, I spotted my boss and coworkers in the crowd and approached them. We ended up sticking together for the rest of the night."

Celine lifted an eyebrow at Reagan's remark.

"What?" Reagan said. "Don't judge me. I didn't ditch Jordan. I got sucked into the carnival games. Besides, I got a text from her telling me not to worry."

"When was this?" I asked.

"Around one in the morning." An hour before the night market ended, when I'd stumbled across Jordan's body.

Was this supposed text a creative imagining in Reagan's head? Or had it been a real response from Jordan—or her murderer?

"My turn," Reagan said, as she pointed toward the archway leading out of the kitchen. "Tell me, what was the message from Elodia?"

My cousin touched her wavy hair and said, "You'll be back at the company soon."

Or not. I quickly amended Celine's exaggeration. "Elodia said she needs some time to think it over." She'd said she didn't easily change her mind, but that still left a glimmer of hope.

"Well, it's a start," Reagan said. "I knew I shouldn't have gone over budget yet again, but how else are we supposed to boost team morale? And Jordan really should've stepped up to bat for me instead of throwing me out. Especially since I got her the job in the first place." She drew her eyebrows together and her mouth turned down, a strange contrast to her usual happy demeanor.

"For what it's worth," I said as I passed by her to get to the front door, "I think you deserve another chance."

She flashed me a tentative smile before ushering us into the hallway and closing the door with a gentle click.

"On to the next roomie," Celine said. "Which is?"

"Genesis," I said. "Sounds like her trio should be playing around here somewhere."

Outside the apartment building, we walked up and down the street but couldn't see any musicians. We decided to stroll around the neighborhood, listening for the strains of music. Within ten minutes, we heard a steady drumbeat. Genesis's signature raspy voice soon rose above the thrumming rhythm.

"Over there," Celine said, stalking down a side street.

Nestled among apartment buildings, an enormous gray house had its garage door open, and the Tresillo Trio stood in its shadowy depths. The house looked haunted and run-down, not in a fake Halloween way, but having been weathered by years of students wandering in and out of its door.

The keyboardist played a cool riff while the drummer softened her beating in order for Genesis's voice to float out in the late morning air. Maybe they wanted to attract the attention of passersby because I noticed a handmade sign nearby that advertised their future public engagements.

Genesis was crooning about someone being in love with a ghost when we walked up the concrete driveway. She finished her stanza but fumbled on the last words. Turning to her bandmates, Genesis said, "I'm gonna take a quick break."

She carried a plastic water bottle with her as she marched toward us.

We stood our ground near the sign advertising the trio.

"Can I help you?" Genesis asked.

"We were in the neighborhood dropping off food and heard you playing," I said.

She uncapped her bottle of water with a vicious twist. "What a coincidence."

"Since we're here, we'd love it if you could chat with us," I said.

"Why? So you can investigate some more?" Genesis gulped from her water bottle and then capped it.

"We arranged that pupusa date for you," my cousin said. "Since we did you a solid, can't you take the time to answer a few quick questions?"

"Fat lot of good that did," Genesis said. "Blake told me I reminded him of his baby sis."

Unable to offer any personal insight on romantic relationships, I turned to Celine for help.

My cousin brushed her hair out of her eyes. "There's plenty more options out there."

"Maybe." Genesis sighed. "What do you two want to know?"

"The timeline," I said. "What happened at the night market, and when did you return home?"

"We showed up at the beginning of the event, and I went straight to the arts area." Genesis gazed up at the sky, as though tracking a cloud. "Sometimes seeing others' creative talents inspires my own."

"Then you went to the food stall, right?" I said.

"Yep. I wanted to see what was taking Jordan so long. Turns out she was chatting with Blake." She crinkled the top half of her flimsy plastic bottle.

"And when did you get home?" I asked.

"I didn't stay very long. Like I told the cops, I was back around one-ish in the morning."

"You don't know the exact timing?" I said. If Genesis could come up with a more precise hour, we might be able to rule her out.

Genesis shrugged and half turned toward the band to leave us, but Celine interrupted her.

"Did you take a Lyft or Uber?" my cousin said. "If so, there should be a log of that."

"Oh yeah." Genesis placed her water bottle on the ground and checked her phone. "Hmm. Guess I got in earlier than I thought, at a minute past midnight." She showed us the timestamp on her phone.

"That's almost a whole hour's time difference," I said. "A huge gap."

"Not that it matters," Genesis said, pocketing her phone and picking up her water bottle again. "A light was on in Sierra's room, and she heard me come home. She's vouching for me. Anyway, I gotta get back to the band."

She returned to the other musicians with confident steps.

"Genesis seems sure of her alibi," my cousin said.

I observed as Genesis commanded the other musicians and then stood center stage.

"We need to go to The Cacao," I said. "It's a local coffee shop not far from here."

"Missing your caffeine hit?" Celine asked.

"Sure, we can grab some drinks, but I was hoping to fill up with info instead. Sierra should be there doing some tutoring." The flyer on her refrigerator had indicated the hours she'd be at the coffee shop and available to meet with pupils.

"So that's her side gig," Celine said. "Let's roll, then."

The main adjective I'd use to describe The Cacao would be "rustic." At the entrance, I admired the exposed rafters overhead and the long wooden bar. The whole place exuded a quaint country charm. Sierra was sitting at one of the round barstools at the end of the counter.

Just as I began to approach her, a guy rammed into me. I toppled over, but Celine caught me before I fell.

"Jerk," she said.

I rubbed my aching side. "He didn't even apologize." An alarming thought came to me. "Wait, you don't think it was deliberate, do you?"

My cousin gritted her teeth. "The slashed tire and now this? Someone's scared we're on to them. I'm going to find out more."

Before I could stop her, Celine darted off. I saw her calling out to the man who'd barged into me, but he didn't pause or even turn his head her way. In fact, it seemed like he'd started picking up his pace, trying to run faster now.

I hoped Celine could catch him. In the meantime, I turned my attention to Sierra. I planted myself on top of the empty stool beside her. "Small world," I said.

Sierra slipped a hefty-looking textbook into an orange backpack and put it to the side. Then she picked up a ceramic mug and sipped from it. "L.A. is a big city with lots of places to drink coffee. How did you pick this one where I happen to be tutoring?"

"Fine, Sierra," I said. "You asked me before to tell it to you straight. I found out about your side gig and dropped by to ask you something."

"Involving the case?" she asked, holding the mug tight.

"Yes," I said. "Now the whole night market enterprise is on the line. They might cut out all future events if there's a hint of an unsolved murder. Anything you say could help."

"I'm listening," she said, with a slight lean toward me.

"It's about Genesis. You're her alibi. What time did she come home?"

"One o'clock," Sierra said without hesitation.

"Are you sure about that?" I asked. "Did you see her in the house?"

Sierra tensed her jaw but tried to cover it by taking a

sip of her cappuccino or whatever frothy drink she'd ordered. "I couldn't fall asleep so early and was in my bed reading to relax when she came back."

"How'd you know what time it was?"

"I checked the alarm clock on my nightstand." She sipped some more.

I pivoted in my stool until I faced her. "What if I told you that the time on her rideshare app clocked her coming home at midnight?"

She wobbled the mug in her hand and placed it down on the unvarnished counter. "I must have read the clock wrong, then."

"From two digits in the hour slot down to one? How could you have made such a mistake?"

She shrugged. "I'm nearsighted."

Sierra still wanted to back up her roomie. No matter how hard I pushed, I doubted she'd change her tune.

"Look, I appreciate you trying to help Jordan, but all these questions aren't actually helpful to the case, and it's just painful. So maybe you should stop it with the internet sleuthing," she said. "Let the police do their job."

"Oh, okay. Thanks for the chat." I slunk out of the seat and met up with an out-of-breath Celine at the door. "I hope your time with the mystery man was more productive."

"Not really," my cousin said. "I lost him on campus. Too many guys around his height carrying black backpacks. But he did drop this." She pulled out a scrap of paper and showed it to me. "Do you think it's code for something?"

At first glance, it looked like a name plus a jumble of letters and numbers: *Young Hall CS50 1500.*

"Who's Young Hall?" she said.

Wait a minute. I had a suspicion. Peeking at the number at the end, I asked Celine, "What time is it?"

"Three o'clock."

"Or fifteen hundred in military time." I pointed to the piece of paper. "The poor guy was in a rush to get to Young Hall. Try looking up the place on a map of UCLA."

Celine pulled up the info on her phone. "You're right, Yale. Young Hall is the name of a building on campus. For the Department of Chemistry and Biochemistry."

I snorted. "The poor guy was late for class. Or an exam. He had probably just finished a tutoring session with Sierra."

This investigation was putting us on edge, and when my cousin's cell phone rang in her hand, I jumped. She peeked at the screen and answered with a tentative hello.

Celine scrambled outside to complete the conversation, and I followed her. As the door swung shut, she said, "Yes, I see. We'll be right over."

"What's going on?" I asked Celine.

"That was Detective Strauss," she said. "There's been a break in the case."

SEVENTEEN

WHEN WE ARRIVED AT THE POLICE DEPARTMENT,
Detective Strauss didn't lead us to any of the interview rooms. Instead, he chose to invite us into his inner
sanctum.

In the open desk area, split into different sections, the
detective wandered over to a metal desk under a "Homicide" sign. He sat on a rolling chair and motioned to two
seats across from him. "Enjoy the department's finest
visitor chairs."

They definitely beat the ones supplied in the waiting
room. These at least had carved arms and cushioned seating. I sank into one of the cobalt-colored chairs, and Celine followed suit.

Detective Strauss waited until we'd gotten settled
before speaking in his bass voice. "I believe I owe you two
an apology."

Celine offered him a smug smile while I felt my jaw go
slack.

"I have some good news," he said, tugging open one of

the drawers in his desk. He plucked out a familiar bottle of gold flakes and pushed it across the metal surface of the desktop to Celine. "I'm returning this to you."

"You don't need it anymore for the investigation?" Celine asked.

"No. When those flakes got tested, they were chemically inert and passed the marks for safe eating."

"Told you so," Celine mumbled as she stuffed the bottle into her purse.

"The technician also informed me that because the gold was so pure, it shouldn't affect someone with a nickel allergy. That only happens when impurities get mixed into the gold."

"This is excellent news, Detective Strauss," I said. Perhaps I should've trusted the law enforcement system more. After all, he'd just cleared Celine—and, by extension, the whole Yee name—from the investigation.

The detective held a paper up and waved it in the air. "If that wasn't enough to declare your innocence, more specialized analysis showed that there was *no* metal absorption whatsoever in Jordan Chang's system that evening."

"Now that we're clear," I said, "does that mean everything will work out for the night market venture?" I'd hated that the investigation had disrupted future plans for a regular event, and despite my dislike of Nik Ho, I held a soft spot for his mother.

"I'm afraid not," Detective Strauss said, slotting the paper into the tiered filing system on his desk. "The murder still occurred during the night market hours according to the medical examiner's report. Until we solve the case, there won't be any public events happening in that location."

"But you now know what happened, right?" I gestured to his multilayered trays. "Maybe the report suggested someone else as the culprit?"

His dark green eyes glittered at me. "If only it were so

easy. We're not certain what affected the victim's stomach like that, so I'll need to go through the case notes and reports all over again."

"Maybe it was something dissolvable." And therefore unidentified in the autopsy and lab reports.

He rubbed his chin in thought, but before I could expand on my musings, his desk phone rang.

Detective Strauss picked it up and said, "Okay, I'll be done soon."

He listened for a few beats before saying, "I see. Well, they're here right now. I'll send them over."

After Detective Strauss hung up, he said, "Turns out there's a visitor waiting for you in the lobby."

As we followed him down a hallway, I mouthed to Celine, "Who could it be?"

"Beats me," she whispered back.

Detective Strauss left us in the lobby, where we found Jacey Chang sitting in one of the hard chairs. She rose from her seat to greet us.

"I hear you're off the hook, given the chemical reports," she said.

"It sure does feel good," Celine said and held her head up higher.

"I hope they catch the real culprit soon," I said.

"It'll be tricky," Jacey said, fiddling with her glasses. "They're not sure what kind of substance is involved."

"I bet something dissolvable," I said, "that doesn't remain in the system."

"My thoughts exactly," Jacey said.

I snuck a glance at the wall clock in the police station. He'd given me forty-eight hours. "I have to ask, Jacey. Is Nikola Ho still high on your list of suspects?"

She took a deep breath to center herself. "I wish. Unfortunately, all I have on him is the green tea he served, which doesn't really damage the stomach lining. It's even less acidic than coffee."

Celine turned her head toward the door we'd exited, her lips turned up in a smile. "Don't worry. I trust Detective Strauss."

That didn't seem to be her tune too long ago, but I didn't correct her statement. She deserved to feel a high after having been officially released from the list of suspects.

"Actually, I think if we put our heads together, we might be faster than the bogged-down police department." Jacey stepped toward us and held her hand out. "Want to work with me and track down the person who's responsible?"

Celine nudged me with her elbow. "We don't have anything else planned for the rest of the day. It might be fun. When else am I going to get a chance to say I solved a case?"

"I don't know," I said. Now that Detective Strauss didn't have my cousin or me in his crosshairs, I much preferred a quieter mode of living.

Jacey clasped her hands together and begged. "Please help me," she said. "Just for this evening. We can compare notes, and then you don't have to be involved anymore. I can't leave this case to that inexperienced detective."

"Detective Strauss is new?" I said.

"He told me this is his first time as a lead detective," Jacey said, "and I don't want to leave the chances of solving my sister's murder to a rookie."

Then what were we—sub-rookies? But I didn't dare remind Jacey of our lack of expertise. "One night," I said. "That's it. It's about time my cousin got to enjoy her vacation."

"Let's meet up at five in front of my sister's apartment complex." Jacey pulled out a key ring. "I've got her spare. We can look around Jordan's room and ask more questions of her roommates if needed." Not knowing of our previous visits to the place, Jacey passed on the address to us.

"We'll be there," Celine said. "Here, let's exchange

numbers to keep in touch since we'll be driving separately." The downside of her fancy rental Boxster car was that it could only seat two people.

———————————

Celine and I showed up at the beige stucco building five minutes before the appointed time. My cousin had even scored a prime parking spot right in front of the building.

For once it felt nice to not need a food delivery pretense. We didn't have to buzz in because Jacey led us through the front glass doors.

Neither Celine nor I needed to knock. Jacey unlocked the door, and it swung open with a groan.

Inside, all the housemates were ensconced in the living room. They paused in their separate actions to gape at us. Sierra, curled up in an armchair, almost dropped the novel in her hands. Reagan, reclined on the couch, pressed pause on the rom-com flick she was watching; an actor and actress paused in the middle of a longing gaze. Genesis was playing music on her phone and had one earbud in but also peeked at the movie.

"We're dropping by Jordan's room in case I missed something," Jacey said. "Let us know if you remember any important info from that night."

The roommates muttered under their breath, with Sierra giving me the stink eye, and returned to their activities.

Jacey motioned for Celine and me to follow her down a long hallway. Three doors remained closed, but the fourth one had an open door. We crossed its threshold, and the first thought that occurred to me was: *This is a very dark room.*

When Jacey flipped a switch, the overhead light attached to a ceiling fan flickered on. It didn't add much brightness, but I could still see that the room was mostly empty.

Jacey must have really picked through Jordan's items. The walls looked bare, with subtle traces of putty left behind in one area. I bet that had been where Jordan had stuck the yin-yang poster.

A battered wooden dresser with a mirror took over almost all of one side of the room. Across the way lay a narrow twin bed, consisting of a bare mattress atop a metal frame. Next to it stood a dusty two-drawer nightstand on spindly legs.

"Wow, it's dark in here," Celine said, moving toward the heavy drapes covering the sole window in the room and sliding them open. Golden sunlight streamed in.

"My sister insisted on blackout curtains," Jordan said. "They helped with her migraines."

"I suffer from those sometimes," Celine said. "In my purse, I always stash some ibuprofen just in case."

"Jordan was into food and drink as a way to ward off her headaches. She swore caffeine helped fight the throbbing."

No wonder she'd been happy ordering green tea at our Canai and Chai stall. Plus, a second dose at Nik's stand.

"Time to compare notes," Jacey said. She leaned with her back to the large dresser as she pulled out her physical stack of notes.

Glancing around for a chair and finding none, I opted to sit on the bed near the nightstand. I sank into the thin mattress. Celine sat down next to me, making the mattress sink even lower with our combined weight.

"Let's go through the suspects," Jacey said, with a red pen in her hand. She'd be a brutal editor.

My cousin pulled out her phone, opened the notes app, and held it between the two of us, so we could both see the screen.

"We have roommates and food vendors on our list," Celine said.

I snuck a glance at the wide opening to Jordan's room. "Do you mind closing that?" I asked Jacey.

She placed her notes down, darted over to the door, and shut it.

"The roommates all have motives," I said. "And two of them were definitely there at the night market, Genesis and Reagan."

Jacey picked up her papers from the dresser and shuffled through them. She seemed to be reading off her own conjectures. "The food vendors were also nearby and could've easily doctored Jordan's food or drink. Except now I've crossed Nikola and you off the list."

"Yeah," Celine said, her eyes on the screen. "We've taken Sierra out of the roommate picture as well. But Genesis could've reacted to Jordan threatening her family about that fire code violation, and Reagan had a falling-out with Jordan because of work stuff."

Jacey ran a finger down her own list. "For the food vendors, Blake and Lindsey are still in the running."

"Is Blake really a suspect?" Celine asked, her eyebrows raised. "The only reason he'd be angry was that she broke up with him, but he seems like one not to care."

"True," Jacey said, "but apparently the guy got super-dumped. Jordan mentioned to me about some Facebook thing she did, but I don't have an account, so I'm not sure what she was talking about."

"Lindsey," I said, grinding the toe of my shoe into the carpet. "She seems like a good culprit out of the vendors. On Instagram, Jordan had tagged her and joked about turning her over to the health department. How dangerous is that liquid nitrogen that Lindsey uses?"

Jacey tapped the tip of her red pen against her chin. "The only thing about Lindsey's involvement is the timing. Didn't my sister post about the ice cream when she first purchased it? So Lindsey wouldn't even know about the threat until after Jordan tagged her."

"Good point, but what if something went down offline? We should keep on investigating," Celine said. She checked the time on her phone. "Are you ladies on the same wavelength as me? How about grabbing some dinner plus ice cream tonight?"

Jacey packed away her red pen and sheaf of papers. "We know the perfect places to eat at." She headed toward the hallway.

To get out of the sunken bed, I had to kick off with my feet and use momentum to stand. Celine seemed to have the same idea because she stood up at the same time with a forceful push, causing me to stumble and grab hold of the nightstand. I jammed my toe underneath the furniture and felt my shoe kick something. Peering in the space under the nightstand, I noticed a small plastic item.

I picked it up. It must've fallen recently since I didn't notice any dust on it. Two caps read "L" and "R." I placed the contacts case on the dusty nightstand and hurried to catch up with the others.

My cousin stood waiting for me in the hallway. "Ready to go? Jacey's already at the front door."

We drove separately to La Pupusería de Reyes. Before we entered the restaurant, Celine made sure to swipe on a layer of fire red lipstick. Then the three of us strolled in together.

Blake groaned upon seeing us and approached with hesitant steps. "How do you ladies know one another? You all live in Long Beach or something?"

"No. We met the night market on Sunday," I said. "When Jacey stopped by our stall."

"Went by mine, too," he said, irritation creeping into his voice. "Asking all kinds of loaded questions about Jordan."

"I'm trying to do right by my sister," Jacey said.

Blake said, "That detective already asked me a bunch

of questions even though I'm innocent. I stayed working at the booth all night long."

Remaining at the food stall didn't mean Blake had an airtight alibi. After all, he did have a troubled history with Jordan, so he could've placed something in her drink when she showed up at his food stall. Especially if he'd known beforehand she was going to attend the night market.

I tried to make my tone casual to counteract my question. "Hey, Blake. Did Jordan know you were working that night?"

He pointed at the menu behind him. "Are you here for food or to interrogate me?"

Celine sidled up to the counter and said in a silky voice, "For your delicious dish, of course."

Had she meant to say "dishes" instead or had she injected deliberate innuendo into her statement? Either way, he seemed to lap up the attention.

"At least one person in your group shows some appreciation," he said. "Pick a table and sit down."

We ended up in the corner at a four-seater. Although Jacey ordered pupusas, I wanted to try something different. Celine must have thought along the same lines because she asked Blake, "What else do you recommend here besides the usual?"

"The tamales," he said.

My cousin tilted her head at him. "Is that really so unique?"

"You betcha," he said. "We wrap them not in common corn husks but in plantain leaves. Once you try it, you'll never go back to other tamales."

"I'm sold," she said.

"I'll try one, too," I added.

Once Blake deposited our dinners before us, we focused on the meal. With him so close by, we didn't dare discuss the investigation, so I lost myself in the savory texture of the corn masa and the spiced filling inside.

Once I'd finished, I asked both Jacey and Celine, "Do you have an actual plan for coming here?"

"Well, we got dinner and showed our faces to intimidate him," Jacey said, though she sounded uncertain.

Celine patted her mouth with her napkin. "Don't worry, cuz."

When we called Blake over to pay our bill, Celine left him a generous tip. At the same time, she said to Blake, "Can I Facebook-friend you? I love meeting people from around the world. And if you're ever in Hong Kong, message me."

"I was wondering where your accent was from," he said, picking up the check tray.

"Can you friend me right now?" Celine asked, a purr to her voice. She gave him her Facebook username.

"Sure," Blake said, pulling out his phone and tapping away on it.

Celine checked her phone and flashed him a dazzling smile. "Got it. Thanks."

We exited the restaurant and clustered around Celine's phone as she scrolled through previous posts where Blake had been tagged.

"There," Jacey said, leaning over the screen. "I recognize my sister's thumbnail pic."

I read Jordan's old post over Celine's shoulder: "'Blake Westby Reyes's idea of a relationship'"—his name was highlighted in blue—"'is three girls fighting over him. I'm so done with this. Consider yourself dumped, Blake. #boyfriendfail'"

"Ouch," Celine said, impressed. "She really called him out."

"That's not all," Jacey said. "Look at that huge comment section."

My cousin clinked on the "view more comments" link.

It turned out that Jordan had also tagged multiple women on the first comment. I assumed these were previous dates of Blake's. They ended up on two sides of a debate: some supported him while others felt upset that they hadn't been as exclusive as originally thought.

"She sure started something," Celine said.

"No wonder he passed out those free pupusa cards at the night market," I said. "He was desperate." Embarrassment burned my cheeks. He'd even offered his business card to me, probably trying to connect to more single women. I must have looked both bookish and available.

My cousin peered at me. "You all right? Your face is heating up."

"It's a good thing we'll be getting ice cream soon," Jacey said. Her mouth set into a grim line.

EIGHTEEN

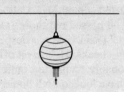

JACEY, CELINE, AND I LOCATED THE ICE CREAM truck on the corner of an intersection in Venice. A street-light lent a halo glow to the vehicle, but nobody seemed to be lining up to buy a frozen treat.

In fact, I saw Lindsey with her head out the window, shouting, "Free samples of ice cream!"

Jacey glided up to Below Freezing. "I'll try one," she said.

Lindsey handed her a cup, but her eyes soon narrowed. It seemed like she recognized Jordan's sister.

"I told you," Lindsey said, "I have nothing else to add."

The two stared at each other in a contest of wills until I stepped into the light. "I'd like to buy a cup," I said. "Coconut, please."

Jacey retreated from the truck, and Lindsey focused her attention on creating my flavor. She went through the motions of crafting the ice cream, including pumping the nitrogen tank. As the billow of smoke rolled out, I said,

"Gee, that seems really cold. I can feel the chill even from here. How low does the temp get?"

"I know what I'm doing," Lindsey said, jabbing a spoon into the finished ice cream mixture.

Celine took over the questioning. She opened her eyes wide and said, "Is it ever dangerous?"

"No." Lindsey scowled. "Like I've said in person before and on social media many times, I use the safest techniques to make my ice cream."

I paid for my dessert, suppressing an internal groan at giving over my hard-earned night market money. It'd been almost a week since I'd gotten laid off. I'd better start looking for a job in the coming days.

Lindsey glanced between Jacey, leaning against the streetlight pole, and the two of us at her window. Thoughts seemed to swirl around in her head. "Enjoy my impeccable ice cream," she said, thrusting the cup at me.

I decided to wait a few minutes before eating it, to ensure that the liquid nitrogen had dissipated. Celine and I joined Jacey at the streetlight, where she held the empty sample cup in her hand.

"What's the verdict?" Jacey asked us.

Celine said, "Lindsey swore she used the safest handling techniques."

"Of course she did." Jacey crumpled the cup in her hand. "Especially if she thought we knew each other. And given her lack of business, there's really no doubt we came together."

I dug my spoon into the coconut ice cream and ventured a small bite. It tasted smooth and rich in my mouth, an edible tropical paradise. "Not only did she deny it verbally, but she said she'd posted something on social media. Can you two check?"

Both Celine and Jacey got to work tracking down the accounts plastered across the side of the silver food truck.

"It's on Below Freezing's Twitter account and their Facebook page that the company uses the 'utmost precautions,'" Jacey said.

"Found it on Instagram, too," Celine said. "She said that she knows what she's doing because she's been in business for three years now and has never received a single complaint."

I peered at my cousin's phone and studied the hashtags: #icecreamforthewin and #EastwoodVillageNightMarket. "When did Lindsey give that statement?" I asked.

Celine checked the date of the post. "Saturday night," she said.

"What time?" I asked. "Before or after Jordan tagged her?"

Jacey used her phone to do a search for Jordan's IG feed, and she and my cousin compared timestamps.

"After," Jacey confirmed. "She may have done it in direct reaction to Jordan's veiled threat."

"Interesting." I whipped my head back to study Lindsey, but she'd disappeared into the interior of the food truck.

"But even if she was miffed about Jordan's remarks, she couldn't have done anything. Jordan had probably left by then, and the ice cream she ate hadn't been doctored."

Jacey let out a disgruntled huff, and I watched her stalk over to a trash can a few feet away and hurl the empty sample cup into it. I spooned more coconut ice cream into my mouth, letting it melt on my tongue, as I ran through different scenarios in my head.

Unable to think of any purpose to staying longer, we walked back to our separate cars, us to the Boxster and Jacey to her dented black Jetta. As Celine slid behind the driver's seat of the rental car, I watched Jacey check her rearview mirror before she merged into traffic.

"At least she won't have to deal with a lot of cars on her way back home," I said.

"How far is Long Beach from here?" Celine asked me. "Is it a quick drive?"

"About thirty miles away. Why do you ask?"

She nodded at the disappearing taillights of Jacey's car. "Do you think *she* could be involved with her sister's murder?"

"I sure hope Detective Strauss would have caught that," I said. "Plus, aren't Blake and Lindsey better suspects? What did you think about our interactions with them tonight?"

Celine started up the engine and roared down the street. "Blake got Facebook-dumped. That must have been a huge blow to his ego."

"Enough that he would mess with Jordan's ensalada drink?"

"Maybe," Celine said. "It had fruit in it, right? You've surely heard of poisoned apples."

I let the wind toss my hair around. "What about Lindsey's ice-cold reception toward us? She seemed to be giving us angry looks the whole time."

"Yeah," Celine said, as her foot pressed down on the gas, increasing our speed. "Defensive much? She assured us multiple times how careful she was while serving her ice cream. But the timing doesn't work out."

Unless . . . I reclined back in my seat, feeling tempted to prop my feet on the dashboard in triumph. "Lindsey could have served the ice cream later. Remember that cup she was giving away to drum up business? Maybe Lindsey lured Jordan back with a laced freebie, and Jordan wouldn't have posted a photo of a tiny sample cup on her social media."

"Huh," Celine said, as she parked close to Fountain Vista. "I didn't think of that."

Inside the apartment, Celine rummaged in her purse and tossed the bottle of gold flakes away. "I'm certainly glad not to be in the hot seat anymore, and I don't need that reminder around."

"Yeah, time for Detective Strauss to sort through his

huge pile of paperwork and sift through the real evidence."

"Life can now go back to normal for me and you," my cousin said.

"Whatever that actually means," I said. "Now that there's no night market to participate in and no investigation to distract me, I need to figure out what to do with my life."

"You're smart. I'm sure you'll think of something."

I didn't often apply that adjective to myself, knowing I didn't have much higher education. I let my cousin's compliment nestle in my heart for a moment before realizing that my lack of marketable skills did leave me in a quandary. "As I see it, I've got three immediate options: pitch in at the restaurant, scour the classifieds, or file for unemployment."

"Why don't you Marie Kondo it?" Celine said.

"Which is?"

She lifted her eyebrow. "Find employment that sparks joy."

"Easy for you to say. You've got the money to do a thousand things until something sticks."

Celine's posture stiffened. "I'm a really good social media influencer."

I could tell I had offended her and tried to make amends. "So, now that you're free from suspicion, do you want me to show you around L.A. some more? Do vacationy stuff?"

"Don't bother," Celine said. "I already have plans."

"You do?"

She sauntered over to the spare room and started grabbing clothes from the closet.

"What's going on, Celine?"

"I'm packing," she said, folding the clothes into neat piles.

"Right now?"

"Yes. Flights to Asia often leave late at night. I think I can rearrange my itinerary to catch the next one."

"I'm sorry. I think I must have hurt your feel—"

Celine put up one hand to stop me. "Yale, the timing works out perfectly. I've been wanting to go back home to my family. Now that the detective isn't jumping down my throat, I can do so. It's as simple as that."

I stumbled out of the room. Weren't Ba and I "family" to Celine as well? Perhaps she'd only stayed as long as she did because of the murder case. Had she even enjoyed the amateur investigating we'd done together?

I peeked through the open doorway. Celine had already filled one of her three purple suitcases. It wouldn't be long before she'd managed to pack everything up. And when would I see her again after she left the country? Would it be another twenty long years of silence?

My cousin soon wheeled her stacked suitcases out of the room.

"Do you want me to take you—I mean, accompany you to the airport?" I asked. It was one of those few times where I missed actually owning a vehicle even though I had a valid driver's license. My mind flashed back to the wind whipping through our hair in the rental convertible. I supposed sometimes a car could serve to create connections instead of severing them.

"Nah," Celine said. "I have to return the Boxster near the airport anyway."

I wanted to say something more. Maybe I could ask to be Facebook friends, but I knew I wouldn't have the initiative to set up a profile, let alone follow through on checking the account on a regular basis. Was it significant that Celine and Blake, a virtual stranger, could be friends on Facebook, but I couldn't?

Moments must have passed while I mused because Celine said, "See ya around, Yale."

She leaned forward, touching our cheeks together and giving air-kisses. I remembered when she'd shared her slip-up story about the celebrity. My cousin had given the pop star the same superficial greeting. I wondered if I'd be the source of one of Celine's stories at a later date—the time when she'd visited her bookish cousin and gotten accused of murder.

Even though I'd read so many books, words failed me now. "Thanks for coming to visit, Celine," I said.

She nodded at me before extracting an envelope from her purse and said, "To cover my stay this week. I also added a bit more to tide you over."

Celine dropped the envelope into my hands and slipped out of the apartment. It felt like such a transactional gesture, and I closed the door with a sigh.

At the stroke of midnight, I called Ba to tell him the news about Celine's sudden departure.

"Yale," he said when he picked up. "I think I know what this is about."

"You heard already?"

"Celine texted me. Thanked me for all the hospitality and said goodbye."

"I can't believe she actually left." I sat on the guest bed and looked around the spare room. It seemed bare without her overabundance of accessories and clothes.

"Celine's like the wind. Blows wherever she wants," Ba said. "You know how she is."

"Do I?" I glanced at the spot where her suitcases had been. "Before this trip, I hadn't seen my cousin in ages."

My dad hemmed and hawed. "We got those Christmas letters from time to time."

"Not the same, Ba," I said. "And Celine's the only relative close to my age."

"You had your school friends," Ba said. His voice dropped lower in register, and he sounded weary.

"Study buddies," I said, smoothing the comforter on the bed. "We all went our separate ways after college." Even after I had returned to Los Angeles, I hadn't bothered to reconnect with those who'd stayed in town or boomeranged back like myself. I didn't want to answer insensitive questions about my failed education. Or my mom. The city was big enough that I hadn't run into any of them anyway, except for Nik.

Ba said, "The years sure slipped by fast. And my brother and his family were so busy in Hong Kong with all their charity events and casino remodels . . ."

I parroted back the words he'd said to me when first discussing Celine's visit. "You told me before, 'Family should be together.'"

Even as I said it, though, I knew it'd been a philosophy he'd borrowed from my mom. She had been the one to keep up with her extended relatives in mainland China by mailing postcards. She'd even coordinated the Disneyland trip.

"You know all our relatives live so far away," Ba said, "and it's hard for them to travel internationally. Besides, the restaurant takes a lot of time to run."

True. After my parents owned Wing Fat, my mom had slowed down with her efforts to maintain family ties. She'd been so tired after putting in the long hours.

"Work shouldn't be used as an excuse," I said. Not to avoid relatives, or even the reality of a devastating loss. "And it isn't everything."

"People can't laze about," my dad said. "Everyone should have a good work ethic. Haven't I taught you anything? That's what this country is all about: initiative, and pulling yourself up by the bootstraps. Money doesn't grow on trees for the Yees on this side of the world."

"Don't you think I know that, Ba?" I whacked the bed, making a thump. "I'm the one struggling to get by on doll noodles, worried about my next paycheck—"

"Wait. What happened to your bookstore job?" he asked.

I stayed silent.

"When did you find out?"

"They told me last Friday," I said, "right before the night market gig."

"Is that why you're so grumpy?" His tone softened. "Look, you can always come back to Wing Fat. Any position you like. You could be hostess, waitress, cook." He paused. "Or even soy sauce wiper-downer."

I knew his teasing acted as a verbal olive branch. I grabbed it tight. My dad was the only family nearby, and I loved him. "The last one's not even a real role," I said.

"It should be. Cleaning up the condiment bottles requires a lot of skill and needs to be well compensated."

"Anyway, I might take some time to think over things."

"The offer stands," Ba said. "No expiration date. I know you like backup plans and structure in your life."

I did indeed. In fact, I lived in Eastwood Village because the region had been planned in minute detail, everything within walking distance. Or, at least, I had enjoyed all that order until my cousin had waltzed into town. She'd offset the equilibrium in my life, even to the point of involving me in a murder investigation.

I thanked my dad for his kind offer and said good night to him. Then I stayed sitting on the bed, cradling the phone in my hands, and mulled.

Taking an active role in investigating Jordan Chang's death had sparked something in me. I'd gone out into the world, beyond my Eastwood Village bubble, and made adventures happen instead of reading about them.

I placed the phone back on the bookshelf and reached for the copy of *Pride and Prejudice* I'd splurged on with my last paycheck. I took it to my own bed to relax and wind down for sleep. However, I found myself rereading the first pages even after several tries. I slid a bookmark in and placed it on my nightstand. Maybe when tomorrow dawned, I'd be able to return to my previous quiet pace of existence.

NINETEEN

I WOKE UP TO THE SHRILL RINGING OF THE TELE-phone from the guest room. Wiping the sleep from my eyes with the back of my hand, I jolted up and raced to answer the call.

Without any preamble, Detective Strauss said, "When did you last see Jacey Chang?"

"Huh?" I muffled my yawn. "Yesterday."

The detective's voice turned sharp. "What time exactly?"

"After eating some ice cream. At night. Maybe shortly past eight?"

"This is important, Yale," he said. "Where was she planning on going after you left her?"

"Um, she was headed home, I think."

"She didn't say she had plans to meet anyone?" he asked.

"No."

I heard a repetitive tapping noise over the phone and pictured him drumming his pencil against his notepad.

"What were *you* doing around midnight?" he asked.

"Talking to my dad," I said.

"Was your cousin with you at that hour?"

"No, actually I'd called my dad to let him know she was leaving Los Angeles. Celine was probably on a flight back to Hong Kong around midnight." I rubbed some more sleep from my eyes. "Why are you asking about the time anyway?"

"Jacey was out around midnight, and she ended up falling down a long set of stairs."

"Oh my gosh." My eyes widened. "Is she okay?"

"She's in the hospital now."

I searched for a nearby scrap of paper and pen to write down the details. "Which one?"

The nice thing about being unencumbered with a job was the freedom in my schedule.

The detective named a hospital.

"In Long Beach, right?" I said.

"Nope. Culver City."

"But that's closer to here." That meant Jacey had remained local after she'd gone out with Celine and me. "When are visiting hours?"

"You might want to give her some time to recover before barging into the hospital," Detective Strauss said. "She suffered some injuries."

"How long was this staircase? Where was she?" I asked, trying to picture local buildings with lots of steps.

"She fell down the Culver City Stairs," he said.

"Oh my." The well-known exercise site southwest of Culver City featured a huge concrete staircase that led up to an amazing overlook. The entire staircase spanned over seven hundred feet in height. A tumble down those steps could prove horrendous. "How hurt is she?"

"She's broken her leg and seems to be suffering a mild concussion," the detective said. "Don't know when she'll be cleared to drive. Without any close relatives nearby, I ended up having her car towed to Jordan's old apartment and leaving the keys with the roommates."

"That's kind of you," I said.

He brushed the compliment aside. "Anyway, I'm trying to find out more details about last night. Where did you go with Jacey?"

"First, we went to chat with Blake at the pupusería," I said, "and then we tracked down the location of the Below Freezing ice cream truck to speak with Lindsey."

"I told Jacey not to chase leads on her own," Detective Strauss said. The previous tapping noise over the phone grew louder.

I still couldn't wrap my mind around the situation. "Why would she be working out at the Culver City Stairs around midnight?" Many exercise enthusiasts didn't go near the place until daylight because of the steep climb.

His voice turned gruff. "I'm pretty sure she was pushed down those stairs, Yale. Call me if you remember anything else."

I sucked in my breath as Detective Strauss ended the phone call.

───

Shaken by my conversation with the detective, I sought a sense of normalcy. I stumbled into The Literary Narnia, to find refuge in the stacks. Kelly, sporting a peach cardigan, was ringing up a customer at the cash register.

In the meantime, I wandered around the establishment. At the new books table, I tried to distract myself with the recent arrivals, but the summaries on the back covers blurred due to my lack of concentration. I ambled along the aisles, picking up a tome or two, and then shelving them back with disinterest.

When the customer said bye to Kelly with a quick "Lovely to see you, Dawn," I headed back to the front.

Kelly shook her head. "Still can't tell us apart."

Dawn bustled over from the back room and stood next to her sister.

"It's no wonder," I said. "You're dressed exactly the same."

The two of them looked like identical twins with their matching cardigans and black slacks.

"These outfits were on sale," Kelly said.

Dawn craned her neck, appearing to look at the surrounding aisles. "Where's Celine?" she asked.

"She flew back to Hong Kong last night."

"Oh." Concern flashed in Dawn's dark brown eyes. "Is everything okay? She sounded ruffled when she last spoke with her parents."

"Beats me," I said, giving the book carousel at the front desk a vicious spin. "She wasn't really talking up a storm to me when she left."

Kelly placed her elbows on the table and settled her face between her hands. "Sounds like a juicy story. Do tell."

"Nothing much to say. She practically *fled* my apartment after I said something about how her family had big bucks."

"We need more details," Kelly said, as Dawn adjusted her spectacles and frowned at her sister.

I relayed to them how I'd felt lost, uncertain of what to do with my sudden stretch of empty hours. My cousin had told me to chase after something that sparked joy, but I didn't have money like her to do so.

Dawn rubbed her chin with delicate fingers. "Sounds like maybe she got offended."

I spun the rack one more time while Kelly raised her eyebrows at me. "She even tried to pay me rent for staying at my place," I said. "Like it was some sort of business relationship instead of family hospitality."

Dawn reached out and patted my arm. "You two had

just been talking about your financial woes. Do you think Celine gave you some extra money to help you out for the time being?"

"I hadn't thought of it that way." Instead, I'd figured it was transactional, or a way for Celine to smooth things over with money, as always. Could the "rent money" have been a gift of generosity from her, with no strings attached?

"It's really a shame we can't afford to keep you around here," Dawn said, shaking her silver-haired head.

Kelly stood up straight and peered past me through the front door. "What about the night market over the weekend? Could that money help your situation?" she said. "It looked pretty crowded to me on Saturday."

"You were there?" I asked. "I didn't notice you around the food stall. You should've come by!"

"No, too crowded for us. Kelly took a quick peek, though, from outside our shop," Dawn said. "We were in here going over our invoices that night, trying to make the sums work for us."

"And you noticed the people milling about?" I angled toward Kelly since she'd mentioned seeing the event.

"I did," Kelly said. "Went outside to get some night air close to eleven. Since I was walking around, I paused on the sidewalk to check out all those neat costumes people were wearing."

The bookstore faced the entrance to the event. Anyone who'd used rideshare to get there would have hopped out on the sidewalk in full view of Kelly—and she had a photographic memory.

I tamped down my excitement and tried to ask my question in a neutral tone. "Did you happen to see a bunch of ninjas get out of a car?"

"Let me think." She narrowed her eyes to gaze past me, toward the front door. "There were some ninjas that night, coming together and separately. I do remember seeing a group arrive."

I tugged at a hangnail on my thumb. "How many of them were there?"

"Three, I think."

Bingo. She'd seen Jordan and her two roommates. "Notice anything odd about them? Did they act pretty friendly or distant with one another?"

She pursed her lips as she thought. "They were too far away to really notice much. But they did walk together. I remember thinking that they could've been triplets in their identical costumes."

"Right." I tried to hide the disappointment from my voice. Of course Kelly wouldn't have spotted anything. It wasn't like she'd been right next to them and had eavesdropped on an important conversation. "Thanks, Dawn and Kelly."

I waved to the both of them and exited the bookstore. Although I hadn't browsed through the inventory or purchased any books, I felt calmer having talked to the Tanaka sisters. They were the true source of comfort at The Literary Narnia.

I glanced back at them and smiled. They waved to me, looking very twin-like with their clothes and cheery faces. It was the kind of snapshot moment that I imagined happened often with a sister.

My thoughts veered toward another sister pair, and I hastened over to the bus stop around the corner. I'd better check the schedule to see when the next one bound for Culver City arrived.

⊏━━━━━━━⊐

I t took about forty-five minutes by public transportation to reach Brock Hospital. The tall gray building, the color of broken dreams, did little to settle my nerves as I entered it.

After ascertaining Jacey Chang's room number and acquiring a visitor's sticker, I scurried over to the correct corridor. It took several tries before I located the appropriate wing in the hospital.

Her room door was wide open, and I peeked inside to find Jacey resting in a hospital bed. Her injured leg was encased in a long white cast.

I knocked on the doorframe before entering. Noticing me, she used a remote beside her to incline the bed upright.

"Welcome to my new home," she said. "Don't you love the minimalist whiteness of the space?"

Glancing around, I did realize that everything came sans color: the walls, the bed, even the rolling table near her. She also didn't seem to have any gifts from friends. I didn't see any plants nearby or get-well cards.

"Jacey," I said, "can I grab you anything to make you more comfortable?"

"No, thanks." She rubbed at her cast. "Guess you heard about the fall."

"Detective Strauss called me. Or rather, questioned me. What happened to you last night?"

She tapped at her forehead with her pointer finger. "It's still a bit fuzzy, but I do remember going to those horrible stairs."

"Not to exercise in the dark, I imagine. Were you meeting somebody?"

"I must have been." She motioned to a white cabinet next to the bed. "My purse is in there. Can you get it for me?"

I handed over her bag, and she pulled out her phone.

"No text messages," she said, "but it looks like I received a phone call around eight thirty."

"Who was it from?"

She squinted at the screen. "I'm not sure."

She didn't have her glasses on, so maybe she couldn't

read the print? I hurried to her side and peered at the phone log. Nope, it wasn't an eyesight issue. A call had come in, but it was listed as "Unknown."

Jacey tucked her phone back into her purse, and I put it away in the cabinet.

"What do you remember about last night?" I said.

"I started climbing the stairs. They were tough, and I had to stop a quarter of the way up. Then, before I knew it, I tumbled down."

"You didn't trip, right?" I asked.

"No," she said. "I knew I needed to be careful going up the steep stairway. I remember aiming my flashlight app at each step to make sure I didn't stumble."

"Then you must have been pushed," I said, like the detective had surmised. A shiver passed through my body. "Did you see anyone around?"

"It was too dark. Everything was in the shadows. Plus, I'd been looking down."

I glanced at the closed cabinet door beside the bed. "What about the phone conversation? Do you remember any of it?"

She shook her head, and the pillow behind her slid down. I retrieved it and restored its previous position.

"This concussion," she said, "blocks memories and gives me an ongoing headache."

I remembered Jordan's room. "Would you like me to close the blinds?" I asked.

"That'd be great."

As I did so, Jacey pushed the button for the nurse's station and said, "Some ice chips, please."

A nurse hurried in within minutes, handed her a plastic cup, and bustled out. With the blinds closed, the room seemed dimmer and quieter. More relaxing for Jacey, I hoped.

I watched as she placed several chips in her mouth. "Yum," she mumbled. "The cold does help my head."

"I'll let you rest now," I said to Jacey and headed toward the door.

Before I made it into the corridor, she called my name. "I do remember something about the conversation," Jacey said.

I turned back around.

"One thing," she said. "The call was muffled, but it was definitely a woman's voice."

"Very interesting," I said.

Jacey placed the plastic cup on the bedside table, rolled it away, and lowered her bed. She seemed tired from our chat.

"Speedy recovery," I said to her.

"Thank you."

After I left the room, I got disoriented by the winding corridors. My missteps, though, took me to the hospital shop. I peered through the large glass windows and paused. Jacey hadn't received any gifts, and I thought I could pass on some cheer.

Inside the tiny store, I debated on what to purchase. I could buy a bouquet of wilted roses or a card with "Get well soon" or any number of balloons. Finally, I ended up with a helium balloon with a smiley face and a rainbow on it. As I paid for the get-well present, the irony hit me. Here I was using my money to pay for a bit of happiness for Jacey, just like Celine. My cousin had given me money to tide me over, to give me a small financial cushion so I could job search a bit more comfortably.

I left the hospital with more appreciation for my cousin and also more insight into the Chang case. Since it had been a woman who'd pushed Jacey down the treacherous staircase, I could narrow down the suspects list. Even though I didn't have Celine's notes app to double-check, I knew I could cross Blake and Nik off.

Nik. I groaned as I remembered the date. Friday had come too soon, and I didn't have all the answers yet.

Maybe I could head off his gossip threat by indicating that I'd reduced the culprits down to three women: Lindsey, Genesis, and Reagan.

⸺⊏▭▭▭▭⊐⸺

I found Nik behind the counter at Ho's. He was pulling a sticky menu from a huge stack and wiping it down when I arrived.

He stopped midwipe and said, "Yale Yee. Are you here for lunch?"

"No," I said, even as my stomach growled. Maybe he couldn't hear it from where he stood. I sure wished there had been other patrons sitting in one of the vinyl booths. They would have disguised my hunger pangs with clinking forks and snapping chopsticks.

"It's Friday," I said, "so I decided to give you an update."

"Find out who did it?" he asked.

"Not yet." I lifted my chin a little. "But I did narrow the suspects down to three."

Nik put down his menu and did a slow, mocking clap. "Wowee. A thirty-three percent chance of uncovering the killer."

Thirty-three and a third, I corrected him in my head. Out loud, I said, "It's not bad odds, so why don't you give me an extension until after the weekend?"

"I don't think so," he said. "Isn't there that stat that murder cases have the best chances of being solved within forty-eight hours? You've blown way past that deadline."

"That's probably mumbo-jumbo you picked up on TV," I said.

"Doesn't matter." Nik finished wiping down the menu and placed it in a much smaller pile of those with cleaner covers. "Ma's meeting up with the owner of The Shops at Eastwood Village on Monday, so if she wants to change his mind about the bad publicity we brought to the shopping center, she needs to deliver the good news pronto."

The kitchen door swung open. "Did I hear you say my name, Nikola?" Mrs. Ho said.

"Hello, Auntie," I said.

"Yale, nice to see you," Nik's mother said. She seemed to glance past me. "Is Celine here as well?"

"No, sorry." I scuffed my shoe against the weathered checkerboard flooring. "She had to fly back to Hong Kong."

"Already?" Mrs. Ho snuck a worried peek at Nik, who turned pink at her scrutiny. "That's a shame."

Mrs. Ho focused her attention on me. "Are you here to chat with Nik? Do you want me to make you two a snack? You must have very fond high school memories to talk about."

Hardly.

Nik piped up. "Actually, Yale has to get going. She's on a *dead*line."

I ground my teeth at his words but managed a smile for Nik's mother. "Thanks for your hospitality, though, Mrs. Ho. Nik was also telling me about your upcoming meeting regarding the plaza. No matter what happens, I thought you did a wonderful job of organizing the night market."

"Thank you, Yale." She placed a weathered hand against her heart. "That means a lot to me. I tried my best to bring in good vendors for games, arts, food, and entertainment."

"Actually, that reminds me," I said. "Could I get a copy of the vendors plus the performers and their contact info? I didn't get a chance to see all of them and would love to learn more about each one."

"Of course, dear," Mrs. Ho said. She reached under the counter as the phone rang.

"One of our many eager customers," Nik said as he picked up the call. He listened for a few moments before saying, "Actually, sir, she's right here."

He handed the phone over to me, and I heard Ba's

voice come across the line. "Yale, I've been trying to find you everywhere. I called your apartment, the bookstore, and now I'm using my restaurant connections."

"What's the matter, Ba?" I said.

"You got a message." His voice sounded alarmed. "Can you come to Wing Fat right away?"

"Yes, Ba."

Mrs. Ho offered me the night market list, and I squeaked out a curt goodbye before sprinting out the door.

TWENTY

I RUSHED OVER TO WING FAT, WORRIED ABOUT WHAT I would find after the disconcerting call from my dad. Ba stood in the foyer of the restaurant, which signaled to me the extremity of the situation. He should have been in the kitchen, presiding over a wok filled with food. Instead, he hovered over the pale-looking hostess.

Instead of standing behind the podium, she was leaning against it for support. My dad used a soothing voice to talk to her and offered her a cold drink of water.

The waiting customers at Wing Fat appeared more irritated than concerned, but my dad said, "Not to worry, it's just dehydration."

I heard several of those milling around mumble about wanting to leave the restaurant, so I stepped in. Despite not wearing the traditional cheongsam, I grabbed tickets from the nearby machine and handed them out. Peeking at the seating chart, I also called out numbers and connected parties with waiters and waitresses, ready to lead them to open tables.

When I finally finished taking over hostess duties and the front room had emptied for a spell, I turned my attention to my dad.

"What happened here?" I asked Ba.

His brow creased. "Someone dropped off an upsetting note."

The hostess, now standing straight, with cheeks displaying a healthier color, moved toward me with a closed fist. She opened her hand to reveal a folded square piece of paper with my name on it.

I unfolded it to find a printed slip in Times New Roman font, stating, *Stay away if you know what's best for you. Look what happened to Jacey.*

I stared at the hostess. "Who delivered this?"

She stammered for a bit and then said, "I don't know."

I checked the dining room and around the entrance, as though the perpetrator could still be found. "Do you remember what they looked like at all?"

"No," the hostess said. "You know how crazy dim sum hours are. There was a throng of people out the door."

I glanced up at the bare corners of the ceiling. For once, I wished my dad wasn't so trusting and had decided to install a security system, complete with cameras, for the restaurant.

"Yale," my dad said, his brown eyes widening with concern, "why would anyone want to send a note like that?"

I felt my mouth quirk. "Guess that's what happens when you stick your nose where it doesn't belong. Celine and I . . ." I tripped over my cousin's name, as the absence of her company struck me anew.

"Were you two looking into the night market incident?" Ba asked.

"Yeah." I'd caused my dad worry. I looked down at the floor, studying the dark swirling pattern in the rich red carpet.

My dad softened his next words. "Yale, you don't always have to rescue people. It's okay to let go sometimes."

For a moment, I wasn't sure if he was speaking about the murder case or about my mom.

He continued, "Who is Jacey?"

"She's the sister of the person who got killed. Last night, she fell down some stairs, and she's in the hospital now."

He reared back.

"I just visited her, though," I added. "She's doing okay. Recovering."

Ba wiped his hands against his grease-stained apron. "If you and Celine were working on this together, is she also in danger?"

"Of course not," I said. "She's on an airplane and untouchable."

My dad reached into his pants pocket for his phone. "Let me just check."

He dialed and left a voice message. Then he texted, slow going on his flip phone, but received no response back.

"Do you think she made it to the airport okay?" he asked me.

I bit my lip and thought through the timeline. She'd have dropped off the rental car before going to LAX. Flights to East Asia happened late in the night, close to midnight. That was around the time when Jacey got pushed down the Culver City Stairs. The killer couldn't be in two places at once. "I bet she's on the plane, Ba. And her phone's turned off."

"I hope so." He checked the dining room and soon turned businesslike. "Ah, it looks like I have many customers to cook for."

After he left, I read the threatening note again. In a way, Celine had been lucky we'd had a disagreement, so she'd be halfway around the world and out of the murderer's reach. Someone—a woman, if Jacey's observations were correct—wasn't happy with our inquiries. I'd be next on her list. This time, neither Jacey nor Celine would be with me. I usually liked working alone, but a thought floated around, about how dangerous it could be doing things solo.

Ba's words echoed in my head. Did I really need to be on the rescue again? Unlike in the past, when I'd rushed home from college to right things, I had options now. I could stop, step away, and let the police handle things. Even the note urged, or rather threatened, me to do so.

But I hated bullies. Stuffing the warning note in my pocket, my hands discovered another piece of paper. I pulled out the contact list that Mrs. Ho had given me. Glancing over at the phone on a lacquered side table, I figured it was time to make some calls.

———

Perusing the list, I decided to skip over the food vendors who'd been highlighted on Jordan's Instagram. I'd questioned them plenty. However, I could ask the arts and crafts sellers if they'd seen a ninja checking out their products.

After a few calls, I found an artist who remembered a ninja approaching him. She'd almost purchased an abstract painting of his, the paint splatters resembling stretched-out musical notes. The woman had even tried to haggle with him over the sum, but he'd held fast to the list price and then she wandered away. The potential buyer of the painting sounded like she could be Genesis. She'd already mentioned to me that she'd checked out the arts area before proceeding over to the food vendors and finding Jordan deep in conversation with Blake. Her testimony seemed true thus far.

Next, I phoned up the games crew. The worker manning the darts and balloons booth recalled a group of young people with a costumed ninja among them. He grumbled that the ninja had cleared out almost all his prizes, including a giant stuffed teddy bear with a velvet bow. "Curse YouTube," he concluded. "Now everybody knows the tricks of the trade."

Finally, I called the performers. Most of them couldn't recall a thing besides their own show, particularly the breakdancer. He didn't remember much, no doubt because he'd been upside down half the time and spinning on his head.

I hoped to extract more clues from the hula guy. At the emergency meeting, he'd voiced what other people had probably felt, that they were being unfairly punished because of the tragedy. He'd also let slip that he'd seen the ninja with some other friends, not just her roommates.

It'd be best if I used a methodical approach. "You said you noticed Jordan Chang with her friends during your show. When was this?" I asked, my pen poised above a guest check pad I'd snatched from the waitressing supplies pile.

"I started at midnight, and my show goes on for forty-five minutes," he said.

I jotted down the times on the blank guest check. "And you're certain you saw a ninja? It gets pretty dark by then."

"She was right in front with her pals, who all wore bright shirts," he said. "Besides, once I start working with the fire, I can see clear as day."

Now I needed to home in on the fine details. "Do you remember anything at all about them?"

"Beats me," he said. "It was a mixed group of men and women."

I tapped my pen against the pad. "Okay, tell me this. What did their shirts look like?"

He hummed a tuneless snippet before saying, "I remember . . . they were highlighter orange with a huge picture of a cell phone with a smiley face."

That would match the Maximal Games logo. I needed to make sure he could identify Jordan as well. "This ninja," I said. "Did she happen to be eating anything?"

"Probably not," he said. "When I'm performing, people stop everything to watch."

The hula dancer certainly had a healthy sense of ego, but I did remember pausing myself to appreciate his brave performance.

He continued, "Although before my finale, maybe they squabbled over something. There was some shouting, and they didn't stand huddled together, friendly-like, at all."

I thanked him for his time and reflected on the discovery. At the emergency meeting for night market vendors, I'd thought Jordan had happily been with the group, but now it sounded like there had been problems. Could Jordan have done something to alienate herself from her co-workers, much like what had happened with Reagan?

I figured I should tell Detective Strauss about this new potential lead and move the case forward. Plus, I needed to report the warning note to him anyway. After indulging in a quick meal of pot stickers, I headed off to the police station.

When I asked to speak with Detective Strauss, the officer on duty in the glass-partitioned booth tried to contact him but failed. "Odd," the policeman said. "He definitely came in and hasn't left yet."

The cop tried again, but the line on the other end kept ringing. Not a moment later, the side door to the hallway swung open, and the detective I'd been seeking marched out.

"Wait, Detective Strauss," I said. "I need to speak with you."

He halted, nodded at me, and we both took seats in the waiting area.

"I have something to show you," I said.

Detective Strauss leaned away from the seat's hard back. "These chairs are awful."

"Yeah, you got the cushy seats in the inner sanctum," I said. "Anyway, I received a note at my dad's restaurant." I transferred over the written threat to the detective's hands.

He read the words and raised his eyebrows. "When did this show up?"

"Around lunchtime. Can you analyze the slip for more info?"

He rubbed the back of his neck. "I'm afraid not. How many hands has this passed through?"

I counted in my head. I'd touched it and so had the hostess. Maybe my dad had even grabbed it before I'd arrived.

"At least three."

"Hard to isolate prints, then."

While staring at the menacing sentences, I asked, "What about the ink? Could you track down the toner?"

"That would be really tough," he said. "Besides, I think I know who's behind the murder of Jordan Chang."

I inched closer to him. It appeared that I didn't have to share about my recent phone calls with the vendors.

"I was actually about to speak with a person of interest when you showed up here," he said.

"Who is it?"

"You and Celine were right. I was trying to figure out why there wasn't a record of any poisoned food in the stomach of the deceased. Nor any toxic metals involved. It had to be a chemical that disappeared or dissolved."

"Who?" I said again, after looking around and observing nobody else in sight. Even the officer behind the glass partition seemed occupied with paperwork. "You can tell me. My lips are sealed."

He hesitated and straightened the lapel of his suit jacket.

"Basically, Celine and I led you on the right track. You kind of owe it to us."

He lowered his voice. "Let's just say that liquid nitrogen does fit the bill. One's stomach can get destroyed by that stuff, in the same manner the autopsy report found. Basically, the stomach will freeze."

A strangled sound came out of my throat.

"Sorry about that last image," he said, and then stood up. "And don't worry about the note. I'm off to find that person now and have a little chat with her."

"Good luck, Detective Strauss."

He nodded at me as he ambled out of the police station. Detective Strauss had managed to achieve success in his first-ever homicide case due to Celine's and my probing ways. I felt proud of my role and decided on celebrating with a home-cooked dinner.

In preparation, I did a simple grocery run. It'd feel great to not eat ramen noodles at home. I didn't want to overextend myself, though. I aimed low and chose to make fried rice.

Fried rice was one of the easiest dishes to cook. Random leftover ingredients were often paired with rice. Since I didn't have anything in the refrigerator to throw together, I'd purchased veggies, eggs, and a dash of bacon. I even lugged out my rice cooker and made fresh rice. Even though fried rice tasted better with day-old grains; they made for a less sticky version.

I relished eating the first homemade dish of more than three ingredients that I'd cooked in a long time. Living alone and on a budget didn't result in lavish meals, particularly when I'd thought my old passion for cooking had faded away.

I'd finished my simple meal and put away the dishes when the phone rang in the spare room. I picked it up to find Ba at the end of the line. He must have taken a break during the lull in the dinner hours to call me.

"Just checking in on you," he said.

"Are you worried about that note?" I said. "I'm a capable adult, Ba."

He issued a soft grunt. "I still want to watch out for you and Celine."

I sat on the edge of the bed in the spare room. "Did she get back to you?"

"Yes. Finally. Turns out she *was* on a plane. She called me back when she reached Hong Kong." He paused, and his voice rumbled low. "FYI, Celine's concerned about you."

"Did you tell her about the note?" I asked, swinging my legs from my perch.

"Yes, with its threatening tone. And how your friend Jacey ended up in the hospital. Plus, the blog post."

I stopped moving my legs. "The what?"

"Some anonymous article on a new website about the night market tragedy."

"Can you tell me the URL?"

He shared it with me, and I wrote down the link.

"I wonder who posted that . . ."

"Please stay safe, Yale."

"Ba," I said, "I went into the police station earlier today, and Detective Strauss has everything under control."

After my confident reassurance, Ba sounded relieved as he ended the call. The blog post Celine had seen that Ba had mentioned rattled me, though.

I traveled over to the clubhouse and made straight for the business center. Like usual, it was empty, and I had my choice of computers. I entered the website link Ba had given me, and it led to a blog called the *Eastwood Village Connection*.

Only one post appeared on the site, but the title of the piece shocked me. It read, "Night Market Murder Points to Local Yee Family." Who had written this piece of trash?

I skimmed it and noticed the phrase "brutal boba," used to describe my drink. When I reread the post, other details popped out at me: green tea bubble drink, light bulb glass beverage container. Besides Celine and the detective, the only person who knew what I'd served Jordan and would be mean enough to write something about it was Nik Ho.

He hadn't wanted to give me an extension earlier when I'd asked for one, but I didn't think he'd follow through on his threat with such heartlessness. I'd understood he might gossip with the other restaurant folks, but I didn't think he'd involve the entire Los Angeles community. In fact, I didn't think he'd had the guts to publicize my supposed guilt to the whole world, but anyone anywhere could access online content. I checked Ho's business hours on the computer, but they'd already closed for the night. I took down the number, promising myself to call Nik in the morning and set the record straight.

TWENTY-ONE

I DIDN'T SLEEP WELL DURING THE NIGHT AND FIG-
ured it had to do with that horrible blog post that Nik
had constructed to tarnish my family name. Early in the
morning, I called the restaurant, but when the line kept on
ringing, I decided to take the initiative. He could hang up
on me over the phone, but he couldn't very well walk
away from me if I showed up on Ho's premises.

At Ho's, the sign on the front of the restaurant read
"CLOSED," but I could spy movement through the glass.
I curled my hand into a fist and banged hard against the
door.

Nik sprinted over, a look of alarm crossing his face.
When he recognized me, he smirked and pointed at the
sign. I knocked harder, possibly bruising my knuckles in
the process.

He unlocked the door and pushed it open a crack. "All
right already. Don't break the glass."

"How dare you print that stuff about me and my family," I said. If I hadn't knocked on the door so hard it hurt my hand, I'd have been tempted to do the same to his gloating face.

"I gave you a deadline, Yale." He gave me a smug smile. "Actually, that post has already gotten a hundred views. Who knew people were *dying* for gossip?"

"It's libel, Nik. And totally fake news."

"What do you mean?" He pushed the door open wider in his disbelief.

"Detective Strauss has someone else in his sights for the murder, so why couldn't you wait a day until things got solved?"

"Who's the new suspect?"

"Lindsey Caine," I said. "Maybe you should amend your post. But leave out her identity. It's still under wraps."

He stroked his goatee. "I don't recognize that name."

"She's the owner of the Below Freezing ice cream truck."

"Why would she want to whack Jordan Chang?"

"I don't think people use that term anymore," I said. "But to answer your question, Jordan posted something on Instagram about maybe reporting Below Freezing to EHD because the ice cream being served there was too cold."

Nik guffawed, and his eyes glittered with amusement. "That's a good one, Yale."

"What's so funny?" I stepped forward with bunched fists. Maybe I could use my nondominant hand to knock some sense into him.

"I remember Jordan ordering the shaved ice." He used his foot to hold the door open and held his hands about six inches apart. "She told me to make the ice a giant size, and she demolished it within five minutes flat. That girl was not afraid of a brain freeze."

I blinked at him. Could Jordan have posted her comment as a joke? I thought back to all her Instagram shots:

my bubble tea, the ensalada drink, the shaved ice, and the nitrogen ice cream.

Reflecting on all those pictures, I remembered she'd missed posting the second green tea she'd imbibed that night. Why hadn't she put up a picture of the drink she'd gotten from Nik?

She was snap-trigger-happy. Jordan also seemed to have a strong preference for the chilly. For a moment, my mind flashed to Jacey in the hospital bed sucking on ice chips. Like sister, like sister, I thought, which also reminded me of Dawn and Kelly Tanaka with their twin-like appearance.

I gripped Nik's wrist hard. "How did Jordan pay for your drink?"

He glanced down at my curled fingers. "Er, by cash. I remember that she took a long time to do so. I thought maybe she kept fumbling because she was gonna cry. She was blinking a lot, maybe to hold back tears."

"Interesting," I said. "Nik, this is important. What kind of purse did she carry?"

"She took out her wallet from a mini leather backpack."

I pressed harder on Nik's wrist, and he winced. "Are you sure?" I said.

"Yeah, because I remember thinking how silly it was for a grown woman to have a backpack purse."

"Oh geez," I said, releasing his arm. "I've got to go."

If my suspicions were correct, it seemed like Detective Strauss was following the wrong trail. Time would be of the essence, so I sprinted the few blocks over to Wing Fat.

The distance between Westwood and the hospital in Culver City spanned only five miles, but using public transportation could easily double the time to get from one point to the other. The fastest mode of travel would definitely be a car—and I would need to swallow my fear of driving one.

When I ran into Wing Fat, not one customer gave me

a funny look. It wasn't due to politeness, though. Despite the starting period for dim sum–goers, we didn't have the usual line snaking out the door. Nobody waited, with their feet tapping, before the hostess and her podium. Yikes. People had already learned to stay away from us, and I knew I could attribute the nosedive in business to Nik's blog.

I passed by the two sparse tables of customers in the dining room before bursting through the kitchen door. The staff stood around, seeming at a loss for what to do without the typical eating frenzy.

My dad stared at me from the stove area. Without a wok in his hands, he looked older and more haggard.

"Hi, Ba. I need to borrow your Camry for some important errands," I said.

"You want to drive?" he said. "It's been a while, Yale."

"I'm sure, and I still have my driver's license."

I'd kept it for identification purposes, renewing it each time through the mail. As luck would have it, I hadn't needed to go into the DMV to take a written or driving test to verify my skills. "Come on, Ba," I said. "I've driven before."

"The last time was years ago," he said, his eyebrows drawing together.

I avoided the subject of Mom's accident and my subsequent nondriving. "It's like riding a bike, right?"

"It's like driving a car," he said, handing me his key fob. "Be careful out there, Yale."

"I will," I said, before scooting out the door and hurrying to the parking lot.

When I got to the driver's side of the vehicle, my hands trembled. Good thing the car had keyless entry. I slid into the seat and took my time adjusting the mirrors to calm my nerves.

It took me a while to figure out how to start the engine, although I'd seen Ba do it over the last few years, after he'd purchased the vehicle. I gripped the steering wheel and backed ever so slowly out of the spot.

Once I made it to the exit of the parking lot, I waited, watching the other cars whiz by on the road. I had to make a right turn into that mass of moving traffic? Only after a car from behind honked at me did I inch out into the street.

At the next stoplight, I swiped my clammy hands on my pants. Could I do this? I gripped the wheel again, tighter this time.

My heart sped faster. What could I do to decrease my tension? I tried to distract myself by focusing straight ahead through the windshield, but the sight of roads with unseen potential terrors unnerved me even more.

I thought back to my time spent with Celine in the convertible. Those rides hadn't felt so bad. To emulate the feel, I rolled down the window. The flowing breeze in my hair soothed me as I maneuvered the car. In this slow fashion, pretending Celine was next to me, I made my way (on surface streets) to Brock Hospital.

Once in the building, I sped past the information area and over to the nurses' station of the corridor I wanted. "Is Jacey Chang still here?" I asked the man behind the desk.

He guided his computer mouse and clicked away. "Discharge should be today," he said.

I sprinted down the hallway, while the man issued a stern warning after me.

In her room, Jacey sat up in bed. She looked stronger than the last time I'd seen her.

"No need to rush, Yale," she said. "I'm pretty slow-moving with this cast on."

"When are you leaving the hospital?" I asked.

She scrunched her nose as she thought. "Should be at least a few more hours. They want to double-check some things."

"Can you delay them? I want to make sure you're as safe as possible, and this hospital is well guarded."

"Why are you so worried?" Jacey said. "Detective Strauss passed on the word to me that he has a solid lead in my sister's case. He won't be letting the suspect out of his sight."

"His lead's not that great," I said, pacing around the room. "In fact, it's downright *mis*leading."

"You think he's wrong?" Jacey asked, giving me a piercing look behind her glasses.

"I got a threatening note warning me to quit snooping, and it said that I might have an accident just like you." I stopped moving and faced her. "Tell me, Jacey. When you questioned everyone at the night market on Sunday night, did you introduce yourself by name?"

"Sure," she said. "I told them I was Jacey, Jordan's sister."

She'd done the same at my food stall. The note given to me had been delivered to Wing Fat, but anyone who'd read the original night market vendors lineup could've tied the Canai and Chai stall to my dad's restaurant.

All those Jacey had questioned would have known her name. The tip-off, though, would come with the answer to my next question. "Did you give any of the vendors your phone number?" I asked.

"What? No. I don't just give out my info to complete strangers." She mock-knocked her head with a fist. "You know, this was before I got a mild concussion."

"Then who around here with connections to Jordan has your number?" I asked.

She drummed her fingers against her cast. "Just her roommates—I don't know many people in this area, only closer to Long Beach where I live."

Yes, my suspicion had been correct. Jordan's phone had been disabled since after her death, out of commission or perhaps destroyed by the perpetrator. That left one of Jordan's roomies who'd contacted Jacey and shoved her down the stairs.

I glanced at Jacey sitting up in her hospital bed, remembering her call for ice chips. Ice and sisters and lookalikes revolved around my brain.

All three of Jordan's housemates dressed alike on special occasions and even for Halloween. They'd each gotten the same ninja outfit to match, and one of them must have doubled for Jordan at the Ho's Small Eats booth, ordering green tea. Nik had basically revealed so to me unknowingly. The ninja who'd come the second time around to his food stall had paid in cash, pulling out a wallet from a mini backpack. The young woman who'd ordered from me and had received a light bulb drink in return had taken her money out of a silk coin purse with embroidered flowers. She'd been the actual Jordan Chang.

I bet the fake Jordan had taken that second green tea and doctored it somehow. She'd slipped something lethal into the drink and poisoned her roommate.

Although I'd previously approached each roomie separately to dig into their alibis, I realized that I needed more objective witnesses. My first stop would be Maximal Games.

I drove over to Hilgard Avenue and managed to find a faraway spot. Not trusting my rusty parallel-parking skills, I bumped up against the curb in a space wide enough for two cars.

After marching up the steps, I used the brass knocker on the door to announce my arrival.

"Hi, Elodia," I said. "Remember me?"

"You delivered that tray of pupusas from Reagan Wood. Delicious, by the way. It lasted me several days."

"We weren't just deliverers," I said. "I kinda know Reagan."

She jutted out her bottom lip at me. "And . . ."

I thought fast, remembering what the game stall person had told me during his call. "Reagan was gushing about all the prizes she won for you at the night market. I just had to see that giant teddy bear she was describing in person."

Elodia giggled. "Oh, yeah. We totally wiped out that booth. Give me a moment, and I'll bring it over." She made sure to close the door and lock it, leaving me behind in the entryway.

I shuffled from foot to foot, trying to come up with a way to ask after Reagan's alibi in a roundabout way.

When Elodia returned, I made sure to admire the teddy bear with the velvet bow. It did seem pretty huge, almost the size of a whole person, so I didn't need to fake my amazement.

"How great that Reagan ran into you last Saturday night," I said. "Or was it Jordan who spotted your group first? I can't remember."

"Jordan Chang?" Elodia twirled a lock of her hair. "You know her, too?"

"Sure. She's Reagan's roommate, after all."

"I didn't see Jordan at the night market," she said.

Guess Jordan hadn't approached the group, like the stage performer had surmised. He must have confused her with Reagan at the time, even with the brightness of the fire for light.

"That's right." I slapped my forehead, mocking my mistaken memory. "It was Reagan who told me she saw your crew during that fire performance, with the hula dancer."

A small smile formed on her lips. "Oh, that guy was hot."

"I'm so glad you let her hang out with you . . . even after her work fiasco."

The smile disappeared. "She really messed up our budget."

"But I heard your latest game is a hit."

"Yeah, should help our financials," she said. "Anyway,

I know Reagan didn't plan on running into me, but she *was* trying to schmooze with me. Get her old position back."

"Did she really hang out and play carnival games with you all night?"

"Of course, because everyone at Maximal Games is into fun." She offered me a sparkling smile.

"Not a single moment when she slipped away to get a treat?"

"I don't know, maybe. I think she might've gone to the bathroom at some point," Elodia said.

Would that have been enough time for her to order a drink and put something in it?

"Reagan didn't act odd or anything that night?" I said. "After all, she ditched her roommates to be with the Maximal family."

"Roommates?" She shook her head. "Reagan told us she'd come to the night market alone. Had all the time in the world to stay with us."

Had Reagan fudged the truth to get an in with the gaming founder? Maybe Genesis had already messaged her saying she'd gone home early, but that still left Jordan . . . unless Reagan had decided to permanently make sure Jordan couldn't hurt her chances of reestablishing ties with Maximal Games.

TWENTY-TWO

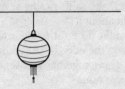

I MOVED REAGAN HIGHER UP ON MY MENTAL LIST OF suspects. She'd been at the night market at the right time. She also had a motive to take Jordan's life, given how upset she'd been over the fact that Jordan hadn't stood up for her at work and had actually been the one to tell her to leave. Also, Reagan could have used the short "potty break" away from Elodia and her ex-colleagues to commit the crime. Nobody really counted the minutes, especially when busy concentrating on winning a carnival game.

What about Genesis? She made up the trio of housemates who'd gone together that Saturday evening. Although Genesis had shown Celine and me the timing on her phone, she could have done so to establish her alibi and caught another ride back to the event. She'd also had a motive to deal with Jordan, especially since her relatives were involved. To double-check her veracity, I decided to travel to The Literary Narnia.

I didn't notice anyone around except for Kelly, the sister I wanted to locate. She stood behind the cash register, straightening the books in the revolving rack.

I rushed over to her. "Kelly, remember you were telling me about how you saw people coming and going during the night market on Saturday?"

"Uh-huh," she said, gazing at me with curious brown eyes. "What about it?"

"This might be vital to the murder investigation," I said, gripping the edge of the counter. "You told me you saw ninjas going together and separately. When did you notice a single ninja?"

She rested her chin on her clasped hands. "Hmm, there was a taxi around the witching hour."

"I knew it," I said, my words gathering speed. "That's around two in the morning, right?"

"I wish," Kelly said. She pulled off her wire-rimmed spectacles and cleaned them with a soft handkerchief. "I'm sixty, not sixteen. I can't stay up that late anymore."

"Oh," I said. "I thought the witching hour was in the wee hours of the morning."

"Not according to Shakespeare," Kelly said. "He thought it was closer to midnight, which was when I saw that ninja near a cab."

A sudden loud noise startled me. I turned toward the back room. "What was that?" Nobody seemed to be in the darkened space in the rear.

"Sorry." Dawn's voice fluttered out to me. "I had to change the light bulb but stumbled off the ladder."

"Are you all right?" I asked, moving toward Dawn's location, when I saw a warm light fill the space in the back.

"I'm fine, just tripped going down the bottom rung," she said, coming out of the room. "It's good to see you, Yale." Dawn enveloped me in a hug. I felt relieved at seeing her move without any telltale stiffness or pain in her joints.

"Please be careful," I said to Dawn.

"When you're the owner, you've got to do odds and ends," she said.

"Co-owner," Kelly said from the register, "and I'm sorry I couldn't be of more help, Yale."

"It at least clears up the timeline," I said and then wished both Tanaka sisters and the bookstore well.

"Maybe you can join us back here if we can get some more customers in through the door," Dawn said.

"Perhaps." I wound my way to the front. "Or maybe it's time to return to a previous passion of mine," I said, remembering my joy at making the grapefruit bubble tea and the simple fried rice dinner.

I got back into Ba's Camry and drummed a beat on the gear shift. Kelly had seen a taxi with a single ninja around midnight; it must have been Genesis bailing out from the night market and heading back home. Their apartment complex. I wondered what traces of evidence it might still hold. I wished I'd been able to rummage in every room when I'd gone there with Celine and Jacey.

If only I could get into the building again and search it at leisure. I stilled my fingers. While I didn't have a way to enter the apartment, Jacey did. She'd been given a spare key by her sister.

I drove to the hospital once more and found Jacey located in the same room. She sat up in bed with pillows propped behind her back and was reading a glossy magazine. I noticed my "Get Well" helium balloon tied to her bedside table.

Jacey looked up and bopped the balloon with the flat of her hand. "I forgot to thank you for this present. It brings a little color to this place. And I'll make sure to take it with me when I get out of here."

"What time will that be?"

She riffled through the magazine. "Hospital paperwork is horrendous, and I apparently need to find a driver.

I can't be getting into my own car with my leg in a huge cast. Plus, I've been trying to stay put in this place as long as possible, like you told me."

"Thanks for that, Jacey. I'm so close to putting the puzzle pieces together in this case," I said, then summarized my interviews at Maximal Games and the bookstore for Jacey.

"Sounds as though you're focusing on Reagan," Jacey said, grimacing. "I kind of like her, though. All bubbly and cheerleader-ish."

"She's got a one-track mind in regards to getting back with Maximal Games. Plus, she was there that night. And"—I'd thought about it on the drive over—"maybe she dropped some dry ice into Jordan's drink."

Jacey scrunched her brow. "Where would she get that?"

"You don't remember?" I said. "They had all these bubbling mini cauldrons with dry ice in them for decoration. Near the game booths."

As an events coordinator, it would've been easy for Reagan to recognize the dry ice, tilt some into tea, and give the modified mixture to Jordan as a refill for her empty light bulb glass.

I said, "I'm not one hundred percent sure, and everything's still conjecture. That's why I need to get into their apartment and really search."

Jacey tossed her magazine onto the bedside table. "You know, I've already been there half a dozen times."

"But were you looking at the roommates' belongings? Or just organizing Jordan's stuff? I'm going to do a thorough combing of the place."

"You'd need an empty apartment to do that."

I tugged at the string of the balloon, pulling it down. "That's where you come in," I said. "You need a designated driver, right? I think Reagan would make a wonderful chauffeur."

"What about the rest of the roommates?" Jacey said. "How would you get them out of the way?"

I let go of the string, making the balloon pop up. "Food, of course. There should be a celebratory dinner for your recovery. Conveniently planned for tonight."

"Sounds like you've got things all figured out." She jerked her thumb toward the cabinet. "Could you grab my cell from my bag? I'll send them a text right now."

I located her phone, and as I held the sleek device in my hand, I thought of Celine and her Instagram shots. "Just one moment, Jacey. Do you think I could text my cousin and say hello? My dad said she already landed in HK."

"No prob. Her number's on my phone from when we spoke with Blake and Lindsey."

"Thanks," I said and scrolled through Jacey's contacts. I clicked on Celine's name and started typing.

I messaged, Ba said you landed safely. I'm sorry I made that comment about the money. Oh, and this is Yale.

It seemed longer than the standard length for a text, but I didn't know much about messaging protocol. I added, Miss you.

Then I waited for a response from Celine.

Some time passed before Jacey said, "Should I send that group text out to Jordan's roommates now?"

"Oh, sure." I placed the phone in Jacey's hand.

Her fingers sped over the keys. "Done," she said.

Not a moment later, and her phone chimed with pings. I wondered why Celine hadn't responded to me with the same speed. I guess twenty years of silence outweighed less than a week of adventures.

Jacey read from her screen and said, "Reagan is free to pick me up from the hospital. She's sending out feelers about the group dinner."

A few beats later, and her phone emitted more noise. "Everyone's in," she said. "They're all coming over here at five thirty. Then Reagan's going to drive me and her roommates to this well-reviewed seafood place."

"Excellent," I said.

Jacey handed her phone back to me and said, "The spare key's in the side pocket of my bag."

I checked her purse and found a set of slim bronze keys.

"The wider one is for the outside door," Jacey said. "Good luck, Yale."

I thanked Jacey for her collaboration and left her bedside. Having another person beside you could not only be helpful but heartening. At that moment, I really missed Celine.

Before I collected any clues from the apartment, I knew I needed to prepare. I spent a long time at the local pharmacy poring over and accumulating a pile of supplies there: a box of nonpowdered gloves and some baggies (both plastic and paper, because I couldn't remember which type I should be using to contain evidence).

Also, I debated whether to buy an expensive Polaroid camera or not. I didn't have a phone, so I couldn't take digital pictures, and I needed photo proof quickly. *Money is options*, I thought, as I added the camera to the mix, and the irony of thinking like my cousin hit me.

I showed up at Jordan's old apartment complex at a quarter to six. Even if they were running late to the hospital, they should have left the building by then.

Although I'd purchased multiple items, I decided to enter the complex with only a single large paper sack. Inside the bag, I'd placed a pair of gloves, a few baggies, and the camera. I figured it'd look less conspicuous entering the building with what could be a takeout dinner as opposed to juggling boxes of supplies.

I strode up to the front door, and unlocked it using the wide key. Nobody gave me a second glance. I felt a wave of relief that the neighbors must not all know each other in the complex. With increased confidence, I headed for the elevator.

At the apartment, I leaned my head close to the door. I didn't hear any sound from within. I stuck the key in, unlocked the door, and turned the knob. The door swung open with a resounding creak.

The inside of the apartment was dark, indicating that all the roommates had left for the scheduled hospital pickup and ensuing celebratory dinner. I made sure to close the front door with its whining hinges and lock it.

I decided to check the common spaces first. Nothing unusual. A sweep of the living room also left me empty-handed.

What wouldn't the perpetrator have tossed away? I came back to Nik's testimony, of how Jordan's double had carried a mini backpack.

I peeked at the wall rack near the front door. Nothing adorned any of the hooks there. It'd be in her room, then.

The first room I opened happened to be Reagan's. I could tell by her fabric bulletin board crisscrossed with pink satin ribbons. They held photos of her with tons of friends, including a few coworkers with Maximal Games shirts. She didn't have any mini backpacks in there. A sudden sense of doubt flooded me. I checked inside her closet and under the bed. Still nothing.

Biting my lip, I decided to check out the other two bedrooms, just in case. Sierra's room had a fair number of sample lotions and creams on her desk. Genesis had opted to keep her room sparse except for framed blown-up posters of famous musicians. Neither of those rooms had a mini backpack.

I paused before the last door in the corridor, Jordan's old room. I'd been there previously, and it'd offered nothing. This time around, the door was closed. I pushed it open . . . to reveal the same scene I'd observed before. Dresser with mirror, bare mattress, spindly nightstand.

I stomped my foot in frustration, which triggered a memory. I'd kicked that contact lens case with my foot the last time I'd been here. My eyes sought the dusty nightstand, and everything tumbled into place as I gazed at its now bare wooden surface.

Snippets of scenes and phrases swirled in my brain. Kelly had told me about seeing a cab at midnight. Dawn had scared me from the back room at The Literary Narnia as she'd changed out a light bulb. I thought about the contacts case and the fake Jordan blinking unusually at Nik. Then I came back to how the real Jordan had winked at me after I'd given her my "*yum*" green tea drink.

I'd mixed up the suspects and tangled up the timeline. Now that I'd sorted everything out in my head, I looked around Jordan's old room. There had to be *something* in here to incriminate the real killer.

I didn't think I'd find anything in the nightstand and placed my paper sack on top of it. The drawers were too shallow to hide much. Yep, all I discovered were dust bunnies.

Then I crept toward the dresser. I searched from top to bottom. There, in the last drawer, wedged in the rear corner, my hands grasped a mini backpack.

I lifted the bag up. It felt light, strangely so. The mini backpack didn't have a zipper but a snap button closure. I fumbled trying to open it. When I finally did, I seemed to hear another faint snapping noise. I wondered if the acoustics of the bedroom resulted in weird echoes.

After opening the flap of the bag, I peered into the interior, desperately hoping to find the source of liquid nitrogen. I'd wanted to discover a small tank in the backpack, similar to the kind Lindsey had employed in her ice cream food truck. I didn't find anything. The emptiness of the backpack mocked me.

Putting my head down near the bag, I examined the lining. Maybe there'd be a hint that something cold and lethal had been housed in it before.

Someone cleared their throat from the doorway. "Looking for this?" she said.

TWENTY-THREE

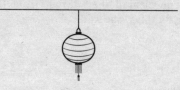

Sierra stood before me and raised a stainless steel container in her thick-gloved hands. It had been the one I'd mistaken for a lunch container when I'd checked on Reagan's alibi and had brought over egg rolls. The "Do Not Touch" sticky note I'd seen made even more sense now.

"You left it out on the counter in plain sight," I said, shocked.

She managed a half shrug. "My roommates know not to touch my stuff. After all, I graduated as a chem major." I guess they'd gotten used to her science projects lying around.

"I assume there's liquid nitrogen inside," I said, trying to suppress a shudder.

"That's right. And this top-of-the-line steel liquid dewar can keep contents cold for weeks at a time." She positioned herself to block off the doorway and any chance of my escape.

"Where are the rest of your roommates?" I tried to peer beyond her and strained to hear their voices.

"Still back at the restaurant. I had to come home because I 'forgot' my phone." She did a half pivot, and I spotted the orange backpack I'd seen at the coffeehouse during her tutoring session hanging from one shoulder. "Oh, oops, guess I did take it with me. Guess this bag's just too cavernous. It can hold both a phone and a canister of liquid nitrogen."

I lifted the floppy mini backpack that I'd discovered. "You planted this in the dresser drawer. It wasn't here before, when Jacey looked. Or she would've found it."

"Of course not. I kept it in my room until tonight, just before we left for the hospital."

"You must have known I'd be coming, but how?"

"Please." Sierra tilted her head at me. "What a flimsy excuse of a celebratory dinner. I figured something was up. And I knew you were part of it, ever since the night at the French fusion restaurant."

I touched my cheek with the palm of my hand, remembering the makeover Celine had done on me. With all those extra layers and fancy clothing, I figured I'd fooled Reagan and Sierra in the powder room. "You recognized me?"

"Not right away," she said, "but how you kept asking questions bugged me. Then Reagan mentioned your unflattering lipstick color, and when you stepped back into the brighter hallway, I knew I'd seen you before, doing that 'wrong delivery' act."

I touched the texture of the mini backpack I now held. Its supple material made it a horrible defensive weapon. Maybe if I kept Sierra talking, I could inch my way toward the nightstand. I bet that Polaroid camera felt pretty hard upon contact. "I still don't get it, Sierra. What's your beef with Jordan? So she called you a freeloader. As the saying goes, sticks and stones."

"She was going to gather the other roommates together for a final decision," Sierra said. She almost hissed out her next words. "But Jordan had already told me in private that she'd started interviewing prospective new roommates."

I held up my hands in a calming gesture. "But you were getting more hours at your job, right? And you had your tutoring gig. You could've worked something out."

"Three strikes, Jordan had told me. This was my third month missing the rent." Her mouth thinned into a tight line. "And the landlord was going to hike up the prices in a few weeks. I begged Jordan to give me more time, but she just wouldn't budge."

"I can see how that'd be rough," I said, wanting to get on her good side.

Sierra's eyes seemed to blaze. "I just wanted to buy myself more time. If Jordan got sick, she'd have to postpone the meeting, giving me more leeway to pay my portion of the rent."

Sierra looked down at the floor. "I didn't mean for her to *die*. I don't know how things got so out of control."

With Sierra lost in reflection, I took the opportunity to inch toward the nightstand.

"What I don't get is how you figured it out," she said, focusing on me again. "Even that detective didn't question me after he discovered that I had an alibi."

"Genesis never saw you," I said. "You 'heard' her come in, but she only saw the light on in your room and assumed you were home." I'd made the inverse mistake at The Literary Narnia. Since the back room had been dark, I'd figured nobody was in there, but then Dawn had surprised me.

"It was great that she could vouch for me."

"Yeah, a lucky break," I said.

"Luck had nothing to do with it. That was all skill," she said.

"You mean, you made Genesis come home?"

"Sure. Knowing her puppy love for Blake, it was only too easy. I knew Jordan was going to try out all the food stands—that's her thing. Blake would be no exception, so I just texted Genesis to make sure she checked on the two of them, hinting at the possibility of a reconciliation."

I took another glacial side step toward the nightstand. "You did an excellent job covering for yourself. For a long time, I kept suspecting your other roommates since you were supposedly out of the equation, having stayed at home, but then the contacts case clued me in."

"How so?" Sierra said.

"When Jordan stopped by my booth, I remembered her pretty violet eyes. An unnatural hue. I figured they were colored contacts because I saw a case here on the bedroom floor, and I also remembered Jacey having put Jordan's old pair of glasses into a donation box at the library." I stared at Sierra's glasses. "I realized that someone must have worn those violet contacts and pretended to be Jordan. Even ordered another green tea in her stead. Only someone who had a prescription could've worn them, although you did fumble with your wallet and blink a lot." What Nik had described to me as intense blinking could be attributed to putting on a pair of contacts with the wrong prescription.

I continued talking. "Why'd you wear them in the first place?"

"Extra caution. I didn't want to be recognized at all that night in case things went sideways," Sierra said. She gripped the steel container tight with both hands. "People would've assumed I was Jordan walking around."

"You know, I did have friends who saw you arrive at the night market at midnight," I said. Kelly had testified that she'd seen a ninja near a cab at that hour. At first I assumed she'd been talking about Genesis, but then I remembered that rideshare companies don't use taxis.

Plus, the time didn't match since Genesis had already been home at midnight. "The police can track your taxi trail."

"It doesn't matter if they do," Sierra said. "I could've decided to join the festivities on a whim. There's no harm in that."

"Speaking of harm, how did you get Jordan alone by herself?"

"Easy peasy. I messaged her to meet me at the fountain. Promised it'd be quieter there," she said. "Of course Jordan agreed. Loud noises and bright lights intensify her headaches."

"And she liked cold foods when she suffered from her migraines." Jordan had exemplified that by gobbling down the shaved ice. "But how did you force her to take the liquid nitrogen?"

Sierra gave me a confused look. "Jordan took it willingly. To combat her heat energy."

Jordan had been into feng shui, with her mini fountain and yin-yang poster. The *yum*—what Jordan had said to me at the booth, when I'd started hawking my wares in Cantonese—was how the word "yin" was pronounced in our dialect, as opposed to standard Mandarin. Jordan had thought she could combat the yang, or *yeung*, energy that caused her debilitating headaches by eating lots of *yum*, or cooling, foods. "Still," I said, casting Sierra a doubtful look, "drinking liquid nitrogen?"

"I billed it to her as a fad beverage. I'm sure you've seen those nitrogen cocktails smoking away on a bar napkin. This new green tea was something along those lines. Thanks for that, by the way."

I startled at her mention of gratitude. "For what?"

"The light bulb glass. I was looking for a nice container that could withstand the low temp of the nitrogen."

"I thought you wanted Jordan to get sick, not die."

"Yeah," she said. "I figured Jordan would stop after a couple sips, but she kept right on going."

Maybe all the exposure to cold foods and drinks had somehow numbed Jordan's sense of the correct temperature for eating and drinking.

"I have heard that sometimes when a drink is so cold, you won't even feel the freeze," Sierra said. "So you see, Jordan basically did it to herself. Obviously I didn't mean for it to happen, but she was a terrible roommate."

Sierra didn't want to take responsibility for her actions, which made her dangerous. I took a bigger step toward the nightstand, and her eyes narrowed at my movement.

"Stop right there," she said.

She moved a few steps toward me, leaving the doorway open. I measured the small gap in my mind, but I doubted I could run past her.

"One thing I'm wondering is why no one spotted Jordan until I stumbled into her," I said. "Even Reagan didn't come looking. You must have really covered all your bases." Appealing to her pride seemed to distract her.

She paused in her forward slinking. "That was brilliant on my part. Leaving her in the shadow of the fountain, under that jutting edge. Everyone gave that area a wide berth because of the wild spouting water."

I did the same myself whenever I walked past it.

Sierra continued, "It also helped that I took away her phone—before I eventually trashed it. I even used it to pretend I was Jordan, texting Reagan and telling her not to worry about me and to hang out with her old work buddies."

"Geez," I said, taking in the entirety of Sierra's confession.

"There's no reason I should get locked up when it wasn't really my fault," Sierra said. "What's done is done, and I need to move forward. I have a future to think about, and I can't let anyone get in the way of that."

"I'm sure we can find some sort of alternative," I said, my voice coming out hoarse.

Her mouth quirked up. "Don't worry, I have a surefire way of keeping you silent. Liquid nitrogen is killer on the skin. I should know, working in dermatology, even though I'm just the receptionist. A little bit is fine to battle warts and lesions, but too much . . ."

I retreated but soon realized I literally had my back against a wall.

Meanwhile, Sierra stepped toward me. "This will damage your mouth so badly, it'll be too painful to move your lips. And then I'll deal with your hands, so you won't be able to write a message either. I really can't have you telling the police all of this."

I swore I could hear my heart thumping, its beating audible. "You're going to kill me."

"Of course not," Sierra said. "You'll be the scapegoat. I'll just damage you enough so you can't communicate properly. After the police find you with this incriminating dewar, all signs will point to you again as the poisoner."

I didn't think the police would buy her frame-up, but I wasn't going to tell her that.

She started unscrewing the lid of the container. Her heavy-duty gloves, though, made it hard for her to twist and bought me some time to think.

The paper sack and its contents, including the heavy camera, were too far away for me to reach. I also knew the rest of the room consisted of barebones furniture. My best line of defense would be to run past her.

"By the way, I played softball in high school," Sierra said. "I have excellent aim." She finally jerked open the container's lid, and the backpack she wore shifted to the edge of her shoulder.

My muscles tensed as I geared to sprint for my literal

life. At that moment, I imagined I heard Celine's voice. Could panic make you hear things? She whispered, "Attack. Go for the slip-off."

I lunged. Instead of aiming to go around Sierra, I listened to the voice. I launched myself to the side of Sierra, yanking her backpack strap hard and then darting out of the way.

She fell over, startled, spilling the dewar's contents on the floor and on top of herself. Sierra yelped in pain, as her shirt became saturated with the chemical.

Someone grabbed my arm and pulled me into the exterior hallway and slammed the bedroom door shut.

"Lean against this door and keep it closed," a familiar voice said.

I focused on the new arrival and found myself gaping at my cousin. "Celine, what are you doing here?"

"No time to answer. Gotta grab something and jam it against this doorknob."

She left me for a moment and followed through on her own advice, securing the door tight with a dining chair slanted at an angle.

Then she called Detective Strauss. When she hung up, she said, "The police are on their way, so even if Sierra tries to climb down the four stories to the ground, they'll be ready for her."

I thought back on Sierra crying out in pain. "I doubt she'll be able to do much after spilling liquid nitrogen on herself."

"That's called karma," Celine said.

I clutched onto my cousin's arm. "I still don't get it. How'd you get here?"

"Simple," she said, disentangling my grip with gentleness. "The door to the apartment was open."

"Rusty hinges," I said, remembering the clanking I'd had to deal with when getting inside the apartment.

"Probably made too much noise, so Sierra decided against closing it, the better to sneak up on me. But how did you know I was even here?"

"Oh, it started with the message you texted me," Celine said.

"The one where I talked about you landing safely in Hong Kong . . ."

"It's also where you apologized and said you missed me," she said.

My cheeks heated up even as I heard a muffled yell coming from inside the closed room.

"Let me out of here," Sierra cried out.

I leaned against the door, and Celine also braced herself on the other side of the propped chair.

"You, um, didn't reply to my message," I said.

"I was on an airplane, cuz," Celine said, "flying back here."

"What? Why?"

"Because I was worried about you. That threatening note sounded horrible. I couldn't believe I'd left you in the lurch . . . and in actual physical danger."

"Aww, you do care about me," I said, giving her a playful tap on her arm.

"That, and Hong Kong was boring. The same old yawn-inducing charity dinners and casino events. No murder cases and excitement. Even the hubbub has faded away about my slip-up—"

"Thanks for that, by the way," I said.

"No problem," she said. "I hadn't realized my faux pas would soon become a fashionable method of attack."

I calculated the numbers in my head. "It might be the adrenaline wrecking my brain, but I still don't know how you made it here so soon. Isn't it at least a twelve-hour flight from Hong Kong to Los Angeles?"

"I traveled across the International Date Line. Leave

today and arrive on the same day," Celine said. "It's airplane magic."

Speaking of magic, Detective Strauss made a sudden appearance in the hallway. He pointed to the door we were leaning against, where the thumping of fists could be heard. "I take it that's where our special guest is."

TWENTY-FOUR

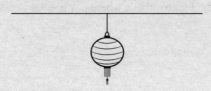

SEVERAL OTHER OFFICERS HUSTLED IN BEHIND DEtective Strauss to stand in the hallway to the bedrooms. I whispered to the detective, "It was liquid nitrogen, just like you said. She's got a steel container of it in the room."

Detective Strauss gave me a curt nod and then commanded one of the other police officers to lead Celine and me to a safer area. The cop relocated us to the living room.

My cousin and I stayed in place, but, unable to see Jordan's bedroom, we inclined our heads toward the action. I heard the scraping of the chair being removed from where it was jammed under the doorknob and the running of footsteps. Scuffling ensued, but within minutes, I heard Detective Strauss let out a satisfied whistle. "Got you," he said.

The next hour passed in both snippets rushed and glacial slow. Celine and I were barraged with questions, first from the police, attempting to assess the situation and re-

create what had happened in the apartment, and then from
the emergency responders, examining us for any signs of
injury.

After giving multiple statements to various officials,
we were allowed to leave the apartment. Celine and I
ducked under a barricade of police tape. The stark words,
reading "Do Not Cross," gave me the shivers.

My cousin didn't display any nerves but whipped out
her cell phone. "I usually take only foodie shots, but I'll
make an exception this time." *Snap.*

We moved down the corridor of the building, dodging
about half a dozen residents in the process. They lingered
in the common hallway and studied the apartment we'd
exited with curiosity.

One bystander asked, "What happened in there?"

Another said, "Is everyone okay?"

Celine and I assured the neighbors that everything was
fine and that the police were handling the situation. We
didn't go into specifics, uncertain of how much we could
divulge to the public at this point. Besides, they'd probably learn about it soon enough in the news.

When we clambered into the elevator, Celine and I
gave each other relieved grins.

"I'm sure glad that's over," I said.

"Same, and I'm happy you made it out in one piece,"
she said.

The elevator rattled and moved down to the first floor.

"By the way," Celine said, "congrats on solving the
case in just one week."

Had it been only last Saturday evening when everything had transpired? I reveled at justice being finally
served, but turned to face Celine. "I didn't do it alone."

She smiled at me as the elevator doors opened and
slung an arm around my shoulder. "Come on, cuz, this is
our stop."

As we made our way across the empty lobby, I stopped

short before a familiar set of luggage. "Are those yours?" I asked, but who else would haul around a stack of three purple suitcases?

"Yeah," Celine said. "I was in a bit of a rush to get here from the airport for the life-and-death situation."

"Don't I know it?" I said, letting out a mock groan. Despite the harrowing experience, it'd also been exciting at the same time. Reading about it with my favorite literary heroine at the helm didn't quite translate to the same experience as living it.

Celine left my side to gather her luggage. Then she pulled her phone out. "Time to get a ride. Can I crash at your place again?"

"Of course," I said, "but no need to call for a ride. I can take you."

I held up Ba's key fob and watched Celine's jaw drop. It felt nice to swap places and be the adventurous cousin for once.

"You bought a car?" she said.

"No, it's my dad's, but he let me borrow it for the day. I'll take you to the apartment, return the car to the restaurant, and then have Ba drive me home."

"That's so roundabout," Celine said. "I'm not even tired. Let's go to Wing Fat now, and I'll say hello to Uncle at the same time."

"If that's what you want," I said, as she rolled her luggage out of the apartment complex.

As I drove to the restaurant, Celine hugged her arms tight around herself.

"What's up with the windows being rolled all the way down?" she said.

"It feels like being in the Boxster. The breeze kind of calms me down while driving," I said, giving her a sheepish grin.

"I've turned you into a convertible fiend," she said, rolling up the window a few centimeters.

When we made it to Wing Fat, the restaurant looked dark. Lights off.

"That's odd," I said. "Isn't there still half an hour before closing time?"

"Let's check in the back," Celine said, and we hurried to the alley behind Wing Fat.

We saw light from the kitchen through the screen door, and I felt my shoulders relax.

"Ba?" I said, leading the way inside.

"Over here," he said, as he shut the door to the large walk-in refrigerator with a hearty shove.

"Celine," Ba said, blinking at her. "I thought you were in Hong Kong."

"I was, but now I'm back to spend some more time with you and Yale."

"That was a quick turnaround," he said.

"Family is worth it," she replied.

"Yale, I'm all done here," Ba said. "Thanks for bringing my car back. I can drop you two off at Fountain Vista."

I glanced around the kitchen. No one else was in sight, and the dirtied cookware all seemed to be cleaned up. Ba must have already wiped down the prep tables as well, given their shiny surfaces.

"Why is everything put away already? And the place shut down so early?" I asked.

He took off his apron and dropped it into the hamper for dirty linens. "It was pretty quiet here all day long. I let the others go home and closed earlier tonight."

"The blog post," I said, my hand curling into an automatic fist. "Curse that Nik Ho."

"What does the Ho family have to do with anything?" Ba asked while Celine said, "What did he do this time?"

I handed the key fob over to my dad. "It's nothing to worry about, Ba. I'll take care of it."

We trailed my dad to the parking lot, where I asked

him if he'd be okay with Celine and me sitting in the back of the Camry.

"No problem," he said. "Enjoy your girl talk." Ba was even kindhearted enough to blast some old Canto-pop music to cover our talking.

In the back seat, I told Celine about my suspicions of the blogger behind the *Eastwood Village Connection*.

"I figured that Nik was the only one who could've written the piece," I said. "Nobody else knew about my light bulb glass and the grapefruit green tea concoction."

"You're right," she said. "We'll have to talk to Nik and get him to take it down."

"I already tried," I said, giving my seat belt a yank. It felt more constraining the longer I spoke. "At his restaurant, I told him that he was sullying the Yee family name. Not that he cared."

Celine glanced toward the front, where Ba was humming along with a catchy song. "Your dad and Mrs. Ho are good friends. Could we use that pull to make Nik stop?"

"It was posted anonymously," I said. "I doubt his mom even knows he wrote it. Auntie Ai isn't really super techy either."

"Well, he got his facts wrong," Celine said.

"I know," I said. "But I'm not sure he really minds, as long as the Ho name isn't tarnished. He didn't budge an inch and even laughed at me when I told him that Detective Strauss no longer thought of us as suspects."

"But now that the detective has Sierra Tang in custody, maybe Nik will change his mind."

"I don't know," I said. "And even if he did, the damage is already done. People are either avoiding or boycotting Wing Fat on purpose."

"Public opinion can be harsh," Celine said, shifting in her seat and gazing at the passing streetlights for a moment.

I wondered if she'd physically separate herself from me now, move away, like she had so many years ago when we'd been in a car. Instead, she surprised me by leaning her head close to mine.

"Don't worry," my cousin said. "We'll get through this together."

The next morning, Celine and I stood at the ready, in front of Ho's, blocking entry into the business. Nik spotted us first, sprinting toward us from the car, while his mom took her time to maneuver out of the vehicle.

Nik stood before us, swiveling his head left and right, with a steely look at us both. I couldn't help but notice that Celine and I stood a few inches lower than him, and I tried to straighten my spine to block his height intimidation.

"What are you two doing here?" he said, his tone unwelcome and his arms crossed over his chest.

I didn't hear Celine's answer because for a moment I focused on Nik's height. It should've tipped me off to the culprit before. Mrs. Ho had mentioned that the ninja buying a drink from their stand had been taller than Nik, and I knew for a fact that the real Jordan stood around my height. Nik's mother had given me this tidbit during the emergency conference meeting. If I'd caught it back then, maybe I could have clued in Detective Strauss earlier. Then Jacey wouldn't have needed to suffer a concussion, and I could have escaped from being stuck in a room with a vindictive Sierra.

Mrs. Ho's warm voice brought me back to the present moment. "Celine," she said to my cousin. "You came back to the United States. Any particular reason?"

Before Celine could even answer, Nik's mother bustled over to the restaurant's door and unlocked it. "Come on in. You must be hungry. I can make you and Nikola a special breakfast. My treat."

I mumbled my hello to her as she marched us all inside the restaurant. She then directed Celine and Nik to a cozy booth. Then she turned to me and said, "Yale, you can sit at one of the stools."

I perched at the counter while Mrs. Ho hurried into the kitchen. As soon as I heard the clattering of pots and pans, I slid off the stool and joined Nik and Celine. I heard the last part of my cousin's sentence.

". . . know you're the author," she said.

Nik leaned back in the booth. "So, what's it to you? The *Eastwood Village Connection* won't affect you at all."

"Yee is my last name, too," she said.

I nudged my cousin, and she scooted over for me.

"You're all the way in Hong Kong," Nik said. "Why do you even care?"

"How about the fact that it's not true?" Celine said, putting her phone on the table. A stylized shot of the crime scene tape she'd taken last night peeked up at us.

"What's that?" Nik said, curiosity making him draw closer to the picture.

"We were there when the real culprit for the 'Night Market Murder' got nabbed by the police," Celine said.

She continued, "I can give you the scoop. Wouldn't that be amazing for your fledgling blog?"

He pushed the phone back to her. "Nah. I'm not really a journalist. I just did it for my family, to make sure we wouldn't be blamed for the mess that happened at the night market."

"Nik," I said, putting my palms flat on the table. "You talk about the importance of family. Do you know what that blog post has done to my dad? Nobody's going to Wing Fat. He even had to close up the restaurant early last night."

If anything, that revelation put a smug smile on his face. Maybe he didn't mind taking out the competition in such a sly way. "Come on, Nik. Have a heart." I reflected on what emotional leverage I could use to sway him.

Leaning back in the booth and mirroring his crossed-arm image, I continued, "What about that meeting with the plaza owner you mentioned to me? If you can show that the culprit is caught, wouldn't that place your mom in a better position?"

"That might help," he said, uncrossing his arms and stroking his goatee in thought. "Will it be enough, though? Reputation is already shot. A murder at the night market wasn't the best publicity for an inaugural event."

"Or maybe it is," Celine said, confidence making her voice ring out loud. "I know a thing or two about the sway of media."

"What do you have in mind?" Nik asked, his brow creasing.

"A new article, making a claim to fame for the East-wood Village Night Market. Log into your blog right now," she said, sliding her phone over to him. "I'll make up a sample draft."

Nik nodded, and before long, Celine had typed up a new post. She didn't show it to me but allowed Nik to look it over. As he read the draft, his eyebrows lifted in his surprise. I wanted to peek at the screen, but that's when Mrs. Ho arrived with food in tow.

She gave me a pointed look, and I darted away back to my lonely stool.

"Don't worry," Mrs. Ho said from across the room. "I'll bring you an individual portion of breakfast."

She kept her word because I soon received a platter of fried-dough crullers, along with a bowl of steaming sweet soy milk to dip them into. She also treated me to a sesame bread *shao bing* sandwich with egg in it. From my spot, I couldn't see what Nik and Celine were doing, but they seemed to be in agreement. Before long, they dug into their delicious breakfast dishes, and so did I.

After finishing my food, I wiped flaky crumbs from my mouth and left a tip at the counter. I felt overly full and practically waddled my way to their booth.

"Everything all set?" I said.

"Yep," Celine said. "Wait until you see what we came up with for the latest blog post."

Mrs. Ho bustled out from the kitchen and started clearing away the dishes.

Nik stood up. "I've got that, Ma."

She swatted at his hand. "What kind of romantic date would this be if you had to dash away from the table?"

Nik and Celine stared at each other in alarm, as Mrs. Ho left them with a satisfied smile on her face.

"That needs to be cleared up soon," Celine said, giving a nod to Nik. Both his neck and face looked flushed. "Anyway, I'd better go before it gets more awkward, and your mom also plots lunch and dinner for us."

When we left Ho's, I turned to Celine. "What did you end up publishing?"

She whipped out her phone, located the blog, and showed it to me.

The headline of the article read, "Yee Solves the Case." I swallowed down a lump in my throat at the gutsy title.

The sensationalist piece meant to drive up interest established me at the center of the story. It felt both flattering and embarrassing to be highlighted. "You make me sound better than I am," I said.

"Come on," Celine said. "Learn to take a compliment, Yale."

I continued to read the post, which indicated that an anonymous source had revealed that I'd played a big role in securing the real culprit in the Night Market Murder. The article, for legal reasons, did not divulge the name of the killer. In the end, the post made it seem like the East-wood Village Night Market had been an amazing affair, rife with adventure, and organized by the incomparable Ai Ho. The article ended with the opinion that it'd be great to have more night market events in the future, to bring excitement to the surrounding community and draw crowds from even farther away.

"Not bad," I said after reading it. "Maybe a tad over the top. I'm surprised Nik gave his approval, especially since he's not at the center of attention."

Celine gave me a devious grin. "He liked it once I put in that airbrushed shot of him in front of Ho's Small Eats."

"And you think this post will really reach people?"

"I believe so," Celine said. "It's already got fifty views and climbing."

"That was quick," I said.

Celine wiggled her fingers at me. "It's all about the spin."

"I wonder if it's working for Ba," I said. "Want to walk over to Wing Fat to see?"

"Sure," she said but shook her head. "I still can't be-lieve you walk—and bus—everywhere. At least take a Lyft or Uber, woman."

"Can't. No phone," I said, emptying out my pants pockets for her to see my credit card holder and keys. "I'm never going to be tech obsessed . . . but I must admit, driving did feel freeing."

"That's the spirit," Celine said, as she looped her arm in mine, and we strolled over to the restaurant.

TWENTY-FIVE

WE SAW THE RECENTLY PUBLISHED BLOG POST already working its magic by the time Celine and I arrived at Wing Fat. A line of people snaked out the front door of the restaurant. They seemed to buzz with uncontainable energy.

My cousin and I circumvented the crowd by sneaking through the back kitchen door.

"Ba," I said, "there's a stream of people outside."

He put down the stack of bamboo baskets he was carrying. Ba greeted us both before saying to me, "The tables are almost all filled inside, too."

"That's great," I said.

"Everyone loves your dim sum," Celine added.

He shrugged his shoulders in response to my cousin. "I'm not so sure about that. Quite a number of people have been asking for something called 'brutal boba.' Have you heard of it?"

Celine chortled with glee while I clapped a hand over my mouth to stop any empathy laughs.

My cousin recovered her composure and said, "That's a special drink Yale made up for the Eastwood Village Night Market."

"Wonderful," my dad said, placing a hand on my shoulder. "Maybe you should continue exploring more recipes, Yale."

"I just might do that, Ba."

I swore I noticed his eyes misting up, but he soon turned away to cook up another dish. For a few moments, I let myself soak in the sensory experience of being in a busy kitchen. I loved hearing the excited sizzle of the oil dancing in the wok and the smell of steamed treats in the air.

I glanced over at the tower of bamboo baskets. They waited, ready to fulfill the dim sum dreams of hungry patrons. My mind wandered to the personality categorization system I'd invented, and I thought about my cousin standing beside me. Which dim sum dish would represent her the most?

I considered and ruled out different options before settling on sticky rice. Perhaps I wouldn't mention that food description right to her face, but I thought the food was fitting.

Something about Celine made people, including me, want to stick with her. She had a luxurious presence, like the similarly beautiful package that contained glutinous rice. Usually, the dish was wrapped into neat bundles with kitchen string, like a food present for diners. The sweet fragrance of the lotus leaves used for wrapping the sticky rice made taste buds spark alive. Plus, once a sticky rice package was opened, it offered a treasure trove of ingredients—everything from fairy-sized dried shrimp to earthy black mushrooms to golden salted egg yolks.

Celine nudged me. "What's going on, Yale? Are you in a food trance? You look hungry again, even after that huge Taiwanese breakfast."

"No way," I said to my cousin. "I'm more than satisfied." I did feel full, not only with yummy food in my stomach, but with the double promise of a bright life and loyal family surrounding me.

"It's nice to see you happy," Celine said. "Glad this new blog post seems to be working. Now that there are no killers to chase or gossipers to silence, do you want to head back home and relax?"

"Sure," I said. "Let's go."

Celine studied my dad's back. "Actually, I need to stay a little longer and chat with Uncle about something. Do you mind going home first?"

My smile faltered a little as I said, "No problem."

Even though I'd taken public transit so many times in the past, it felt odd as I clambered aboard the bus. Perhaps I'd been spoiled by having easy access to a vehicle. I felt very alone on the stiff seat and stared out the window as the bus chugged me back to Eastwood Village.

I managed to shake off my melancholy by lounging on the settee and diving into Jane Austen's world. Celine had spoken the truth. The past week had been a whirlwind of activity, and I deserved some relaxation.

I'd paired my reading with a steaming mug of honey ginseng tea by my side. Time passed, and I'd reached the middle mark in both the novel and my cup, when the phone rang.

I picked up the call and heard Detective Strauss on the other end of the line.

"Yale," he said. "I'm glad I caught you at home. It's hard to get in touch when you don't have a cell."

"That's half of the allure," I said.

"Anyway, are you free for me to swing by?"

"Of course, Detective Strauss." I couldn't help but add,

"I certainly hope it'll turn out better than the last time you visited me."

He cleared his throat. "Yes. I'll be updating you on the happenings with the case. And Jacey Chang will be with me. If we could meet in the lobby downstairs, that'll make it more manageable for her with the crutches."

"Certainly," I said.

"See you in about ten minutes."

I spotted the two of them right away from my seat in the fake library area. Detective Strauss wore his usual dark suit ensemble, except he carried a small cardboard box in his hands. Jacey looked unstable with her new crutches, and I was grateful our lobby had automatic doors for entry.

I'd already placed three overstuffed chairs in a triangle formation so we could better converse. I sat with my back to the wall of pretend books, so I didn't have to stare at their false covers.

Jacey moved with slow motion toward me, her crutches tapping against the hard floor as she shuffled along. Detective Strauss made sure she'd settled in before placing the box beneath the remaining chair and taking a seat.

I said hello to them both before asking, "What's the latest, Detective Strauss?"

"The case is wrapped up," he said. "I let Lind—er, the previous person of interest, go. For some reason when I questioned her, she kept apologizing about a flat tire and her dislike of busybodies."

Oh. That explained the flat tire we'd had with the rental car.

Noticing my frown, the detective said, "Do you know something about that?"

"Nope. Anyway, it's been patched," I said, forgiving

Lindsey on the spot. "I'm eager to hear more about the murder case."

"I'm only telling you now," he said, "because we recently released a statement to the press."

"Is Sierra locked up?" I asked, uncertain of how fast the justice system worked.

"Legal proceedings are in progress," Detective Strauss said.

"You found that steel dewar she had on her?" I said.

"We definitely took that in as evidence," Detective Strauss said. "It still had traces of liquid nitrogen in it."

"Why did she keep the chemical around for so long?" I said.

He scratched at his jaw. "From what I gathered, Sierra wanted to keep some for the future. Plus, she plain hadn't gotten a chance to get rid of the contents responsibly, what with the constant presence of her roommates and Jacey."

"What can I say?" Jacey said. "Jordan had a lot of belongings in that small space." Her voice wobbled at her sister's name, and she looked down at the floor.

"Sorry again for your loss," I said, wringing my hands at her obvious show of grief.

She raised her head and looked up at me. "At least justice is being served."

"That's right," Detective Strauss said. "From Sierra's phone records, we managed to trace the call she'd placed inviting Jacey to meet with her at the Culver City Stairs. She'd masked the caller ID by using the star-sixty-seven trick, but cell companies still keep records."

"That not-so-anonymous phone call might indicate she's involved with Jacey's incident," I said, "but how does it implicate her in the murder?"

"The phone again gave us leverage." He glanced over at Jacey. "When Sierra ran out on dinner with her roommates, they saw her stepping into a cab to get to the apartment."

"Taxis seem to be her preferred way to get to places," I said. "She took one to the night market, too."

"I know," Detective Strauss said. "When we called the taxi company for more information, they had a record of all her recent rides."

"You took away her alibi," I said.

"Yes, that was the last straw for her. Plus, she had the liquid nitrogen in her possession, and the dermatology office confirmed that they were missing supplies. Those facts all broke her down, and she confessed to us at the station."

"Well done, Detective Strauss."

"Same can be said for you." The detective slid out the box from underneath his seat. "By the way, you can have these investigative tools back."

He handed me a familiar-looking paper sack.

"You needed a whole box to carry that?" I said to Detective Strauss in a teasing tone.

"No," he said. "The plant is from Jacey."

"What?" I said, as the detective pulled out a potted plant and passed it along to Jacey to do the official honors.

She presented it to me. "Thanks, Yale."

"How do I take care of this?" I asked, studying what looked to be a miniature tree about a foot high with a twisted trunk and broad green leaves growing from it.

"Money trees are resilient," she said. "I'm sure you can look up the care and handling of it online. Note the five leaves on each stem. They stand for the different elements."

I recited them from memory. "Water, wood, fire, earth, and metal."

"They're valued in *feng shui*," Jacey said, using the Mandarin pronunciation of the concept. "I thought it a fitting gift for you for helping bring closure for my sister."

Some shuffling steps sounded beside us, and a new voice piped up. Celine appeared at my side. I'd been too

busy studying the leaves to pay any attention to the swishing open of the building's doors.

"That's gonna bring you good fortune," my cousin said
to me. She waved to Detective Strauss and Jacey. "So,
what's this intimate convo about?"

Detective Strauss summarized how Sierra Tang had
confessed to the murder of Jacey Chang, and Celine did a
congratulatory fist pump.

After her excitement died down, I turned to Jacey. "Do
you know how the roommates are handling the news?"

"It's hard on them," she said. "We literally stumbled
onto the cleanup scene last night after we stopped dinner
short to figure out what had happened to Sierra. She'd
disappeared and wasn't answering her phone. By the time
we got back, the police had taken Sierra away."

Detective Strauss spoke up. "We cleared out the apartment as fast as possible. Even offered hotel vouchers if any of
the ladies didn't feel comfortable staying there for the night."

"Jacey," I said, "wasn't Reagan supposed to drive you
home?"

"She wasn't in any state to use a car after the news
about Sierra. Besides, with all the excitement of last night,
I decided to postpone the trip," Jacey said. "I ended up
using one of those hotel vouchers myself because I wanted
to stay as close as possible to the action. I needed to see
everything come to a tidy conclusion."

"Do you still need a ride to Long Beach?" Celine said
with a gleam in her eye. "Yale and I can help you out."

"Really?" Jacey said. "Detective Strauss was going to
work it out with one of the other officers and drive me to
Long Beach, but I'm sure police resources could be used
in better ways."

"Detective Strauss"—Celine stood before him—"if
you don't mind dropping Jacey off at her hotel to start
packing, we can handle the rest of the transportation."

The detective agreed and gave Celine the name of the place where Jacey was staying. Then he hovered near Jacey's chair to help her up.

I said to Celine, "I hope you understand what you're agreeing to. In the meantime, let me dash upstairs and put this plant and paper bag away."

"I know what I'm doing," Celine said, giving me a wink. I wondered if her plan involved driving Jacey's car to Long Beach and then taking rideshare back, not that I minded. I hadn't seen Celine all afternoon, and I missed her company.

When I came back downstairs, only Celine remained in the lobby.

"Come on," she said. "It's off to the hotel."

I followed her, and we ended up in front of a shiny blue Boxster. Only then did I understand her motivation to drive Jacey to Long Beach.

"Joyride, huh?" I said, buckling into the passenger's seat.

"A quick one to her hotel."

In the short trip to Jacey's temporary lodgings, I stayed silent and enjoyed the ride. The wind tossed my hair with gentleness, and I breathed in the new car scent.

"You lucked out," I said. "They sprayed some kind of fancy air freshener in here. It doesn't even smell like a rental."

She gave me a mysterious smile as she parked in front of a nondescript chain hotel. "We're here."

Celine and I assisted Jacey with her packed duffel bag and stored it in the trunk of her black Jetta.

After we'd settled Jacey into the passenger's side of the car, making sure to push the seat back to give her extra leg room, my cousin turned to me. "Open your palm," she said.

I complied, and she placed the key to the convertible in my hand.

"You take the Boxster," she said, "and I'll drive Jacey and her Jetta to her house. Let me just punch the directions into the GPS for you."

My cousin fiddled with the navigational system of the Boxster while I frowned at the on-screen help.

"Do I really need to use that?" I asked.

"It'll provide you clear turn-by-turn instructions," she said. "Give it a go. Tech can be helpful."

I thought about what Detective Strauss had said, how Sierra had confessed to the crime only after they'd gotten evidence off her phone.

"Okay," I said, "but could you change that brash male voice?"

"How about a British woman giving you directions?" Celine said.

"That'll do," I said. "But make sure you drive slow just in case. I want to follow you."

Celine chuckled. "Don't worry, Yale. I don't think you'll have any trouble catching up to a Jetta."

Maybe I'd gotten used to driving, given the test run in my dad's Camry the previous day, but I didn't experience any hiccups along the way. Sometimes I even liked the British voice coming out of the guidance system and pretended that I was a special agent. Still, I made sure to keep sight of the taillights of the black Jetta ahead of me.

Both our cars arrived at Jacey's apartment in one piece.

Celine carried the duffel bag into the cozy home, and I was relieved to note that Jacey had a first-floor unit. She wouldn't have to navigate any treacherous steps with her injured leg.

In the open doorway, Jacey leaned against her crutches and thanked us for our help.

Celine gave her a gentle hug. "You sure you don't need anything else?"

"No, I've got friends and neighbors around who'll pitch in with errands and groceries. Plus, there's always food delivery."

"We're pretty good at that task. Right, Yale?" Celine's eyes flashed at me with mischief.

Not knowing our undercover escapades as food deliverers, Jacey replied in a serious tone. "Well, ordering from Westwood is a bit far for me, but maybe I'll stop by when I'm in the area."

"Please do," I said. "After your leg fully heals."

We said our goodbyes to Jacey and offered her warm wishes for a quick recovery.

At the blue Boxster, I offered to switch places and let Celine drive.

"Nah," she said. "You should keep doing it. Driving is like working a muscle, so you need to train it."

"Are you sure?" I said. A thought bubbled up to the surface of my mind. "Does your rental insurance even cover me?" I guess I should've thought of that before agreeing to drive to Long Beach.

"I mean, it's your car," she said with a grin. "You should definitely be able to drive it."

I had to lean against the side of the convertible to process her news. "What are you saying?"

"I spent this afternoon discussing with Uncle which vehicle to buy you and how the insurance would work out."

"You bought me a car?" I said. Straightening up, I ran my fingers across the sleek blue side. "This one?"

"You're getting it." Celine tossed her hair. "You looked really happy driving around the other day. I thought, 'Why not?'"

I didn't know how to respond. I'd spent so many years utilizing public transportation. Was I ready to give up my old habits? Then again, I'd driven prior to my mom's accident, and I'd done it all day yesterday. I didn't lack the skill but maybe the confidence.

Celine's eyes dimmed. "I'm not sure what the dealer's return policy is, but if you . . ."

"Sorry, Celine. It's just that this is so generous. I'm still processing the gift."

I remembered that money equated to love in Celine's world. Was she trying to express her care for me through this purchase? "Okay," I said. "I accept. Thank you."

Celine gave me a lopsided grin. "Oh, it's not all for you," she said. "You gotta take me around Los Angeles and show me the sights, remember? My initial tour got derailed because of the murder situation. So, what's next on the list?"

***

I'd planned everything and timed our outing for sunset. Armed with a wicker basket and a picnic blanket, I'd chosen Angels Gate Park for our destination. As we climbed up the steep hill, a chilly wind raked our bodies. I'd advised Celine to bring an extra jacket for this very reason, but I found I didn't mind the cold so much when I focused on the breathtaking building before us.

The gorgeous bright-colored pavilion held the Korean Bell of Friendship. Although the huge bronze bell represented the amity between South Korea and the United States, I also thought the rich symbolism could be applied to my and Celine's relationship.

We took our time inspecting the pyramidal roof of the pavilion and its accompanying twelve columns, each boasting a carved animal from the Korean zodiac. Then we stood in the shadow of the giant bell, with its roughly seven-foot diameter.

After admiring the building and its bell, we found a grassy spot on the hillside to face the Pacific Ocean. The sunlight had already shifted from golden to cotton candy colored as we'd explored the unique structure.

I set out the blanket, and we settled on top of it. Celine kneeled with her knees together, while I sat cross-legged. When I pulled out the steamed vegetable buns we'd be having for dinner, my cousin oohed.

"Where'd you get those beauties?" she said.

"I did a quick jaunt to Wing Fat to pick them up from Ba," I said. "While you were freshening up and deciding what to wear for tonight."

She gestured at her polka-dot shirt and cropped chino pants. "It takes time to put together a cute ensemble."

"FYI, Wing Fat was super busy," I said, "especially after the news about Sierra's arrest came out and corroborated the *Eastwood Village Connection* blog post. I barely managed to nab a few buns from the kitchen."

"If only we also had some bubbly to celebrate," Celine said.

"I have just the thing." I pulled out two cans of Apple Sidra. "I mean, at least there's fizz."

"These are perfect," Celine said, popping the tab on one of them. "You swung by an Asian market, too?"

"Ho's. I met up with Nik. Business is starting to boom at his mom's restaurant, too, since her name was also mentioned. Not only that, but the plaza owner personally called her and said that he's had requests to make the local night market an ongoing weekend event. He's hatching plans to make that happen."

"This is amazing," Celine said. She held up her can and toasted to the good news.

We sipped our fizzy apple drinks in unison.

"So," Celine said, "are you thinking about running the Canai and Chai booth on a regular basis at the new and improved night market?"

I gazed out at the distant water, as though searching for

an answer in that vast expanse of ocean. "I *am* starting to enjoy cooking again."

"It'd be a good fit."

I reached over, plucked a blade of grass, and tore it in half. "Running a food stall alone is a tough task."

Celine blinked at me. "Who says you have to be by yourself?"

"I think Ba's got enough on his hands, managing the restaurant seven days a week."

"Don't forget about this Yee," she said, pointing to herself.

I dropped the grass, and the wind carried it away. "How long are you staying this time?"

"To the max, until the end of my visa," Celine said.

I'd read somewhere that a tourist visa lasted at least several months. "It'll be great to have you around," I said.

"Yeah, well, Ma Mi and De Di are starting to get worried about the political climate of Hong Kong. Plus, I'm making a splash over here, what with the new blog I'm working on with Nik."

I nodded at the glowing sky around us. "It's nice to share this with family." I paused and added Celine's moniker for me. "Thanks, cuz."

"No prob," she said. "And I wouldn't call us cousins, maybe more like sisters. Which reminds me, I got you something from Hong Kong."

"Really?"

She handed me a small tube of lip balm. "Made from wild coconut oil. The color's called Sunset. Reminded me of Los Angeles and our fun outings."

"Thanks, Celine." I cradled the lip balm for a moment with a small smile before slipping it into my pocket.

Under the pastel sky, I realized how much my life had changed in a little over a week. On a Friday not too long ago, I'd labeled myself a single woman who, in possession of a paycheck's fortune, had searched for escapism in a book. Now I didn't think of myself as so alone in the world, and I'd expanded my definition of good fortune to include family and a restored passion. Moreover, I didn't need to dive into a book in order to find adventure. I would live out my own story, and I couldn't wait to watch it unfold.

Acknowledgments

AUTHOR'S NOTE: For dim sum references, I took my inspiration from the cookbook *Hong Kong Dim Sum*, edited by Dennis Au. The spelling of Cantonese words came from a mix of my own pronunciation with some guidance from *Understanding Chinese* by Rita Mei-Wah Choy. Toxicology report insight was given to me by Detective Jeff Locklear; any errors are mine.

I'm so glad I get to write this new L.A. Night Market series—thank you, readers, for joining Yale and Celine on their delicious detecting fun. It would be putting a cherry on top if you posted a review, requested a copy at your local library, or posted on social media (bubble tea selfies!) about *Death by Bubble Tea*. Reader support means a lot to us authors. Feel free to also connect with me through my newsletter (sign up on my website at jenniferjchow.com) or on Twitter and Instagram: @jenjchow.

Speaking of support, I'm indebted to everyone who continues to cheer me on. Gratitude goes to the 2020 Debuts of Color, Asian American Writers' Workshop, Dru Ann Love (Dru's Book Musings), Ellen Whitfield (Books

Forward), Lori Caswell (Great Escapes Book Tours), the New York Public Library, the North Brunswick Public Library, Pen Parentis, and Suzy Leopold (Suzy Approved Book Tours). Bookstagrammers, bookstore owners, and journalists have been so kind to my Sassy Cat Mysteries, and I hope you'll enjoy this new series as well. Yay for @booksaremagictoo, @booksloveandunderstanding, @literallybookedsolid, @lovemybooks2020, @milesofpages, @rachaelbookhunter, @rajivsreviews, @readingwithmere, @readingwithmrsleaf, @subakka.bookstuff, @tarheelreader, @yamisbookshelf, Bel Canto Books, Book Carnival, Creating Conversations, Fountain Bookstore, Green Apple Books, Murder by the Book, Mysterious Galaxy, Mystery Ink, Tattered Cover Book Store, Book Riot, BuzzFeed, CrimeReads, Murder & Mayhem, PopSugar, and many more!

I would not have stuck with writing if it hadn't been for a solid community. I've been blessed with great friends from Sisters in Crime and I am honored to serve on the national board as vice president. I'm also grateful for the camaraderie at Crime Writers of Color, and I appreciate the insight from members of Mystery Writers of America.

Chirps of delight for my wonderful blogmates at Chicks on the Case: Becky Clark, Cynthia Kuhn, Ellen Byron, Kathleen Valenti, Kellye Garrett, Leslie Karst, Lisa Q. Mathews, Marla Cooper, and Vickie Fee. Also, I'm thankful to have contributed to and been part of the talented community at the Writers Who Kill blog. Huge thanks to my fellow Berkley sisters for your encouragement and inspiration: Abby Vandiver, Denise Williams, Lyn Liao Butler, Mia P. Manansala, and Olivia Blacke. Hurrah to my critique group, who have seen me through the ups and downs of publishing: Lisbeth Coiman, Robin Arehart, Sherry Berkin, and Tracey Dale.

The night market premise would not have existed without my fabulous agent, Jessica Faust. Thank you for being excited about this idea and honing the concept with me. Happy to have the BookEnds team on my side!

For the amazing illustrated cover of *Death by Bubble Tea*, I owe huge thanks to artist Jane Liu—wow! Thank you also to Judith Murello Lagerman for the art design. Sprinkles and cake to my extraordinary cover reveal collaborators, Hannah Mary McKinnon/First Chapter Fun and @nurse_bookie. Confetti and balloons to all the amazing authors who agreed to blurb this novel—thanks galore!

Angela Kim, you are the superstar of editors! I'm constantly grateful for your brilliant corrections and suggestions. Thank you for saving me from myself many times over. A million thanks to the copyeditor and proofreader, who work hard to make me sound coherent and keep my plot timelines straight. Cheers for the marketing and publicity team, including Stephanie Felty and Natalie Sellars, and all the amazing people at Berkley.

Friends, thank you for posting photos of my books in the wild, coming to events, and buying my novels. Hurrah for Barb, Elizabeth, Eunice, Grace, Liz, Lois, Peggy, Samantha, the Zartmans, and others. Special thanks to R for letting me exaggerate our rivalry!

Family, it was fun (but also work) to own a restaurant. Thank you for all the fond memories. Special thanks go out to Uncle Vincent, Aunt Diana, Steph, Melissa, Brian, and Pam.

Dad, Mama Lim, Melo, Michelle, and Stan: I'm looking forward to more celebrations involving great food!

Finally, my dear loved ones: thanks for appreciating and complimenting my cooking. Steve, it's always a joy to have you by my side for every adventure, including the foodie kind!

Recipes

Grapefruit Green Tea with Boba

(SERVES ONE)

Grapefruit tea:

1½ cups jasmine green tea
½ medium grapefruit
¼ cup boba
2 teaspoons maple syrup

Simple syrup:

½ cup water
½ cup sugar

Boil 1½ cups water and make jasmine green tea; let steep.
  Juice the grapefruit half.
  Cook boba according to package instructions (I like
using the five-minute quick-cooking variety).

Make simple syrup: bring ½ cup water to boil and remove from heat; stir in ½ cup sugar and let dissolve; cool.

Add cooked boba to simple syrup (this keeps the tapioca balls from sticking together and adds sweetness).

Pour tea into glass. Stir in grapefruit juice and maple syrup.

Add desired amount of ice to tea or refrigerate to chilled.

Scoop up boba and place in drink.

Spicy Cucumber Salad

6 Persian cucumbers (washed)
2 cloves garlic
1 tablespoon soy sauce
1 tablespoon black vinegar
½ tablespoon sesame oil
¼ teaspoon chili (I like to use Laoganma's
   Spicy Chili Crisp)
Salt to taste

Slice or use mandoline to cut cucumbers to approximately ¼-inch thickness.

Peel and mince cloves of garlic.

Place cucumbers and garlic in a bowl.

Add soy sauce, black vinegar, sesame oil, chili, and salt.

Mix together and refrigerate for at least ten minutes before serving.

Keep reading for an exclusive look at
Jennifer J. Chow's next L.A. Night Market Mystery

HOT POT MURDER

Available from Berkley Prime Crime
in spring 2023!

ALL HAPPY HOT POT GATHERINGS ARE ALIKE; each unhappy hot pot event is disastrous in its own way. It started off early with the invitation from Nikola Ho. Continuing his trend of irritating me ever since we were middle school academic rivals, Nik had now single-handedly ruined my plans for a quiet Thanksgiving dinner with my nearest and dearest beside me. The holiday was one of the few times that Ba actually shut down his dim sum restaurant, Wing Fat, and focused on family. Even though it'd been quieter in recent years with just the two of us sharing slices of turkey, I'd still appreciated the time spent with my dad. This year, it'd be even livelier with the presence of my cousin, Celine, who'd flown in from Hong Kong last month. Although she and I had had two decades of silence between us, we'd mended our ways recently, especially while clearing our shared Yee name from police suspicion when someone had died at the night market event where we'd run our food booth. The murder and its subsequent resolution had placed the inaugural

Eastwood Village Night Market on the L.A. dining map. It'd ended in the creation of an exciting food event every weekend in the planned community of Eastwood Village.

I loved living in the area. Everything had its place and order. All essential services were within walking distance of my apartment (and Celine's current residence while living in the States) at Fountain Vista. I could stroll to my two favorite spots, the Eastwood Village Public Library and The Literary Narnia, my beloved bookstore and previous place of employment, until I'd rediscovered my passion for cooking.

Nik hadn't bothered to officially invite me to his Thanksgiving banquet. He didn't send me a card or call me on my landline (Celine was still trying to convince me to get a cell phone). To be honest, I wasn't even sure I'd made it on the list of expected attendees. He'd actually asked Ba to come, but added a plus-one option, which Ba had changed to plus-two. I bet Nik's mother, Ai Ho, wanted my cousin to show up as the extra guest. She had rosy-hued dreams of Celine staying in the States and settling down with Nik.

The Thanksgiving gathering had been billed as a meeting of minds for the local Asian restaurant business community. They even had an official title for their group: Asian American Restaurant Owners Association, or AAROA.

Nik had called together a group meetup because of the dwindling members of the association. To be fair, there weren't that many Asian restaurants in West Los Angeles— many of them stayed in distinct geographic locations like Chinatown and Thai Town. Others had branched off to the San Gabriel Valley or even Westminster, down in Orange County. The ones who stayed in business in the region either didn't have time to join AAROA or maybe felt like the restaurant owner connection wasn't necessary. Nik's mother

thought the tie was essential and wanted to promote cooperation among the younger generations of restaurateurs. I
half wondered if she'd thought up the original idea of a
Thanksgiving meal to promote unity among the business
owners.

At the onset of the idea, though, Nik and I had clashed.
Once I'd known about the revised Thanksgiving, I offered
up Wing Fat as the logical place to gather. We had plenty
of space for guests, even though I knew that the group
currently numbered only six people. Wing Fat had a
whole banquet room, a partitioned space, to fill up with
people and food.

Nik declined our offer and said everybody should meet
up at his mother's restaurant, Ho's, and he won the argument. I was surprised the Thanksgiving meal wouldn't be
at Jeffery Vue's restaurant, actually. I figured as the president of AAROA, he'd be ready to jump in with the meeting location. Then again, maybe he didn't want to deal
with the cleanup on his day off. Plus, I'd heard from Ba
that he was rearranging his priorities and currently focusing on his dating life.

Despite the contentious venue, Celine's ambitious
social-media-influencer inclination to "put a shine" on the
event meant that my cousin and I had arrived early on
Thanksgiving to decorate the restaurant in advance of the
dinner. She stood in front of Ho's carrying a large cardboard box, while I tapped on the glass door.

Nik came and greeted us with a half-hearted wave.
Although it appeared like he'd just woken up, I knew his
signature bedhead look took meticulous styling. He'd
mastered the effort in high school and then added
bleached strands and a goatee to the hair mix post-college.

He pushed the door open to let us in. "If it isn't the
deadly Yee duo."

"Very funny," I said, although I hadn't seen any humor

in the situation when I'd literally run into a dead body with my food cart during the night market event around Halloween. "Can't believe you wrote that I made 'brutal boba.'" Nik had run a column in his *Eastwood Village Connection* blog about how the night market had turned deadly, perhaps due to my fatal recipe.

"Who are you to complain?" he said. "People were lining up at Canai and Chai last weekend for your signature drink."

I stopped a sigh from escaping my lips. Who knew what would catch people's fancy? Night market–goers did like ordering my grapefruit green tea with boba, those chewy tapioca balls, for the fun of it. Maybe they felt like they were daring death, even though the police had cleared my drink of any suspicion after they'd arrested the real killer.

"Ho's Small Eats didn't do so badly either," I said, referring to the food stand that Nik and his mother ran, a neighboring stall to our own. I'd seen a line snaking before them, people eager to eat spiced popcorn chicken and enjoy freezing cold shaved ice.

Celine dropped her box on the long counter of Ho's, and it landed with a heavy thump. "Less talking, more work," she said. "It might take a miracle to transform this place in only one hour."

I studied the restaurant, again reflecting on the fact that a 1950s diner had previously been in this location. Ho's still retained the red vinyl booths and checkerboard flooring. They'd even kept swivel bar stools lined up along the counter. "This place has never really screamed 'Taiwanese' to me."

"It's the authentic food cooked in here that draws in our customers," Nik said in an irritated tone. I wasn't sure which hurt him more: that I'd put down his family's restaurant or because I knew the dishes he referred to didn't come from his own hands. Mrs. Ho still didn't trust her son to do more than serve and wipe down the tables.

I leaned toward the kitchen door. In fact, I could hear some banging around in there. Maybe she'd already started preparing. Dad should also be there, and maybe Roy Yamada. All members of AAROA, they'd bonded over their stories about immigrating to America and also the fact that they'd all lost their spouses within the past ten years. Mr. Yamada had been widowed the least amount of time. His wife had died last year after an aggressive bout with cancer.

Celine clapped her hands together twice to get Nik's and my attention. "Here's what I'm envisioning," she said. My cousin was a foodstagrammer, and while she loved her food shots on Instagram the most, I could see her creative brain working as she laid out her Thanksgiving design plan. She wanted to decorate the tabletops with scented spice candles, arrange a line of painted pumpkins along the counter, and pin a garland of colorful walnuts against a wall.

"How do you know so much about Thanksgiving, anyway?" I said. "Isn't it an American holiday?"

"I live in Hong Kong," she said, "not Antarctica."

"We're not even having turkey per tradition," I said as I shook my head at Nik.

"News flash," he said. "Nobody likes turkey. Usually it comes out too dry."

"*I* like turkey," I said, grabbing a few orange candles and bunching them together on a table. "I'm not sure why we have to do hot pot anyway." I liked steaming veggies and meat simmering away in hot broth as much as the next person, but I had looked forward to the holiday's typical stuffing and candied yams.

"My restaurant, my rules," Nik said as he lined up a few pumpkins along the counter.

I wanted to make a sharp retort about his mother really owning the place when the front door swung open. Jeffery Vue, wearing a faded black suit and tie, had arrived.

"Friends, how can I help?" he said, sweeping his hands wide, their huge motion mimicking his booming voice. Jeffery had been president of the Asian restaurant owners' club even back when I'd started helping out after my abbreviated time attending college. I didn't think he ever wanted to leave the position. He was a social man who loved gatherings.

On my dim sum personality assessment scale, I'd thought of him as resembling a *char siu bao*, or barbecued pork bun. He had the same kind of rotund appearance as the steamed treat and overflowed with sweet talk. Lately, he'd snared the woman of his dreams with his honeyed mouth. He'd taken his merry time to do so, according to his own internal calendar.

The man was in his forties, about ten years older than me, but I still used a respectful title to greet him. "Hello, Mr. Vue, good to see you," I said. "Did you bring your date?"

I tried to peer behind his broad body to catch a glimpse of her. I didn't know anything about the mysterious lady. No one in the association had met her yet.

"She wasn't free this evening. Family obligations of her own," he said.

"A shame."

"Thank you for showing up early, Mr. Vue," my cousin said. Celine moved toward him in her goldenrod sweater dress with suede boots, which she told me she'd selected to match the autumn season. "You can assist with the garland." She handed him a clear jar full of prepainted walnuts in various colors.

He accepted the container and blinked at its contents. "What am I supposed to do with these?"

"Put holes in them," Celine said, "and string them together. The drill and twine are in the box on the counter."

Jeffery had picked up the tool when the door to Ho's

burst open as though by a strong gust of wind. Derrick Tran barreled through. "I'm here," he said.

"Hello, Veep." Jeffery raised the drill in his hand in greeting.

Derrick flinched at the movement. "I have a first name you can use, Jeffery."

"But it's so much quicker to say Veep," Jeffery replied.

Derrick had been second-in-command in the association almost as long as Jeffery had been number one. I didn't think the titles in the organization mattered much, though, because I couldn't see the difference in their duties. All the members of the group seemed to pitch in to get the word out about local Asian restaurants.

"Maybe I won't be the VP in a few months," Derrick said. "Voting is coming around, and new leaders start in January." Worry lines creased his pointy forehead, making him appear like the pot sticker personality I'd dubbed him. He'd always seemed an overdone example of the pan-fried version, too crispy and with abundant sharp folds.

"Don't you worry your remaining hairs about that, Veep," Jeffery said as he powered up the drill and bore a hole in a scarlet-colored unshelled walnut. "Because I'll remain in charge."

Celine stepped in between them and said, "I'm sure you can figure out how to work together. In fact, why don't you both assist with the walnut garland? Mr. Vue, you can continue with the drilling. Once he's pierced a few, Mr. Tran, you can begin stringing them together."

"I know my way around a power tool as much as Jeffery," Derrick said, grabbing for the drill.

I didn't think Celine's attempt at mediation was working, and I abandoned my role crafting the centerpieces. "Why don't I step into the kitchen and help Mrs. Ho? Someone can take over my duties."

The two men blinked at me but didn't relinquish their combined hold on the tool. Without waiting for a resolution, I hurried away.

I loved the perfume of a well-kept kitchen. The fragrance of soup and the sound of bubbling broth greeted me in Ho's inner sanctum. Nik's mother stood over a large silver pot, sprinkling in spices. At five feet tall, she almost needed a stepstool to cook at the range.

"Smells delicious, Auntie Ai," I said, using the familial term to greet her.

She turned from the stove. "Yale, come," she said. "Join our little trio. We'll always welcome the next generation to pass down our tricks of the trade. Otherwise we'd be more like the AARP than AAROA."

"I can also get Nik in here," I said, but Mrs. Ho waved her oil-spotted hand in the air.

"No need," she said. "Better that he spend extra time with Celine."

I didn't have a response, not wanting to burst her hopes of the two of them getting together.

Ba called me, and I shuffled to his side. He was bent over a box of tofu at the prep counter.

"Can you help me?" my dad said. "I'm in charge of veggies. A lot of them. While Ai Jeh"—he'd appended the *jeh*, or "sister," term to her name—"makes the bone broth. Roy, who's coming out of the fridge right now, is going to handle all the meats." Ba sometimes used the plural form of a word to talk about it, his one verbal tell of having emigrated from Hong Kong decades ago.

"Hi, Mr. Yamada," I said to the bald man stepping out of the fridge. He had plastic trays of meat in his hands, along with a clear plastic bag of raw shrimp, unpeeled and complete with antennae and eyes.

"Yale," he said, squinting at me. "It's been a long time. How was university? You went to your namesake, right?"

"No." I felt my cheeks heat up. "Actually, I stayed local." I didn't tell him that I'd halted my plans to transfer from community college and returned to Los Angeles because my mom had suffered from respiratory issues. Both she and Ba had needed me.

"I wanted her at Wing Fat," my dad said before plopping a second box of tofu before me. "She got our cooking genes."

Mr. Yamada placed his provisions on the far end away from our vegetables. "The lucky Yee family," he said. "Mother, father, and daughter. All good cooks."

While he wandered away to rinse the shrimp in a colander at the sink, I whispered to my dad under the sound of the rushing water. "Maybe it really is better for us to spend this meal with more than just our family. Make it less lonely for others."

Ba glanced at the back of Mr. Yamada's head. "It's tough to have nobody around. No spouse or child. The holidays can be rough."

I grabbed a sharp knife and sliced open the package of tofu with a flick of my wrist. "Agreed." This time of the year sometimes draped us with a veil of sorrow.

Ba and I worked together, side by side, creating tofu cubes on separate cutting boards. I liked the rhythm of cooking together, and unlike my time at Wing Fat, when I'd frozen up over a wok, this felt safe. It didn't feel like usurping my mom's role but like father and daughter bonding instead.

Mr. Yamada and Mrs. Ho became occupied with their own tasks, and for a while we had a harmonious work arrangement. We made our own music, with Nik's mom stirring her broth, Mr. Yamada slicing the meat, and us Yees chop-chopping away.

A hot pot meal required a lot of prep work. The ingredients must be washed and then cut into bite-size pieces. These included veggies, ranging from enoki mushrooms to napa cabbage to Taiwanese lettuce. As the handler of the meat, Mr. Yamada would cut the beef, pork, and lamb into thin slices. And, of course, the broth added flavor to the mix, enhancing the taste of the steamed items. The fact that Mrs. Ho had used bones to construct her soup would only intensify the deliciousness of the meal.

Anything associated with cooking, even the prep grunt work, pulled me out of my worldly troubles. I couldn't believe I'd resisted the call for so long. I'd stopped cooking because of my guilt over replacing my mom at Wing Fat. That, and because of the tie to my mom's accident; she'd died while driving to pick up a cooking ingredient for me. I still felt a slight shame at the whole incident, but like Celine had told me, my mom's heart attack hadn't come from doing me a favor but from underlying health issues. I still needed to remind myself of that on a regular basis.

The cabbage pieces on my cutting board kept growing, and I centered on the increasing pile, in a zone of peace. Until the knocking jolted me out of my steady rhythm.

The harsh banging on the back door startled all of us. Since Mr. Yamada was the closest to the exit, he washed his hands and checked on the newcomer. Unlike at Wing Fat, where the screen door to the alleyway remained open while cooking, releasing both the warm air and luscious scents to the outdoors, Mr. Yamada had to unbolt the back door of Ho's.

On the threshold of the kitchen stood a woman in her thirties with brown skin, her dark hair in a single long braid running down her back. "How dare you lock me out?" she said.

I didn't recognize her, but Mr. Yamada stumbled back. "Ah, Ms. Patil. You're a little early for the dinner."

"The one I wasn't invited to," she said, her hands on her hips.

Mrs. Ho turned down the flame on the range and shuffled over to the doorway. "Misty," she said. "You're very welcome here. There must have been a misunderstanding. Maybe the email went to your spam folder."

"This is not the only time emails have been 'lost,'" she said. "I had to learn about this event on a local blog."

I raised an eyebrow at my dad, who shook his head at me. He must not have realized there'd been advertising of this Thanksgiving gathering either.

Who could have known about this private meal? I wondered if we'd have people showing up, looking for a free dinner. Then I glanced at the sheer amount of food near us. This would be more than enough for several rounds of hot pot.

Ba wiped his hands against his apron. "Let me introduce you," he whispered to me.

Misty had walked into the kitchen now, and the door shut with a clang behind her. My dad and I strode toward her.

"Good to see you again, Ms. Patil," Ba said. "By the way, this is my daughter, Yale. She just joined the cooking ranks."

"Call me Misty," she said, as she stared down the length of my frame with a calculated look. "It's nice to have another young female chef around."

I shook hands with her, and her previous anger seemed to dissipate.

"What else do we need done here?" she asked.

"The food prep is almost done," I said. "But I'm not sure how the decorating is going in the dining room."

After I uttered those words, I heard the distinct whine of the drill. Then a scream shattered the air.

Ready to find
your next great read?

Let us help.

Visit prh.com/nextread

Penguin
Random
House